# IT'S COLD AT THE END OF THE BED

# IT'S COLD AT THE END OF THE BED

Peter Johnson

Matador
Unit E2 Airfield Business Park,
Harrison Road, Market Harborough,
Leicestershire. LE16 7UL
Tel: 0116 2792299
Email: books@troubador.co.uk
Web: www.troubador.co.uk/matador
Twitter: @matadorbooks

ISBN 978 1803130 798

British Library Cataloguing in Publication Data.
A catalogue record for this book is available from the British Library.

Printed and bound in Great Britain by 4edge Limited
Typeset in 11pt Minion Pro by Troubador Publishing Ltd, Leicester, UK

Matador is an imprint of Troubador Publishing Ltd

For Chrissie
with love

All that matters is love and work.
Sigmund Freud – attributed

# PART ONE

...girls were still something of a mystery.

# TRANSITION

## Oakwood Primary School

*Summary Comment – Sam Martin*

Sam has made good progress in some subjects this year but his confidence wavers when he is out of his comfort zone. When he applies himself, he shows potential but he needs to stick at the task and be more consistent if he is to do himself justice. He is at his best in PE. His enthusiasm and skill in all sporting activities are impressive. The teams at West Park High will be strengthened by his presence. He can sing too but is rather shy about showing it! He is a kind and friendly boy who is supportive of younger children and helpful to both his peers and adults. We shall all miss his cheerful smile around the school and wish him well for the future.

*Melissa Jones* Head Teacher

*Summary Comment – Charlotte Woods*

Charlotte has worked hard and made excellent progress in all subjects. She has reached a high standard across the board and is an outstanding academic prospect. Well done, Charlie! She is a good artist and athlete too, a girl with a wide range of talents who is well equipped to compete with the best in any environment. Her ability, dedication and maturity have marked her out from the rest of her year and she has not always found it easy to make friends, so we hope that she will find more like spirits at Chelston Grammar. We wish her every success in the future.

*Melissa Jones* Head Teacher

# 1

It was a tense moment for Sam Martin when he came second to Charlie Woods in the Year 6 fifty metre dash. His father was upset. He had told him in his pep talk before the race that Martins didn't lose, so to be beaten by a girl was an added insult. Sam would like to have won. He was a competitive boy, and good at sport, but he didn't mind that much. He rather liked Charlie, although girls were still something of a mystery. She was the prettiest girl in his class and they got on well. It wasn't his fault that she was taller than him and had longer legs. She was clever too and destined for the Girls' Grammar School. Sam had a place at West Park High. Despite his mother's efforts to make him work harder, eleven plus exam success had eluded him.

After his father had voiced his opinion on his performance within earshot of other parents and pupils, Sam made a welcome escape to get ready for the sack race.

"You shouldn't be too hard on him, Paul. This is meant to be fun, not a preparation for the Olympics."

"He's got to learn to push himself. He'll never be a serious sportsman unless he really wants it."

"For god's sake, he's only eleven."

"They start young these days and he's got potential. It would be a shame to see it wasted."

"It will be if you carry on putting pressure on him." Jill walked away before she was drawn into a public performance of an argument they had already rehearsed on too many occasions.

Sam was watching and could see the tension from the way his parents were standing – stiffly, and with their faces too close to each other. They seemed to argue a lot these days. Maybe they weren't happy, or perhaps it was because he was getting older and beginning to notice that parents didn't always follow their own guidelines about how to behave. Mrs Jones, his favourite teacher, had mentioned in class that adults sometimes did things that were not a good example to children. He understood what she meant. Sometimes his father was an embarrassment at sporting occasions. He looked overweight and unfit compared with the other dads at mini-rugby and made the most noise. He talked as if he knew everything about the game but never helped with coaching or refereeing. Since his mother had let it slip that Sam shouldn't believe everything his father said about his sporting exploits, he had become less in awe of him.

A whistle blew, and the first group of sack racers made their way to the starting line. Sam was next to Charlie. She smiled at him and something stirred which gave him an inkling of what it meant to be attracted to a girl. He smiled back shyly and busied himself gathering the top edge of the sack firmly in his hands, ready for the off. It was a tight race, memorable for two things in Sam's mind: hearing his father shouting, and seeing Charlie fall as she stretched to overtake him in the last few metres.

"Well done, Sam," Paul bellowed from his position near the finishing line.

"It's only a sack race," Sam said under his breath as he walked over to see if Charlie was OK. Her pride was more bruised than her body, and what Sam noticed about the incident was that Charlie's parents left her alone to sort herself out. There was no fuss. He liked the fact that they were treating her in a grown-up way.

Charlie dusted herself down and adjusted her ponytail. "Mum's brought drinks and some snacks. Do you want some?"

"Yes please," he replied, happy to have the opportunity to spend more time with Charlie. He caught sight of his mother hurrying across the field to get home and change for work. He was proud of her being a senior sister at the local hospital but preferred it when she wasn't on night duty.

Refreshments with the Woods family were enjoyable and Sam was amused by the attention he received from Charlie's little sister Sophie who insisted on showing him all the things she had brought in her brightly coloured backpack. It felt good when Mrs Woods praised him for being patient with her. And Charlie seemed pleased too. The arrival of his father was an unwelcome interruption.

"Come on Sam, we need to get home. You're not in any other races, are you?"

Mr Woods greeted him with his hand outstretched. "You must be Sam's Dad. How do you do. I'm Philip Woods, and this is my wife Clare."

"Paul Martin. Pleased to meet you both."

"There are a couple more races to watch and then we're going to look at the artwork in the classrooms. Would you mind if Sam stayed with us for a little while longer?"

"Sophie won't forgive us if we let him go now... And I think the Head prefers the pupils to stay to the end," Clare added. "We can drop him back home later, if you're happy with that Paul."

"You're not interested in seeing the artwork, are you, Sam?"

Sam wasn't sure about the art, but he definitely wanted to stay with Charlie. He breathed in deeply and looked down at the ground. "I would like to see it, if I can, please, Dad?" he replied, bravely putting extra emphasis on 'would'.

Sam's response took Paul by surprise and, with the Woods family looking at him in expectation, it was difficult to say no. "I suppose it'll be alright, if Mr and Mrs Woods don't mind." It was clear to everyone that he would have preferred to take Sam home.

Clare made the most of the opportunity. "Not at all, Paul. We'd be delighted."

It was a memorable moment for Sam. Being with Charlie had given him the courage to speak up. He beamed with pleasure as they wandered off to explore the classrooms and look at the cardboard mobiles, dumpy playdough figures, approximate family portraits and, their favourite, a group of sand sculptures in a tray. Charlie took pride in pointing out her picture of an athlete sprinting on a tartan track, but Sam was glad she didn't comment on his clumsy attempt at a horse in the top corner of the display which, he thought, was the work by the less talented artists in the class. She's so good at everything…

*

Sam noticed that it was Mrs Woods who did the driving on the way home. His Mum hardly ever drove when Dad was in the car unless they were returning from a night out. The gated entrance was open when they arrived and the gravel crunched loudly as they went through. They parked in front of the double garage and Mr Woods helped him to get his stuff out of the boot. Dad was waiting by the front door looking a bit red in the face and made his usual joke about not needing a doorbell even for pedestrians.

"Sorry we're a bit late, Paul. We treated the children to a pizza. I hope you don't mind."

"Not at all. It was good of you take him."

"He's been a pleasure to have. He and Charlie get on very well."

"He's talked about her a lot. A sporting rival, it seems." He grinned. "Would you like to come in for a drink?"

"That's kind of you, but we ought to get back. The girls have a busy morning at the Athletics Club tomorrow. Goodbye Sam. See you again soon, I hope."

"Bye. Thanks for having me." He was careful to remember his manners and wondered if there really would be another chance to see Charlie. I'll talk to Mum about it tomorrow, he decided.

"Typical builders house," Philip said, too loudly, as they drove away.

"Dad!" Charlie exclaimed.

Clare winced at the comment. "You shouldn't say things like that in front of the girls. They really like Sam."

"Sorry," he replied sheepishly. "He's a nice lad. We had a good chat about his mini-rugby. He's going to West Park, you know. You could well be teaching him next year."

"Well, I'm sure I'd enjoy having him in my class."

*

"You seemed a bit down this evening. What's the matter?" Clare asked.

Charlie was reading in bed. "Nothing."

"Sad to be leaving Oakwood."

"Not really."

"So, what is it?"

"Nothing."

"I don't believe you."

"Well it's true."

"I like Sam."

"He's OK."

"Sophie likes him too."

"Now we're going to different schools, I probably won't see him again."

"Well, you never know, and I might well be teaching him at West Park."

"He said I only won the race because I'm taller than him."

Clare smiled. "He'll get over it."

"It's OK being tall but I don't want to be a giant."

"You won't be. You've had your growth spurt early. I bet you'll end up about the same height as me."

"How do you know?"

"There's a rough calculation you can do which is quite a good predictor. Add my height to Dad's – that's five foot eight and six foot two – take away five inches, then halve it."

Charlie had the answer in a blink. "That's five feet eight and a half."

"Just right. A little bit taller than me."

"I'll be able to wear high heels like you then."

"It's a bit early to be worrying about that, but yes, you will."

Charlie was reassured by her mother's confidence and moved on to something else that had been bugging her. She spoke quietly from half under the duvet.

"Could we ask Sam round?"

Clare managed to avoid smiling at Charlie's discomfort. "Of course, we can. I'll contact the Martins. There are people at the Athletics Club who know them. I should be able to find out their number."

"Cool. Thanks Mum."

Charlie sat up and gave her mother a hug before returning to her book, pleased that at least her last day at Primary School had been one to remember.

# 2

Sam was itching to talk to his mother about his outing with the Woods but he had to wait until the next day before he had the chance. As usual on a Saturday morning, his father had gone to the office. He always seemed to be working these days. Mum had told him that since Dad had taken over the family business, he had more responsibility and was keen to prove that he could run it as well as Grandad had.

"So, it sounds as if you had a good time with Charlie and her parents."

"Yeah, she's cool."

"And you went round the class exhibitions. I'm pleased you did that. Life's not all about sport you know."

"My picture wasn't much good."

"It was fine. I had a look at it in between the races. You can't be the best at everything."

"Charlie is."

"She's a lucky girl, then. As far as I'm concerned, the important thing is to try your hardest at everything you do."

"Dad wasn't really interested. He just went home."

"It's not his thing, Sam."

"He could have had a look, couldn't he?"

"Well, yes, I suppose he could. Anyway, he supports your sport… Tell you what. Let's barbecue tonight. To celebrate the start of your summer holidays."

"Mm, that'd be good," he nodded, but then put Jill on the spot with another awkward question. "Do you wish I was going to Grammar School?"

"No. You'll be happy at West Park. It's a good school."

"Charlie's Mum teaches there."

"There you are then. A teacher you already know."

"If I'd worked harder, I could have gone to the Grammar." There was a dejected look on his face. "Charlie probably thinks I'm stupid."

Jill put her arms around him. "Oh, darling, you're not. Please don't talk like that. You'll make me sad." She squeezed him and kissed him on the forehead. "Charlie hasn't said something unkind to you has she?"

He pulled away. "No, Mum," he said firmly, worried that he might have given the wrong impression. "It's just that, I like her."

"Well, I'm sure she likes you too."

"I won't see her now we're going to different schools." He paused. "Can we have her round?"

"I'll see what I can do, but I can't promise anything. You've got your rugby camp next week. Then we're away in Majorca, and the Woods are bound to have plans."

Sam was disappointed but he understood the problem.

"Charlie's Dad teaches at Chelston. They've got a house in France and go there for the summer."

"Teachers holidays. Nice work if you can get it," Jill mumbled.

Sam was resigned to not seeing Charlie again any time soon and went to fetch his basketball from the garage. He eyed up the hoop to the side of the house and began another attempt to break his record for the number of baskets without a miss.

*

It was mid-afternoon before Paul returned from the office. Jill was not amused. She had expected him to be home for lunch and had resorted to ironing and listening to the radio to keep calm. It usually worked but a loud crash from the front door confirmed her worst suspicions.

"Another visit to the pub on the way home, I suppose."

"Just a couple of pints with the lads. Where's Sam?"

"Up in his room."

"What's he doing there on a cracking day like this?"

"Reading."

"He should be out getting some exercise."

"He was outside most of the morning if you must know. And it's good for him to do some reading," she added, too loudly.

"No need to get tetchy."

"You may have forgotten, but I was working last night and I've only had a couple of hours sleep."

"Maybe you should give up that job and come and work for me. I could do with more help in the office."

"I don't want to work in your fucking office. I've got my own career."

"I'd pay you more."

She stared at him. "I can't believe you said that. It's not about pay. I love being a nurse and I'm proud of the work I do. I'd rather jump off a cliff than spend all day filing invoices and sending out bloody estimates."

Sam peeked round the kitchen door just as his mother turned towards it. He had only come down to get a drink and a biscuit and wished he had gone back to his room when he heard the argument. She looked at him and then dropped her head into her hands. They used to laugh when Mum read him *Mr Angry* and put on a cross face, but this was the real thing. He quickly shut the door and escaped to the garden.

He picked up his football which was resting on the lawn, tested it out with a press of his thumb (it needed a bit more air) and began the keepy uppy challenge. He was at his most content in the company of a ball and spent hours playing solitary games to improve his skills. He wasn't at his best that afternoon and managed only two high scores, but it helped him to recover from the shock of seeing Mum in such a state. Maybe I'd have been better if I'd pumped up the ball before I started, he said to himself.

Jill eventually came out to find him. He was still there with the ball going up and down, up and down, up and down, but he lost control when she walked into his eyeline.

"Oh, Mum," he whined. "I was just about to get fifty."

"Sorry darling." She hugged him and breathed in the sweaty boy smell. "I'm sorry you heard us arguing. I'm ashamed of the things I said."

Sam could feel her trembling and was shocked that she was so upset. He couldn't think of anything to say and just held on until he unwrapped himself and broke the silence.

"I'm hungry."

Jill laughed. "That's what we need. Food."

*

Sam was famished by the time the barbecue was ready. He polished off a steak burger, a chicken thigh, a baguette filled with Cumberland sausages doused with huge amounts of tomato ketchup, and some salad to please Mum. Strawberries and ice cream followed to complete one of his favourite meals. Comfort food Mum called it.

His parents seemed to have put the row behind them. Perhaps it wasn't as serious as it looked, although he could still picture Mum's angry face. She was a bit quiet but Dad was in a good mood enjoying his 'glass or two of red', a phrase which usually meant most, if not all, of the bottle. He stood at fly half as the target for Sam's spin passes while Mum watched patiently and sipped the champagne which Dad had insisted on opening.

"Now we'll do left to right. If you're going to make a decent scrum half, you have to pass well off both hands."

Sam enjoyed the times when he had his father's full attention and he was enthusing about his rugby skills. He worked hard to show him that his left hand was improving and wasn't too upset when Dad told him that he had a long way to go before there was any chance of playing for England. It was a phrase he had heard many times before but it had begun to present itself as his own ambition, not just his father's. He was wearing his replica England shirt which had become his pride and joy. Sam often thought about pulling on a genuine one in the dressing room before playing in an international match. The excitement was almost too much to bear. Imagine what it must feel like in real life... That night he dreamed of scoring a brilliant try against Ireland to secure the Grand Slam for his country.

\*

"Where's Dad?"

"He's gone to see Grandad. He'll be back for lunch."

"Why don't we see him very often? He doesn't live far away."

"You know he's not been well for a while now. His cancer's getting worse."

His parents had explained the situation when the treatment started but the sad truth was that Grandad had never shown much interest in him. Sam had the impression that he didn't like children very much.

"And to be honest Sam, Dad and Grandad aren't getting on very well at the moment."

"Why not?"

"It's all to do with the business now that Dad's taken over."

Sam was pleased that Mum had been honest about it. Mrs Jones had encouraged them to ask questions, 'always politely', she stressed, 'to understand what's going on around you.' Maybe this was one of the reasons Mum and Dad were arguing more than they used to.

"Can you tell me more about Grandpa, Mum."

It seemed strange to be calling him Grandpa when he hadn't lived to be one, but it was how Mum had always referred to her father when she told stories about him. Sam didn't mind if he'd heard them before. They made it feel as if he really knew him and Mum nearly always found something different to keep his memory alive.

"He was a kind man and a wonderful father. He would have enjoyed being a grandparent and seeing you grow up. He loved Auntie Sue and me but I think he would have liked a boy."

Sam smiled. "Why?"

"He was keen on football and I wasn't particularly interested in it – or most other sports, come to that. Neither was Auntie Sue."

"Is that the only reason?"

"Well, men usually want to have a son to bring up to be like them and carry on the family name."

"Like Dad."

"I suppose so," Jill responded cautiously. "But I don't think it's necessarily a good thing. Children should be allowed to be who they want to be."

"Did Grandpa let you and Auntie Sue be who you wanted to be?"

"Goodness, we are full of questions today," Jill said with a smile. "Yes, he did, but he made it clear that he expected us to work hard at school so we could get to university. He didn't make too big a fuss about it, but he would've been disappointed if we hadn't. Fortunately, we both did."

"Why was he so keen on it?"

"He left school after O levels – that was the exam they did before GCSEs – and regretted it. His parents weren't very well off and he was under pressure to get a job. He wanted us to have what he called a proper education and go on to have successful careers but never saw either of us graduate. He would have been so proud."

Jill wiped her eyes with the back of her hand and Sam looked away while she composed herself. Talking about Grandpa sometimes made her upset, but it also made her happy. It was confusing.

"When he talked to us, he made us feel as if we were the only people in the world that mattered."

"What sort of stuff did you talk about?"

"All sorts."

"What?"

"Cars," Jill plucked from her paternal memory bank.

"Cars!" Sam was wide eyed with surprise. This was new.

"He taught me to drive. We didn't have the money to splash out on paying for lessons so he stuck L plates on his old Ford and took me out every Sunday morning until he thought I was ready for my test. He was really patient and gave me confidence. I passed first time. We used to dream about the cars we would buy if money was no object."

"I wish I'd met him."

"Now you're making me sad again."

He wanted to say something to please her. "I like it when we talk about things."

"So do I, even when they're serious."

"Dad and I talk a lot about sport."

"It's his big thing. He loves it." She grinned. "And so do you."

# 3

Charlie was putting up with the usual parental analysis of her end of term report, this time with the added significance of her move to Chelston. She enjoyed the praise she received for her academic success but soon tired of hearing the comments she had already read for herself. Having both parents as teachers was OK but they were too keen at times and she wanted to move on to other things she had been thinking about.

"Will you have to teach me next term, Dad?"

"Don't you want me to?"

"It'll feel weird."

"I could put you in one of the other science sets if you prefer."

"I'd still hear what the other girls think of you."

"They'll probably say good things, so you shouldn't worry," Clare said supportively.

"That'd feel creepy."

"Don't be ridiculous. You don't mind people saying he's a good coach at the athletics club, do you?"

"That's different. Most of them are boys."

Clare sighed. "Your logic escapes me, Charlie. Sometimes you're just plain awkward."

Charlie was beginning to enjoy herself. "D'you think mixed schools are more friendly?"

"Not necessarily."

"You told me that you like working in a mixed school."

"I do but that doesn't mean it's guaranteed to be friendlier than a single sex school."

"You said having lots of girls together isn't always a good thing."

"What's going on in that head of yours?"

"It'd probably be more fun having some boys around."

"Well, you'll just have to meet them out of school, won't you."

"I wanted to see Sam this holiday but that's not going to happen."

"I'm sorry, but you know that holiday plans and sports camps made it difficult for his Mum and me to find a date."

"Couldn't you have tried a bit harder?"

"Now you're being rude, Charlie. I tried my best."

"Sam could come and stay with us in France."

Clare shuffled in her seat. "I'm not sure that's a good idea."

"Why not?"

"We don't know him very well," Clare responded lamely.

"I do, and you said you liked him. So does Sophie."

"I know, but it's too short notice. We're driving down on Wednesday."

"He couldn't come then anyway. You said he was on his rugby course that week."

"So he is. I'd forgotten."

"He could fly out later."

"He's too young to fly on his own."

"It says on the internet that airlines have an unaccompanied child service."

Clare's neck reddened. Having a clever daughter was turning out to be more of a problem than a pleasure.

"We'd be at the airport waiting for him."

"He's not coming this summer and that's the end of it," she snapped.

Charlie looked at her and said nothing. There was an uncomfortable pause in the conversation.

"Well, we might think about inviting him next year if you're still keen."

Charlie had made her point and wanted to escape without further discussion.

"Can I go up to my room now?" It was her father who sent her away with a surreptitious wave of his hand.

*

"That was terrible, Philip. I know we've brought her up to voice her opinions but she's pushing things too far. I just wanted it to be us and the girls for the summer."

"She's heading for adolescence. It happens to all teenagers."

"She's only eleven."

"Too advanced for her own good then," he replied.

"You're being totally unhelpful. She's going to be a real

handful if she carries on like this, and it'll be me who has to deal with it."

"She's growing up fast and she's strong willed but you're used to managing difficult teenagers so you'll be well equipped for the onslaught."

Philip's attempt to make light of the situation went down badly. "That's not funny. We have our share of demanding students but West Park is a good school. Don't you worry. I'll carry on teaching at the sharp end while you make sure all your clever Grammar School girls get their As and A*s."

"It's the right place for Charlie and we must do what's best for her," he replied brusquely.

"I'm not convinced it *is* the right place. Chelston's all about exam results and there's more to education than that."

"What's brought this on, Clare? I thought we'd dealt with Charlie's choice of school long ago."

"This whole business with Sam has made me think about it again. It's a co-ed world out there and I'm concerned that she'll leave Chelston without the social skills she needs."

"It's a bit late to be worrying about that now."

"She struggled with friendships at Oakwood and didn't get on with the other girls going to Chelston. You know how bitchy they can be. God, it's so much easier to have clear views about what should happen to other people's children."

"She'll be fine, Clare. She's a tough girl. There's nothing she won't be able to handle."

"She's more sensitive than you think." Clare paused before raising another concern. "And what about her running? They have no interest in sport at Chelston."

"She can do that at the Club." Philip casually dismissed the point. "Look Clare, you're getting this out of proportion.

We've been through all this before and we've made the right decision…When the time comes, we might make a different one for Sophie."

"God, I can't bear the thought of having the same debate again."

*

Upstairs in her bedroom Charlie was reading *Harry Potter and the Order of the Pheonix*. Harry's adventures were entertaining but they failed to distract her from the pleasing thought that she had got the better of an argument with her mother.

# PART TWO

...behaving like Romeo in straight jeans and Nike trainers.

# YEAR 11

## West Park High School

*Summary Comment – Sam Martin*

We hope that all will be well when the results are out. He has shown pleasing commitment to some of his subjects but the overall impression is uneven. He would have greater success if he could achieve a better balance between his efforts in the classroom and those on the pitch, but he is to be congratulated on an outstandingly successful sporting year, especially his selection for the England Schools U16 Rugby XV. He impressed everyone with the unassuming way in which he dealt with his success. We are pleased that he has shown interest in staying for the Sixth Form and hope that he will find stronger academic motivation when he has fewer subjects to contend with.

*Rob Barnes* Head of Year

# Chelston Girls' Grammar School

*End of Year Summary – Charlotte Woods*

Charlotte has achieved outstanding academic reports right across the board, hence we are expecting an excellent set of GCSE results. She deserves them for her hard work and impressive commitment to all her subjects. She is a potential Oxbridge candidate with a great deal to offer in the Sixth Form. Although she tends to stick with one or two firm friends there is no doubt that she has the strength of character to be a successful leader in the school community if she puts her mind to it. I wish her well for the two exciting years ahead.

*Teresa Clarke* Head of Year

# 4

"Look Mum, it's Charlie Woods. She was at Oakwood."

Sam handed her the local paper in which Charlie was pictured with two other girls from Chelston Grammar who had achieved ten A*s at GCSE. Jill glanced at their typical results day pose with broad smiles and flimsy sheets of paper held up in triumph.

"Yes. I remember you were upset that her Mum and I couldn't find a time to get you together in the holidays."

Sam nodded. It was one of those childhood memories that still irritated him. He shrugged his shoulders in response.

"She's very pretty, don't you think?"

He couldn't resist another look and peered casually over her shoulder trying not to show too much interest.

"Didn't she beat you at Sports Day?" Jill grinned. "Dad was grumpy about it and gave you one of his lectures."

"She used to be taller than me," he said defensively. "I won the sack race."

"I'm not sure that's a great claim to fame for an under sixteen Rugby International."

"S'pose not," Sam reluctantly agreed, irritated with himself for falling into his mother's trap.

"You said she was clever. She's certainly proved it."

It was hard to believe that it was over five years since that Sports Day. Sam remembered being with Charlie, Sophie and their parents as if it was last week. A lot of stuff had happened since then.

"We're not up there with Charlie but me and Lily've done alright. We're good for the Sixth Form."

"Don't take it the wrong way. I'm really proud of your results…and Lily's."

The stress on really sounded a bit false but he didn't mind too much. There was no way he expected to be in the same bracket as Lily and Charlie. He'd done better than he expected considering the amount of time he'd spent playing sport.

"Have you seen anything of Charlie since you left?"

"Yeah, a couple of times in town and at a party. Lily wasn't too impressed when I got chatting to her."

Jill smiled and nodded. "Mmm. I can understand that."

"Her Mum's a great teacher. Got me my A grade. That's why I chose biology A level."

"Lily's doing that one too, isn't she?"

"Yeah, another good reason for me to do it," he grinned.

*

Sam and Lily had been going out for over a year. They were constantly together and had become known as the Year 11 married couple, but he didn't care. Going out with her was the biggest thing that had happened to him, up there with winning his England U16 cap. His mother was unsure about the relationship at first and teased him for behaving like Romeo in straight jeans and Nike trainers. Lily won her over in the end. She had a smile to melt even the hardest of hearts and gorgeous legs which she showed off to full advantage in skirts and shorts which, his mother admitted, brought back vivid memories of her younger years when she pushed Grandpa's patience to the limit by wearing skimpy outfits to go clubbing. Sam's trump card was that she was impressed by Lily's ambition to be a nurse which had never wavered since she was given her first outfit and medical box as a toddler. Lily enjoyed her social life but worked hard and influenced Sam in the right way. She needed good GCSEs and at least three grade Bs at A level to gain a place to read a degree in Nursing and had already researched Cardiff and Southampton as possible university choices.

Sam had to admit that Lily's determination to join the Sixth Form and gain some good grades had made him think more carefully about his future. His decision became more complicated when after his game for England against Wales (one of the best performances by a young scrum half his coach had seen at under sixteen level) he was offered a Sixth Form Sports Scholarship at Wellington College, one of the top rugby schools in the country. It was a huge boost to Sam's confidence. His father was so excited that he got a bit ahead of himself and immediately had his sights firmly set on Sam becoming a professional and gracing the turf at Twickenham in the Six Nations Championship. Sam wasn't too upset with him. He was, after all, his greatest fan.

Mum was pleased too, especially with the school's expectations for strong academic as well as sporting commitment. There was one problem. He would have to board and he wasn't sure that he wanted to. Wellington was an amazing school, but he would miss his local friends. Surely though, he would make new ones, and if the old ones were worth having, he wouldn't lose them – or would he?

"You'll soon forget about us when you get in with those posh bastards and rich girls."

Jack's comment hurt. Sam was shocked by its underlying aggression which made him feel as if he was going to join a different tribe. Other boys in the group nodded in support and one sneeringly added, "And you won't be able to keep a close eye on what Lily's up to." Sniggering and jeering followed.

Sam found it hard to imagine not seeing and touching Lily nearly every day and he worried that she would inevitably find someone else if he was away. She would never be short of offers. When they discussed the move, she understood his dilemma but her support carried an upsetting undercurrent.

"Like, I'd miss you, but I don't want to stop you in case I get the blame if you end up wishing you'd gone."

"So, you don't care what I do as long as I don't blame you for anything."

"I don't mean it like that."

"That's what it sounds like."

They rarely argued, except about their tastes in music, so this was a big deal for both of them.

"I wish I'd never had the offer. I'm fucking stressing out over it."

They were walking side by side in the local park and had reached the children's play area, not the ideal place for a passionate gesture but Lily put her arms around him and pushed him against the fence opposite the wooden climbing frame. She kissed him. Not one of those frantic tongue explorers when they became overexcited and tore at each other, but slow and sensuous with both her hands working gently in his hair. He could hear the squeals of excited children and imagined he could feel disapproving parental stares boring into his back, but they didn't stop the stirring in his trousers.

Lily stepped back and looked at him with her eyes on fire. "That's how much I want you to stay."

Decision made.

Sam was worried about telling his father but managed to impress him with a mature analysis of the situation regarding his rugby ambitions. Lily helped him to rehearse his lines.

"I'm on the talented player pathway with national coaches keeping an eye on me so I don't have to go to Wellington to achieve my next target of making the U18 squad."

"It's the chance of a lifetime but you've obviously thought it through…As long as you're sure."

"I am, Dad."

"What about your A Levels?"

"I'll do them at West Park."

He smiled. "Lily's got nothing to do with this, has she?"

"Nothing at all, Dad."

*

Looking back on that final day at Oakwood was a sad reminder of the early problems that led to his parents' decision to separate. It was upsetting at the time, just a few weeks before his GCSE exams, but things were better now. Living with Mum and seeing Dad when he wanted to, turned out to be a reasonable arrangement. They went out for a meal together every other weekend and he sometimes stayed over. Sam thought Dad must be lonely rattling around on his own in the big house but he never asked. From what Dad said, he seemed to be spending more and more time at the office. Mum reckoned he might as well be living there.

He had set them up in a new house near to the hospital, not far from school, and on a regular bus route. Sam could get to places on his own and appreciated the independence of not having to rely on lifts from his parents. It was a comfortable three bedroomed new build on a small estate which had received a design award.

"Something Dad's yet to achieve," Mum said when she read the details. An unnecessary comment, Sam thought at the time. Tension between them was much reduced once they were living apart but there was still some point-scoring going on and divorce seemed inevitable although he discovered that Dad hadn't totally given up hope.

"I'd have her back tomorrow but I don't think she'd be interested," his father admitted during one of their evenings together.

Sam got a blunt reply when he asked his mother if it was possible. "Not a chance. It wouldn't work."

At least he knew where he stood, and when Mum started dating again (how weird that sounded) Lily took delight in reminding him how attractive she was.

"She's cool. Get ready. Sooner or later, she's going to find a new man…Sooner I reckon," she added with a grin.

# 5

Charlie was proud of her new addition, a pleasing way to celebrate her results. She was proud of them too. Everyone had expected her to do well but you still have to do the work. It was really irritating when teachers said that GCSEs were easy for clever girls. 'Wait till you get to A Levels. They're a proper challenge.' People like that didn't appreciate the hours she'd put in to get those A*s. Mum and Dad were pleased but she had felt the pressure of their expectation throughout the year. They didn't say much but she knew what they were thinking. Anything below an A would have been a disappointment to them. It was good to have it all behind her.

She would have to put up with going out for a family dinner tonight. Dad had insisted on booking the same table as he had when they all went out on his birthday.

"It's an important occasion. Your results were exceptional."

A bit dramatic, she thought. It would be a boring evening but Dad had promised wine and she could look forward to going out with Riya tomorrow. This time her brother Adi was tagging along. He was really fit and was starting at uni next term. She would enjoy getting to know him better.

Clare noticed the stud straight away. "Oh, Charlie what have you done?"

It was Mum's downbeat, tired sounding voice, the one she used when she was trying to stay calm.

"Riya has one."

"She's Indian."

"Actually, she's English."

"You know what I mean. They're part of her culture."

"So, why can't they be part of mine?"

"Thank god you didn't have a septum ring," Philip chipped in unhelpfully.

"I almost did, but I think this looks better," she said, turning her head and pointing proudly at her latest statement.

"I can't disagree with that."

"I'm glad you like it, Dad."

"That's not quite what I said, Charlie."

"It's titanium, which is the safest for sensitive skin – a bit more expensive but worth it."

"We're obviously giving you too large an allowance."

"Mine's about average – just below in fact. We've done a confidential class analysis."

"You've got an answer to everything."

Clare moved the conversation back on to health concerns. "You know it could cause an infection and leave scarring on the skin."

"Yes, I'll have to keep it clean – just like my ear hoops."

Charlie was quick to remind her mother that she had suffered no ill effects from previous piercings. "According to Ayurveda, having the nose pierced on the left side coincides with the reproductive organs and helps to reduce pain in childbirth."

"You're not trying that out any time soon, are you?"

"Of course not, Dad. Mum and I went through all the sex and drugs conversations *years* ago."

It was true, if a little overstated. Charlie liked to exaggerate time and statistics for effect.

"I'm going up to change."

She strode out of the kitchen flicking her hair back with a flourish as she went. Clare and Philip looked at each other with resigned expressions on their faces – not an unusual occurrence after conversations with Charlie.

"I suppose you deserve to be a little bit pleased with yourself when you've just achieved results like hers," Philip suggested.

"She's too spiky for my liking. No-one likes a smart arse. I think we've been too slack."

"It would've been a disaster if we'd been more confrontational. We've done our best and underneath the bolshie exterior there's a lovely girl trying to get out."

Clare wasn't convinced. "I just wish she'd stop testing the bloody boundaries all the time. I think I've lost her."

"No, you haven't. She needs you now more than ever. And she's coming out to dinner with us tonight," he added enthusiastically.

"Oh, lucky us. How kind of her to spare the time for a family celebration of *her* success."

Philip winced. "Then let's be pleased she's coming, and that she's done well."

"She's so self-centred…so entitled."

"Get ready. It won't be long before Sophie's in the zone."

"Thanks very much. That's just what I wanted to hear."

"Sorry." He paused. "It's hard being a parent, isn't it?"

Clare nodded and managed a smile. "And we don't do any training for it. God knows what it must be like to be a single parent with no-one else to share the burden."

*

Her parents and sister had been waiting in the hall for several minutes before Charlie came downstairs. She did her best to move like a fashion model in her shortest skirt and a skimpy top, cut low enough to make anyone at the pub stop and stare.

"I know it's a warm evening, Charlie, but I hadn't expected you to go out with quite so much skin showing."

Charlie was livid and made it obvious with her fiercest scowl. Dad's weak attempt at humour was typical. She hated it when he made comments about her clothes.

Then Sophie made things worse. "Your late and you look like you're in a girl band. We're only going to the pub."

Charlie's eyes flashed with resentment. She wanted to kick her father and strangle her sister. Her mother tried to soften the impact of the two annoying remarks.

"Why don't you take a jacket, darling, in case it gets chilly later." She unhooked Charlie's black leather jacket from the hatstand (it wasn't the ideal choice, but at least it covered up some of the exposed areas) put her arm round her shoulders and steered her through the front door to the car.

"We'll sit in the back, and let Dad and Sophie talk about football."

As soon as they were in the car Charlie turned away from Clare and started to fiddle with her phone. It was the last straw.

"Look Charlie, I know it must be a dreadful prospect for you to have to spend an evening out with us and your sister, but I'd appreciate it if you would show us all a little respect and behave properly."

Charlie looked up and shrugged her shoulders.

"And you can put your phone away when we're in the restaurant."

*

Considering its inauspicious start, the evening went surprisingly well. Charlie remembered the waiter – he was young and very good looking. Her mood changed when he gave her a smile of recognition and showed them to their table. She took off her leather jacket, hung it on the back of her chair and tucked her legs safely under the table. She could see Mum breathe a sigh of relief once her thighs were hidden.

Dad asked the waiter (I'm Rory and I'll be looking after you this evening) to bring over a bottle of sauvignon blanc straight away. Rory returned and put on an elaborate show of opening the bottle and pouring the wine which was clearly designed to impress. Charlie couldn't help noticing how tight his trousers were.

"You're staring," Sophie observed.

"So were you," Charlie responded, irritated once again by her little sister. Not so little now and getting worse by the day. I'm not sure I can stand this for the whole of the summer, she thought.

"That's enough ogling ladies. I want to propose a toast."

"Who to?"

"My brilliant daughter."

It was pathetically formal but at least Dad was making an effort. Despite her cynical view of adults, Charlie enjoyed being treated like one.

"Nice wine, Dad."

"It's good for us all to be out together, and we're proud of you."

"Even me," said Sophie.

*

When they arrived home the girls, 'had to catch up on their messages.'

"But you were on your phones for the whole journey home." Philip's protest fell on deaf ears and they both disappeared up to their rooms mumbling thankyous over their shoulders.

Having negotiated the evening without too many alarms Philip and Clare treated themselves to a nightcap. They sat quietly and let the whisky do its work. Clare broke the silence.

"Did you see the way the waiter was looking at Charlie?" she asked nervously. "I didn't like it."

"I was more concerned about the way she was looking at him."

"Well, he was rather dishy," she smiled. "Trouble is, she hasn't got the experience to handle the attention she's getting."

"I wonder if she realises what she's doing when she dresses like that."

"I'll have to talk to her."

"Better you than me."

"Your attempts at witty comments don't help, you know." She paused. "Do you think one day she might learn to laugh at herself?"

"God, I hope so."

Their worries tumbled out.

"Do you want a top up?"

"Why not. Yes please."

The shots were larger this time.

"You know, I've always had it in the back of my mind that Charlie would be better off in a co-ed environment, but now I kind of feel relieved she's at Chelston."

"It's the right place for her. Our Oxbridge preparation programme is way ahead of the other schools in the area. Now she's doing A Level she'll have to put up with being in my class. I'm going to be involved whether she likes it or not."

# 6

"Mum's with someone."

"See, I was right," Lily said triumphantly.

"No need to sound so pleased about it."

"What's the problem? It was bound to happen."

"I've never met him."

"So what. It's not your choice, Sam. It's good for your Mum to have a new man in her life… as long as he makes her happy," she added with a suggestive grin, followed by a giggle. "Who is he anyway?"

"He's a consultant at the hospital."

"Has he got a name?"

"Mike Ashcroft," he replied grudgingly.

"So, you know that much."

"Yeah, and he's married with twin daughters in year 8."

"Oh, my god. Didn't see that coming."

"Mum told me last night. She's been seeing him for a

while but his wife's found out and asked for a divorce. It's like she only mentioned it cos she had to…"

Lily squeezed his hand as they reached the point on their journey home from school where they usually separated. "Do you want to keep walking for a bit?"

"Yeah, that would be good. Give me some more time to think. It's serious. She said she's in love with him."

"You know, there's nothing *that* unusual about having an affair. These things happen."

"Why didn't she tell me?"

"She just has."

"Too fucking late."

"Are you jealous? Not being the most important man in her life anymore."

"That's a shitty thing to say. Are you on her side or something?"

"It's not about being on anyone's side but I'm just saying that your Mum's got every right to lead her own life. She'll be doing her own thing once you've moved on."

\*

Sam arrived home later than usual, went straight upstairs and shut himself in his room. He was angry. Talking to Lily should have helped, but it hadn't.

There was a knock at the door.

"Sam. Please speak to me. I didn't mean to hurt you."

No response.

"I've bought a couple of steaks. Let's talk over dinner."

Silence. He wouldn't forgive her that easily. Attempted bribery with one of his favourite meals was pathetic. She was obviously feeling guilty. Serves her right.

"I know you're upset but we really must get this all out in the open."

Still no reply. If it's that important why has it taken so long?

"OK, I'll put the jackets in the oven. I'll do the steaks when you come down."

He heard her footsteps on the stairs. If she's assuming that's it, no problem, then she's wrong. He tried to concentrate on his biology homework (he always wanted to do his best for Mrs Woods) but failed miserably. This wasn't a trivial thing she'd kept from him. It was a big deal, and he wouldn't forget it. Those weekends away with friends, extra nights on duty, the two day course in London… How many of them were lies?

But he would have to speak to her sooner or later. He was seeing Dad at the weekend and he wanted to know if he knew before they met.

An hour later pangs of hunger and the need to find out more led Sam down the stairs. He was still angry but the desire to hurt had weakened and a WhatsApp from Lily – *you MUST talk to her* – provided further encouragement.

"Why didn't you tell me before?"

"I wasn't sure where the relationship was going, so I waited. Then it got more serious and everything happened so quickly. I wanted to tell you but I kept putting it off. I couldn't face it."

"Why not?"

"I don't know. I knew I had to but I just couldn't. I suppose I was worried what you'd think of me." She hesitated. "Once I'd left it too long it got harder."

Sam threw his head back and rubbed his eyes with the heels of his hands.

"Look, I'm sorry. I should have told you. I do understand why you're angry. I wish I could turn the clock back. We've always been open with each other about the important things."

She raised her hand as he was about to speak.

"Before you say it, I know this *is* important. I got it wrong. I'll always regret not telling you sooner but I can't promise that there won't be other things that I keep to myself in the future. Have you told me everything about you and Lily and what goes on in your lives?"

Sam was stopped in his tracks. No, he hadn't. Some of the nights when Mum was away had provided opportunities for Lily to stay. They hadn't been honest with her parents or his mother about the arrangements but he wasn't going to admit to that now. Anyway, she probably knew. Not much escaped her notice. He recalled the heavy hints about contraception soon after he started going out with Lily. Best just to avoid the question.

"Does Dad know?"

"Yes. We had a drink together after work last week."

"How was he?"

"Not good." Jill paused. "I've asked him for a divorce."

Sam shook his head, said nothing, and Jill pressed on.

"He didn't look great. It was only six o'clock but he'd already been drinking. For quite a while I reckon. I think he's gone beyond just having a few beers with his mates."

It wasn't a surprise to Sam but he was keen to give his father the benefit of the doubt. "He's always enjoyed a drink. That doesn't mean it's a problem."

"I hope I'm wrong but he's under a lot of pressure at the moment. The business is struggling."

"He's never mentioned it to me. More stuff I don't know about. I'm not a kid anymore."

"I know you're not but surely you can understand why Dad wouldn't want to worry you with his business problems."

Sam thought for a moment. He could, but he was still angry at being treated as if he couldn't be trusted with important things. "So, what are the problems?"

"A big development he was working on has fallen through because of a planning issue. He didn't give much away but I know he invested a lot of money in the land. I think he's overstretched himself."

Jill changed the subject and tried to sound more encouraging. "He's looking forward to taking you to squad training at the weekend."

Sam felt sad. His anger at Mike Ashcroft's arrival on the scene was briefly put in the background by his worries about everything going wrong for his father.

"He's not so embarrassing as he used to be."

They couldn't help smiling. That and the need to avoid letting their meal get cold provided a helpful break from the conversation. Sam gobbled his food with nervous energy while Jill ate with slow concentration on the accurate slicing of her meat and the enjoyment of inspecting the medium rare interior before popping in the next mouthful. Sam finished well ahead of her and looked vacantly around the kitchen while waiting for her to catch up. He couldn't stand up and do anything until Mum had finished. He didn't want to give her the opportunity to criticise him for his table manners. She had always had a thing about those. He wished he hadn't rushed. The silence, welcome at first, became excruciating. Eating had given him something to do. His mother seemed to be getting calmer as he became more agitated.

At last, she put her knife and fork together and sat back in her chair. "Mike wants to take us out to dinner so he can meet you."

What should he say? He wasn't ready to accept the situation and move on obediently as if nothing had happened. Yes, she had apologised but was that it? What did she expect? All forgiven. Get over it.

"To be honest, I'm not sure I want to meet him. I'm still getting used to the idea that he exists."

"I know it's difficult for you but he does, and as he's going to be part of my life you'll have to meet at some stage. The sooner the better for all of us."

"Mum," he whined. "It's not as easy as that. You don't understand… Not a fucking clue," he shouted as he pounded up the stairs.

As soon as he reached the haven of his room, Sam began to regret losing his temper. A row with Mum was rare. He disliked confrontation except on a rugby pitch where he relished the contest and would never back down. He needed to talk to Lily. It wasn't too late to call but he had to calm down first. He sat on his bed, stared at his feet and breathed in deeply just like he did on the changing room bench before a match.

Lily answered quickly. It felt as if she had been waiting for the call.

"Hi, Sam. How'd it go?"

"Not good. We had a row."

"Not surprising. She feels guilty and you're angry but you'll have to keep talking. It's the only way. Mike isn't going to go away." She paused. "I've spoken to my Mum about the situation."

"Why'd you do that."

"Why not for chrissake?"

"I don't want everyone talking about it."

"Trust me. They won't," she said impatiently. "By the way, my Mum's not everyone. She knows you and likes you."

"Sorry."

"She says if your Mum's got a second chance at a serious relationship, she has to take it. If Mike makes her happy why shouldn't she?"

"What about me?"

"Oh my god Sam. That's so selfish. You'll be leaving school and moving on at the end of the year. Busy playing rugby if all goes well. Your Mum will be on her own. She needs to look after herself. Can't you see that?"

He could only shrug his shoulders. "She wants me to meet him."

"Of course she does. You must."

"She's changed."

"So have you – and me. People do."

Sam found Lily's attitude hard to take – lecturing him like an older sister as if the situation was no big deal. Why couldn't she be more sympathetic? He had fallen out with his mother and now he was arguing with his girlfriend, all because of someone he'd never even met. He moved on – wounded.

"I've got to talk to Dad. I need to know how he feels about it."

"You do that. But it won't change anything."

"See you tomorrow."

# 7

Prior to going to the training weekend Sam had convinced his father not to book into the same hotel as the players, coaches and selectors – a potential embarrassment out of the way – and explained that they would not have much time together except in the car on the way to and from the Midlands Club which was hosting it. He also broached the tricky subject of what his father was going to do while they were there.

"I'll be busy with the squad from Friday evening until midday on Sunday."

"Don't worry about me, Sam. I've brought some work with me and I'll watch the training sessions."

"What, all of them?"

"Why not? It'll be good to see national coaches at work."

"Promise me you won't get too close. This is a bigger deal than the U16 stuff. It's not cool to have your Dad hanging around. We're close to being professional players. A lot of the guys will have offers of Academy contracts in the next few months."

"Including you I hope."

"I hope so too, but…" He struggled to get the words out. "This is so hard. Look Dad, I'm glad you're taking me. Your support means a lot but I don't want you to-to interfere."

"What do you mean, interfere?"

"You say things. People can hear."

"I can't help being proud of you."

"It puts pressure on me, you know."

"What does?"

"Your expectations. Worrying about what you're going to say. I'll do better if I can't see or hear you."

"God, that bad, is it?"

Sam nodded.

"OK, I'll keep well away."

A surge of relief gave Sam the confidence to go further. "And promise not to speak to any of the coaches."

"Promise." He paused. "So why haven't you told me this before?"

You knew, Sam thought. Mum told you. More than once, but it wasn't worth bringing that up. Maybe it would make a difference now it had come from him.

"It was too difficult, Dad. I just couldn't."

*

Jill was at work when Paul picked Sam up on Friday after school. Better that way. It was awkward on the rare occasions when the three of them were together. In the current situation it would have been even more tricky.

He thought of his mother's comments when he saw his father's red face and caught a slight smell of mouthwash as he got into the car. He tried to put his worries behind him as they settled into the journey and talked rugby, mostly focussed on Sam's chances of getting an Academy contract. He found it easier to have conversations with his father when they were in the car sitting side by side. Not having to make eye contact made him feel more confident and he was on fertile ground discussing Dad's favourite subject.

Mum was less keen. Although she had grudgingly accepted that Sam's main ambition in life was to be a professional rugby player, she wasn't convinced that it was the right environment for him and he suspected that she secretly hoped he wouldn't be quite good enough. The training weekend was an important step in his quest to get a contract. He needed to perform well. One or two clubs had shown some interest but he decided to keep that information to himself. No point in raising Dad's hopes until he had something more concrete.

It was a relief when Dad asked about Mike Ashcroft. Sam wanted to have the conversation but was nervous about starting it.

"So, what do you think of this Ashcroft guy?"

"I've never met him."

"Oh. Your mother didn't mention that."

Dad usually referred to her as Mum. 'Your mother' was a sign that he was annoyed.

"I'd never heard of him until last weekend."

"So, I was just a few days ahead of you then. She's been living a bloody lie for months."

He switched on the radio, turned up the volume and concentrated on his driving with fierce intensity. It was as if he had joined a race a lap late and needed to catch up. Sam began to take surreptitious looks at the speedometer until they hit eighty five on a busy stretch of dual carriageway. He had never dared to comment on his father's driving before but he was frightened by how close they were to the vehicle in front and couldn't help himself. "We're in plenty of time, Dad. No need to rush."

A convenient set of lights at a major junction slowed the traffic down and forced a return to some sort of driving normality.

"Sorry Dad but…"

There was a strained silence for several minutes before anything else was said but at least it served to calm them down.

"There was no need to apologise Sam. My fault. I was driving too fast… She's asked for a divorce, you know," he added with a tremor in his voice.

"Yes, she told me."

"Truth is, it was only a matter of time. We've been living apart for a while now. Getting back together was never going to happen. I was kidding myself. What Mike bloody smart-arse surgeon has done is to give her the incentive to ask."

"Mum wants me to meet him. Lily says I should."

"You sound as if you don't like the idea. I get that but I'm afraid Lily's right. If your mother's serious about him, and she says she is, then you can't pretend he doesn't exist. Neither can I, come to that."

*

After the unwelcome arrival of Mike Ashcroft into his life, a stonking row with Mum, some less than sympathetic responses from Lily and surviving Dad's scary attempt to emulate Lewis Hamilton, settling into the hotel and meeting old friends and new faces from the rugby circuit was a breath of fresh air. The atmosphere was heady, full of camaraderie and competitiveness. These were the best players in England for their age and every one of them was dedicated to the idea of making a career out of the sport they loved. Gossip about who was going where, which clubs were recruiting for which positions and who had already been offered a contract dominated the conversation. It helped Sam to clear his head of the family complications that had upset him during the last couple of weeks. For the next two days he had to concentrate on making his mark during training and coming across as the kind of personality who could cope with the challenges of professional sport.

Paul had dropped him off at the squad hotel and while getting Sam's kit out of the boot he reiterated the promise to keep his distance. Their knowing smiles suggested that something had changed to bring them closer. His father inched forward and for a moment Sam thought he was about to get a hug but it didn't quite happen. "Good luck, son."

He quickly grabbed his bag to cover up his embarrassment. "Er. Thanks Dad. What's your plan for tonight?"

"Not a lot. I'll have few drinks before dinner. See who's around. There might be a hen party in the bar if I'm lucky."

Sad. But he couldn't worry about Dad now. It was rugby that mattered and he wasn't going to let anything get in the way. His PE teacher had drummed into him that dedication and concentration under pressure were the hallmarks of the great players. "If you're going to make it, it's the top few inches that really count." Sam was determined to make sure that his top few inches were fully engaged for the challenge ahead.

"See you on Sunday."

"I'll be here at one, OK."

"Fine."

*

His father was true to his word. Sam was amused by the thought of him straining at a self-imposed leash. At one point on Saturday afternoon while the scrum halves were being put through their paces, he almost laughed out loud when he spotted him leaning casually against a tree beyond an adjacent pitch trying to appear inconspicuous. He also kept well away from the touchline during the series of competitive match sessions which completed the day's work. It meant a lot that Dad was doing his best to stick to their agreement. Recent events had made Sam realise that having his support mattered more than he cared to admit.

Sam had heard the night before that an academy coach from Bath would be watching the training. This was a club with a location and reputation which excited him. What an opportunity! He was already highly motivated to perform at his best but the possibility of joining Bath gave him an extra incentive to work his butt off and ensure that his skills and fitness were noticed.

At the end of the afternoon he was heading back to the changing rooms when he was approached by a man wearing a Bath tracksuit top. His face seemed familiar but Sam couldn't place him. The sight of the Bath logo was enough to make his heart beat faster. Keep cool. For fuck's sake don't embarrass yourself. This could be the most important conversation of your life.

"Hi, Sam. I'm Mitch James." Sam wiped his sweaty palms on his shirt before shaking hands. "You may not remember, you were with a group of your mates, but we met briefly after the U16 match v Wales. You had a good game that day."

"Thanks."

"Being Welsh I was a bit disappointed that you played so well."

His warm smile helped Sam to relax a little but he could still feel the weight of hope and expectation pressing down on him.

"And you looked in good shape today, too."

"Thanks." No other words would come, but what else was he supposed to say?

"Have you sorted out what your plans are after you're A levels?"

The big question. Be calm. Talk sensibly. "I'd like to give professional rugby a go if I get the chance."

"Well, I just might be able to help with that."

*

They talked of nothing but rugby on the journey home. The family tensions were forgotten in the euphoria of Sam's success.

"I can't believe it Dad. It's a dream come true. He knew a lot about me. Even my offer from Wellington College."

"He'd obviously done his homework."

"I start pre-season training after I finish my A Levels."

"I'm really chuffed for you Sam but just a word of caution. It's not a done deal until you've got something in writing."

Sam didn't let Dad's business caution dampen his enthusiasm. He knew that formal details had to be tied up and Mitch had told him that this would be sorted out within the next few weeks.

"Mitch James is dealing with it, Dad. I'm sure it'll be OK."

"You going to tell your mother tonight?"

"Yeah, and I'll call Lily."

They arrived home in good time having enjoyed a calmer journey than the previous one. Jill opened the front door while Paul was helping Sam to get his bags out of the boot. Memories of their tense week were still fresh but the weekend success had changed Sam's mood. He had come to the conclusion that he would have to get used to the new situation and try to make peace with Mum.

"Hi Sam. Hello, Paul. Journey OK?"

"Yeah, not too bad."

"Thanks for taking him."

"No problem."

"Do you fancy a cup of tea?"

Mum's trying hard, Sam thought.

"No thanks. I'd better head home. I've got some work to do for tomorrow."

Paul turned towards Sam who was standing on the pavement with a bag either side of him. His arms reached out and Sam responded, awkwardly at first but then with more enthusiasm. It was the first time they had hugged for years.

# 8

"I suppose I've got a load of washing to do."

Sam grinned as he nodded. "The blue bag's the dirty stuff."

"It's about time you learnt how to use the washing machine. I've been too soft on you."

"No problem. Show me now."

Jill's eyes widened in surprise. "You're in a good mood."

"It's been a good weekend."

"It's a long time since I last saw you and your Dad hug."

"Yeah, it is."

"How did it go?"

"Fine."

"You obviously got on alright."

"Yeah, but we were only together when we were in the car. Dad watched but kept out of the way and left me to it. He was virtually hiding behind a tree at one point hoping I couldn't see him. So weird."

"Nothing too embarrassing then."

"No. He was OK." It felt as if his mother was searching for something that had gone wrong. "Actually, we got on really well."

Sam hoped she wouldn't ask questions about Dad's reactions to the Mike Ashcroft situation and felt a sudden spasm of guilt when he remembered that he hadn't asked him how things were at work. It soon passed. There was no way that he would have received a straight answer. Dad tended to keep things to himself as far as his business dealings were concerned.

He was keen to tell Mum about the contract with Bath but wondered what her reaction would be. He didn't expect her to be over the moon like Dad but hoped she would be pleased for him despite her reservations. He decided to wait until after six o'clock. She was generally more relaxed with a glass of white wine in her hand.

"I'm going upstairs, Mum. I need to call Lily."

"What about the washing? I thought you wanted a lesson."

He was already three steps on his way but saw the smile on her face as he looked round. A good sign. He smiled back.

"Alright, go on. But I'm definitely going to show you next time."

*

"I've been offered a contract with Bath."

"Cool. Well done. Have you told your Mum?"

"Not yet."

"Do you think she'll be OK with it?"

"I'm not sure. It's what I want to do. She knows that."

"I think she'd prefer you to go to uni."

"I knew you'd bring that up. Look, you want to be a nurse and I want to play rugby for England. We both have our dreams."

"Mine will happen and yours is unlikely."

"That's harsh," he replied sharply. She should be pleased with his success. He was used to hearing the blunt truth from Lily but this was unkind point scoring, a side to her personality which he didn't find attractive. Was it his fault or were her A Level aspirations getting to her? Maybe both.

"You told me that the step up to being a full time professional was, like, massive. Very few make it."

"Yeah, that's true," he admitted. "But I'll never forgive myself if I don't give it a go."

"Can't you play rugby and go to university?"

"Some do but I don't think it'd work for me. I need to concentrate on one thing to have any chance of making a success of it."

"So, you're telling your Mum tonight."

"When I've poured her a glass of wine."

"Good tactics."

*

"I have to give it a try, Mum. I'll regret it for the rest of my life if I don't."

"It's not the career I'd have chosen for you but it's a great achievement. If it's what you want you must go for it."

"Thanks Mum."

"I knew it was coming, so I was ready. Bath's not too far from Cardiff either. That's Lily's first choice isn't it?"

"As long as she gets her grades."

"Oh, she'll get them. I don't think there's any doubt about that. She's a very determined girl." She paused. "Promise me one thing."

"Yes," he replied immediately without thinking what he might be agreeing to do.

"Please get the best A levels you can. They might be useful one day."

Sam nodded. It was a promise that he took seriously. He wanted to do well and hoped he wasn't too late to put in a burst and prove the doubters wrong.

Jill sipped her wine. "Now, about Mike."

That didn't take her long. He would have liked a little more time to discuss his future, especially now the way forward was clearly mapped out, at least for the next year or two. He had to meet Mike but his plan was to keep him at a distance, part of Mum's new life but preferably not his.

"He wants to take us out to dinner on Friday night and asked if you'd like Lily to join us."

Sam thought about it. In some ways it would make the evening easier but was this Mum's idea? Lily would charm him in her usual way but what if she liked him and he didn't? That would make life complicated. He didn't really want Lily's opinion unless it was the same as his. Anyway, there was no reason for her to meet him so soon. He'd make up his own mind first.

"Just the three of us, if that's alright."

"OK." She shrugged her shoulders and failed to hide her disappointment. "Mike and I were talking about you and Lily this weekend."

Sam wanted to say 'why' but could only manage a low pitched, "Oh."

"You know I'm very fond of Lily so please don't take this the wrong way. You've hardly had a day without seeing each other for the last couple of years. It won't be the same when you go your separate ways. Long distance relationships are difficult."

This was nothing new. Lily had brought up the subject when she was putting in her UCAS application and they had discussed it several times since. Sam resented the idea of Mum having conversations with Mike about him and Lily. It was none of his business. Was this what he would have to get used to?

"We're not stupid, Mum. We know it'll be different. Being in Bath will make it easier. You said that yourself."

"Yes, you'll be closer than you might have been but you'll both be busy doing new things and it'll be hard."

"We'll have to get used to it won't we. A lot of people do," he replied impatiently.

There was a strained atmosphere for the rest of the evening. Sam's hopes of an easy return to the pre-Mike relationship with his mother were undermined. He had never met the man but it felt as if he was already having an unwanted influence on his life.

*

They met at *The Coach and Horses*, a popular old coaching inn with an excellent restaurant. It looked to Sam like a place for special occasions. He had never been but discovered that Mum had eaten there several times in the last few months. They were already at the bar having a drink when Mike arrived twenty minutes late. He was tall and well-built but skinny light blue jeans and a classic blazer with brass buttons was not a good look as far as Sam was concerned. A pink shirt with too many buttons undone and a pair of highly polished pointed black shoes added to the impression of an older man trying too hard to look cool. His hair was grey-tinged, long and swept back over his ears in a theatrical style. Sam had been taught to beware of first impressions but he often found that his early instincts about people were pretty accurate. In this case he was immediately struck by the feeling that Mike was someone who thought a lot of himself.

"Hi Sam. I've been looking forward to meeting you."

"Hi."

They shook hands firmly. Mike kissed Jill on the cheek and turned to wave at the barmaid to catch her attention. "The usual please Sally and another one for my guests. Is the table ready?"

He spoke louder than necessary and drew the attention of several other customers gathered in groups near the bar.

"Yes, Mike. It was ready for the time that you booked it," she replied bluntly.

Sam smiled. I like her, he thought. She doesn't take any bullshit.

"Let's go and sit down then."

Mike steered them through to what he called his favourite table and held Jill's chair while she sat down. Sam wondered if he always did, or was it just for his benefit?

The drinks and menus arrived.

"Wouldn't you like something stronger, Sam?"

"No thanks. Coke's fine. I'm driving."

"Your mother's lucky to have a chauffeur."

"To be honest, I don't do it very often."

Recommendations were made about the choices on offer and Sam was pleased to see that it was a traditional menu so he wasn't pushed out of his comfort zone by foody language he didn't understand.

"Don't hold back, Sam. Big occasion this. No expense spared."

Was he supposed to feel grateful or impressed? Sam decided on the smoked salmon starter followed by sirloin steak and triple cooked chips. He wondered why they needed cooking three times. Chips were chips, weren't they?

"So, I hear last weekend went well. Congratulations on the Bath offer."

"Thanks."

"I hope you know what you're letting yourself in for. Us orthopods see a lot of collision injuries through rugby."

Sam saw his mother wince. He kept quiet. What could he say? Of course he knew.

Mike carried on digging an even deeper hole. "Too tough a game for my liking. I've always preferred football myself. I was pretty good at it. Played in the first team. Got Full Colours. Got them for cricket as well but after school the medical career took over and I didn't have the time to play sport."

Sam was unimpressed. If he was so good why didn't he find the time.

"How do you keep fit then?"

If Mike was disconcerted by Sam's question, he didn't show it. "I'm ashamed to say that I don't do enough. I jog occasionally but that's about it. I'm lucky to have the sort of metabolism that burns off the calories."

"It's not fair," Jill intervened. "Doesn't matter what he eats or drinks, it makes no difference… Rose and Grace want to meet you," she added randomly.

Mum was obviously keen to change the subject.

"Yes, Sam they can't wait. Apparently, you're a bit of a legend at school."

He wasn't sure whether Mike was trying to be funny or complimentary but he smiled politely and asked how they were enjoying school. That'll please Mum, he thought.

"They seem happy and their reports have been good."

Sam expected Mike to respond in greater detail but he seemed more interested in inspecting his wine, swirling it round with an elaborate flourish and sniffing it as if he was an expert.

"A good nose," he announced before taking a sip. "Mmm, excellent. Mind you it ought to be. It's the most expensive on the list."

As the evening progressed Sam wondered how the twins would be affected by the family situation. He'd found it hard enough when Mum and Dad split up in less dramatic circumstances so it wouldn't be easy for them. It was embarrassing that his mother was involved. They won't like her for what she's done, he thought. What she saw in Mike he could only guess but he knew enough to understand that there was no accounting for taste.

*

Lily called soon after he got home.

"How'd it go?"

"OK."

"Come on. What does that mean?"

"OK. The pub was good and he paid."

"For god's sake. What did you think of him?"

"A bit of a plonker. Sad. He tries to look younger than he is."

"Is that it?"

"He's too pleased with himself and has a voice that booms out. He had a go at rugby too. That pissed me off."

"You were never going to give him a chance."

"He also had too much to drink and drove himself home. Mum was always strict about Dad not doing that."

"You'd already made up your mind."

"That's not fair. I hadn't."

"So, prove it. Tell me something you liked."

Sam paused. Did she have a point? Had he put up a barrier before they even met? Probably, yes, but the fact was that he didn't fucking like him.

"Hey, you still there?"

"Yeah. Give me a chance... Er – he told me his daughters think I'm a legend." He grinned as he said it and imagined Lily's face at the other end of the phone.

"Well aren't I *so* lucky to be going out with an eighteen year old legend."

# 9

Sam was true to his word. In the final months at West Park High he worked hard at his books, harder than he had ever done. He surprised his parents and Lily, but more significantly, himself. The security of having written confirmation of his Academy Contract and the knowledge that the first stage of his professional rugby career was in place had given him confidence and strengthened his commitment to A levels. He began to think, 'I can do this'. Mrs Woods had always believed in him but other teachers began to notice his improvement. He did have some academic bones in his body after all. He might just get some decent grades. They were pleased to have the school's best sportsman showing commitment to his work. It was a good example to other students.

Lily was determined to secure her grades for Cardiff so she kept him at it but it meant that they saw each other less often.

"After what your Mum said we need to prove we can manage being apart from each other."

Sam sometimes wished he hadn't told her about that awkward conversation but on the plus side Lily's opinion of Mike had turned out to be similar to his. She'd admitted it after meeting him when she came for Sunday lunch at home.

"You were right, Sam. He's totally up himself, a bit creepy. So, you weren't against him just because he stole your Mum."

Sam laughed at the time. They both did. He enjoyed hearing Lily admit she was wrong (it didn't happen very often) but he was sad that Mum had chosen someone he couldn't respect. It was an expression Lily used again when Mike was first invited for a long weekend. Overnight stays had already become more regular and Sam resented this extended intrusion into the family home. To him it was another unwelcome sign of Mike's growing influence.

"He's stolen her for the whole weekend, has he? Or has she stolen him?" she added with a grin.

"It could be either, I suppose," Sam grudgingly admitted. "Shit. I can't wait to leave home."

"Your Mum probably feels the same."

Another blunt assessment which Lily swiftly softened with an invitation. "You'll have to come and stay at mine then… if you like."

Being at Lily's was always a breath of fresh air but this time it was a lifeline. It meant that he could get out of the way. 'Get out of the way.' It was sad, but that's how he felt. Mike's smug presence was hard to take and the thought of what was going on in the bedroom down the corridor made him squirm. Headphones pumping out loud music was his go to solution but the disturbing images wouldn't go away.

Lily's parents knew the situation. They were kind to him and made him feel welcome. They had accepted the fact he and Lily were sleeping together and were relaxed about them being at home.

"You're both grown up now, Sam. We trust you."

Those three words were huge. It was so good to be treated like an adult.

The big question was inevitable but it still made him angry when it came.

"Do you mind if Mike moves in Sam. The rental on his flat runs out soon and he might as well live here rather than carry on paying out whatever it is a month. It's a waste."

He did mind. She might have waited until after his exams. It wasn't long before they would be over and he'd be off to Bath to start his career. Why couldn't they wait until he left? And how could he say no? He was being put in an impossible position. Nightmare.

"I don't really have an option, do I? It's not my house."

He knew it was a confrontational response and that the subsequent frost would take time to thaw but he couldn't hold back. If ever there was a moment when he felt overtaken in his mother's list of priorities, this was it.

"I'm sorry you feel like that Sam. I was hoping we could make Mike feel welcome."

The conversation ended there and Mike moved in a week later.

*

The forthcoming exams gave Sam a good excuse to keep out of the way. He spent hours in his room, working, chatting to Lily on the phone during his breaks and dreaming about the exciting times ahead. Lily was strict about Saturday being their only day off and insisted that he should take work round to her place if he was staying overnight.

Sam also found refuge at home with his father. He felt guilty that he hadn't spent more time with him in the past but Mike's arrival on the scene had brought them closer together and given him the incentive.

"You can stay here whenever you want Sam. It's great to have someone else in the house. It's a bit lonely coming home to an empty place every night. Lily's always welcome too, you know," he added with a wink. "She's been a good influence on you."

It was sad to see Dad looking worn out and depressed. He had never seemed to have many friends, not ones that Sam knew anyway. Mum had often said there were work colleagues and pub mates but no one close. Sam hoped that he could cheer him up by being around more often and Mum didn't seem to worry about seeing less of him. She had other things on her mind – mostly Mike.

He made himself comfortable in the bedroom which had been his ever since his parents first moved in. It felt odd coming back to it when they separated but he was younger then. Now he appreciated it, especially with the advantage of an open invitation to Lily. Dad was working extraordinarily long hours and much of the time Sam was left to his own devices but it did make him feel more independent compared with living at Mum's. He enjoyed the freedom of being trusted to get on with his own life.

Dad's attitude to academic work had changed. "It's good to see you working hard at your A levels. I hate to admit it but your mother was right. I was too keen on your sport and didn't encourage your academic efforts enough when you were younger."

Sam smiled. "Yeah, you were really keen. Sport was fun but being in a classroom was a struggle. Academic stuff didn't really matter to me."

"When did it first start to matter?"

"Hearing the under sixteen coaches talking about the dangers of 'putting all your eggs in the rugby basket.' They were always going on about young players risking too much if they didn't give themselves options other than rugby."

"Your GCSEs were good."

"OK, but I didn't really do myself justice. I should've done better."

"Better late than never."

"Yeah. I'm never going to be an academic but I'd like to prove that I'm not totally stupid."

"You're not. I'd employ you any time."

"You're biased."

"Course I am but that doesn't mean I'm wrong. Anyway, you've got more exciting things ahead of you than working for a small building company."

"How's it going? You seem to be working all the time."

"Following your example," he replied with a smile. He paused long enough for Sam to suspect that he was about to get the usual evasive answer. "It's tough times but we'll get there… Let's have a beer."

# 10

As Sam walked through the entrance to the school holding Lily's hand, he felt the same emptiness in his stomach and heaviness in his legs as he had two years before when he collected his GCSE results. The buildings matched his mood: bleak yellow bricks, flat roofs, ugly windows and peeling paintwork. He hadn't thought about it before but now he had left he realised that they were in desperate need of a makeover.

He could have received the results by email but Lily thought it would be more of an event if they went into school and met some of their mates so he and a couple of the other guys got permission from the Academy Manager to go back home to get their results. It was also a chance to see Lily after three weeks apart. He had never been so nervous. This was scarier than going out to play for England. What if the results went badly? He wouldn't want to see anybody if they did. Perhaps this wasn't such a good idea after all… Too late.

For Lily, it was a place at Cardiff at stake. In Sam's case it was the fear of failing to do himself justice again, especially after having worked hard for the last four months. If that happened it would confirm that he really was stupid.

"Shall we open them together?"

"You go first," Sam replied.

Lily looked nervously at the slip of paper in her hand. A smile appeared. She screamed with joy and threw her arms around him. "I've done it. AAB."

"That's awesome Lily."

Now the pressure was really on. Lily's success had made his results matter more. He fiddled nervously with his envelope.

"Come on Sam," she said impatiently. "Get on with it."

His hand was unsteady as he unfolded the print-out and it took him a while to focus on the details. He looked stunned.

"What's the matter?"

He handed the paper over for Lily to read. "ABC. Like, that's good, isn't it?"

He smiled with relief. "Really good. Better than I was expecting."

Just for a moment it crossed his mind how well he might have done if he had shown full commitment throughout the course but it soon passed. He had proved to himself that he wasn't too bad at the academic stuff and was chuffed.

Lily was buzzing. "We both got As in Biology. Mrs Woods is amazing."

They hugged each other again. It was a moment to remember for the rest of their lives. Students were milling about in the main classroom block in various states of excitement. Fear, joy, screams, tears, misery, laughter, panic, relief – uninhibited emotions were on display after weeks of tension.

Mrs Woods appeared. "Well done you two. Great results."

Lily was still beaming with excitement and it was an added pleasure to see Mrs Woods so soon after receiving the good news. Not all the staff came to school when results were out but she had a reputation for being the most conscientious of teachers. She was admired by everyone.

"You got us both As, Miss. Thanks so much."

"I'm proud of you both. In fact, the whole of your set did well but what a brilliant year for you two. A place at Cardiff, a contract at Bath and those results. Wow." She grinned conspiratorially at Lily. "I must admit that I was confident about yours right from the start, Lily, but Sam's were more like a last minute try to win the match."

They all laughed. Sam thought it was a fair comparison. It was easier to enjoy a joke at your own expense when it was the result of success.

"How did Charlie do Miss?"

"Very well thanks Sam." He noticed the understated way Mrs Woods answered. He guessed she wouldn't want to appear too proud of her daughter's results when she was with her own pupils. But he wanted to know her grades. All those A*s at GCSE must have led to something special.

"What did she get?"

"Four A*s," she said quietly.

"That's awesome. She's brilliant. Tell her well done from me, Miss."

"Thanks Sam. I will."

Once he and Lily had calmed down and spoken to a few friends Sam texted the good news to his parents from outside the school gates.

*ABC for me and AAB for Lily*

Sam's Mum responded immediately. *So proud of you!!! And Lily x*

But nothing came back from his father.

They decided to walk home and chat quietly on their own to enjoy the feeling of satisfaction at their success. The future was sorted, well at least in the short term. They both agreed that the final year at school had been tough. Life as they knew it was about to change but what was happening next was uncertain. Sam's early offer of a contract at Bath had been a great help but Lily's hopes had only been confirmed in the last hour. Thank god that was all over.

"You were super keen to know Charlie's results. What was that all about?"

"Just being polite."

"You fancy her, don't you?"

"I've hardly seen her since her since I left Primary school."

"You were all over her when we saw her at that party."

He grinned. "She did look fit."

She stopped walking and flicked her hair in annoyance. "That's so the wrong answer."

Sam enjoyed the moment. "You weren't jealous, were you?"

"Piss off."

He took refuge by looking at his phone. "Dad still hasn't got back to me."

"Carry on like this and it'll be me ignoring you."

*

It was Saturday night before Sam heard from his father. He was back in Bath in the pub celebrating his results with some of the academy lads when his phone pinged.

*Well done on the A levels. I may have been a bit of a tit at times but I'm proud of you. Dad*

Sam was touched by the words but they seemed odd. It didn't sound like him.

But it was only a text. He shouldn't read too much into it.

# 11

"You're not going to do anything too adventurous to celebrate your results, are you, darling?"

Charlie could read her mother like a book. She loved her and thought that as parents go, she was above average. However, she was prepared to admit that she found it difficult to resist the temptation to wind her up with occasional impulsive gestures.

"I thought I might have another tattoo. Adi and I are going into town to check out some designs."

"*Please* promise me you won't have one on your face."

"Don't worry, Mum. It's going on my back." She twisted round and tapped the bottom of her spine. "Adi says they look sexy just down here. He thinks the one on my ankle's boring."

"At least I won't have to look at it."

"Not unless I'm in my bikini or a crop top."

"Do you have to do everything Adi says?"

Charlie thought he was beautiful, everyone said so, even Mum had admitted it in an unguarded moment. The girls at school thought she was lucky to be going out with someone two years older and already at university. He had introduced Charlie to student life in London and she was grateful for all he had taught her, but her parents had never really taken to him. He was too smooth and had a touch of arrogance that jarred. His family were highly motivated by material things and Adi was no exception. His ambition was to make a shed load of money and to enjoy all the benefits it provided. Charlie understood that this was not a philosophy of which her parents approved. In her heart she agreed with them but Adi was ideal as a first serious catch and gave her street cred to die for.

"Actually, I've not made my final decision. Adi's got a bit of a thing about tattoos. He finds them arousing."

"I'm getting too much information now, Charlie." She paused. "It's important not to give a man everything he wants, you know."

Occasionally Mum came out with something worth remembering. Charlie tucked it away and moved on.

"How were *your* results?" She knew that would change the mood. She and Sophie sometimes felt that Mum's pupils were more important to her than her daughters.

"Thanks for asking. They went well. Very well actually. Four As out of twelve in the set and no fails. One of the As was a pleasant surprise from Sam Martin. Remember him."

"Of course I do. I bumped into him at a party a while ago. He was with his girlfriend. I'm not sure she was happy that we talked for such a long time. It was good to see him."

"She got an A too. She was the one who encouraged Sam to work harder. He did much better than expected. He's going to be a professional rugby player."

"He was mad keen on sport when we were at Oakwood."

"He's grown into a really nice young man."

"One of your projects?"

"All my pupils are projects. No favourites."

"But some more enjoyable to teach than others." Charlie smiled. She mustn't overdo the teasing and needed to get on to the problem that was worrying her.

"There's something important I need to talk to you about."

"I can't imagine what that might be."

"Dad will be horrified."

"That's a strong word. He's usually reasonably balanced about things."

"Not this."

"Oh, for god's sake Charlie, spit it out."

Charlie took a deep breath. "I don't want to go to Cambridge."

"Ah."

"I'd rather go to Imperial. Dad's bound to blame Adi and it's not his fault. It's totally my decision, and he won't believe me."

She spoke in a rush to get the bad news out as quickly as possible but she knew that Mum who was not totally persuaded by the idea that Oxbridge had unrivalled superiority might have some sympathy with her view. It didn't suit everyone and there were plenty of other fine universities in the UK. Mum had enjoyed the buzz of living in London as a student at King's and took great pleasure in reminding Dad that her first was worth more than his Desmond Tutu.

"OK, so convince me that I should believe you."

"I know all about the advantages of going to Cambridge and all the crap about the distinction of attending one of the ancient universities, but I'd prefer to be in London."

"Why?"

"When I went for interview in Cambridge, I couldn't get excited about the idea of studying there. The city centre was beautiful but crawling with tourists, and it felt small and a bit up itself. I just don't want to go there... And Imperial also has a world class reputation for engineering," she added for good measure.

"Dad will be disappointed, Charlie. He wanted you to follow in his footsteps."

"I know. He taught me and prepared me really well, but, if I'm honest, getting in seemed to be more important to him than me. We never talked about whether I would actually enjoy it. And it really isn't about Adi, I promise. It's just that I'd rather be in London. It's more exciting, and Imperial's one of the best and most diverse universities in the world."

"You don't have to convince me of that."

"Do you think he'll understand?"

"I'm sure he will – in the end. Leave it to me. I'll talk to him. He's very proud of you, you know. And he will be wherever you go."

*

"It's that bloody Adi. He has too much influence over her. I thought we'd brought her up to be an independent young woman."

"She is, and she's showing it by making her decision. And I can assure you it's *not* about Adi."

"So why has she left it until the last minute?"

"Sometimes, Philip, you're surprisingly dim. She knew you'd be upset and is worried that you'll think she's let you down."

"Well, I am upset. It's the chance of a lifetime to go to Cambridge."

"But it's her life not yours. This isn't about you."

"Why can't she take a gap year to give herself more time. It's a huge decision."

"I thought you didn't believe in gap years. You've always said they're an indulgent waste of time."

"Yes, but this is different. It's her whole life at stake."

"That's ridiculous, Philip. You're not thinking straight. She'll be going to one of the best universities in the world."

Philip had nothing more to say and shrugged his shoulders in defeat. "OK. Whatever I say is clearly not going to make any difference. So, what's the plan?"

"We're going to sit down this evening, have a glass of wine together and give our full support to her decision."

*

Charlie hugged her Mum with real enthusiasm after a much easier conversation than she expected. Dad was disappointed but understood her decision. He said a few words in support of his Alma Mater but also praised Imperial and gave her his blessing with one proviso. "I'm expecting you to get a first, like your Mum."

"How did you do it, Mum?"

"Actually, it wasn't that difficult. There was a bit of bluster but nothing serious. The fact is that he admires you and respects your wish to make your own decision. You're eighteen now."

The magic eighteen. More responsibility just because of a birthday. Charlie didn't feel much different from when she was seventeen but there was something special about being allowed to take responsibility for your own life.

# 12

Jill had just got up to make Mike a cup of tea and take a shower when she saw the patrol car pull up across the road. She had watched enough crime dramas to know that police arriving at your front door early on a Sunday morning were unlikely to be the bearers of good news. Concern for whoever was about to receive the visit turned to fear when the policewoman checked the number on Jill's gatepost, waved over her colleague and walked purposefully to the front door. The worst-case scenarios went through Jill's mind in seconds. Had there been an accident? Was Sam alright?

The bell rang. It seemed much louder than usual and made her jump even though she knew it was coming. She instinctively retied her bathrobe, tighter than usual.

"Good morning, Madam. Are you Mrs Jill Martin?"

"Yes."

"I'm PC Sian Jones and my colleague is PC John Stapleton.

I wonder if we could come in and speak to you. It would be better said inside rather than on the doorstep."

Alarm bells rang even louder. "This sounds serious."

"Yes, I'm afraid it is."

"Come through to the sitting room." Jill could feel the tension in her neck and shoulders as she steeled herself for whatever disaster she was about to discover. Mike came downstairs barefooted and dressed in jeans and a T-shirt. Jill was glad he was there.

"Do sit down. This is Mike Ashcroft…my partner." She had never called him that before, but it seemed the right thing to say. PC Jones had a strong but kind face and PC Stapleton looked about the same age as Sam, and nervous. He had clearly not experienced many visits like this before. Jill felt rather exposed with just a bathrobe to cover her but sat as primly as she could manage next to Mike on the sofa.

There was an expectant pause while everyone settled. PC Jones spoke formally but softly. "There's no easy way to say this Mrs Martin but I'm sorry to inform you that a man whom we believe to be Mr Paul Martin was killed soon after eight o'clock last night in an incident at Witham Station where he fell under the London bound train. Your details were on his phone. At this stage we are unable to speculate on exactly how it happened. We have yet to complete all our enquiries and there will have to be an inquest to establish the cause of death. We would be grateful if you could agree a time to identify the body."

*

"It was definitely suicide. Two witnesses who were on the platform saw him jump."

"Oh my god, I'm so sorry." Lily reached across the table and squeezed Sam's hand.

"It's horrible. This kind of stuff happens to other people."

He paused to scratch his head and rub his eyes.

"Your Mum's worried about you, Sam. She said she can't get you to talk about it."

"It's hard with Mike there."

"Let's go for a walk round the reservoir. We need to get out."

They often had their best conversations when they were out walking. The local reservoir was a beautiful area with nature trails and the calming effect of water to help him relax. He remembered outings there with Mum when he was a toddler learning about birds and watching the anglers casting for trout. Dad had offered to pay for him to have fishing lessons but he hadn't taken them up. He wasn't patient enough, Mum said.

It was a still day and large stretches of water were mirror flat, gently disturbed here and there by fishermen in hired boats searching for a catch. Brightly coloured life jackets stood out against the blue-grey wash. The trails were busy with walkers but Sam felt comfortable in his own space with Lily holding his hand. She said nothing. The atmosphere would do its work. He would speak when he wanted to.

"I was crazy about ducks when I was young. Used to love feeding them. Mum bought special food. Bread's supposed not to be good for them, you know."

"It's the swans that I love. Like when they take off and their wings slap the water."

As if on cue, one did, and they stopped to watch and listen. It landed with a theatrical splash, leaving behind a line of ruffled water.

"Clever of you to plan that, Lily."

She kissed him lightly on the cheek. "No limit to my talents."

"You know, he sent that text just before he jumped. I've checked the time on my phone. They were his last words to me – to anyone. He may have been embarrassing at times but he was still my Dad. We were getting on as well as we've ever done."

*

Two pews in the crematorium were all they needed. Sam sat between his mother and Lily while the chaplain from the hospital where Jill worked did his best to sound as if he knew his father from the notes they had given him. They were not a church going family but Aunt Sheila and Mum thought it was important for someone with a dog collar to be involved. He felt awkward about Mike being there but Lily told him that it was right for him to come and support his Mum. Whether he liked it or not, Mike was now part of her life.

Mrs Woods was there. It was weird to think that the last time he saw her was on results day. So much had happened since then. "Thanks for your letter Miss. It was kind of you to write." Sam couldn't recall receiving a proper hand written letter before but he would never forget this one.

"The girls send their love. We were all devastated."

She slipped away after the service but her support meant a lot.

The congregation, such as it was, gathered for drinks and sandwiches at a local pub, the same place as they used for Grandad and Granny Martins' funerals. Sam remembered there being far more people at those. He was sad to see such small numbers. They emphasised how lonely Dad must have been since the family split – probably longer than that, now he thought about it. Aunt Sheila chatted to them about the problems of winding up the business and sorting out his father's will. It sounded as if his finances were a total mess but at least Mum wouldn't have the worry of dealing with it.

The Academy Manager had been kind and understanding. "Take as much time off as you need Sam. Rugby's of minor importance when something appalling like this happens."

Sam wanted to repay his trust by keeping fit and being strict with himself while he was away but Lily persuaded him to have a beer. "Come on, Sam, a couple of drinks won't hurt."

In the event he had far too many and ended the day depressed and dulled by alcohol.

*

"How was it, Mum?" Charlie asked.

"Awful. I sat there trying to imagine what it must feel like if someone you love jumps in front of a train."

"I can't believe it. It's horrific. What must be going on in someone's head to make them do such a thing? Poor Sam. Do you think he'll ever get over it?"

"I'm not sure you ever get over a suicide. He looked shell shocked to me. Just as everything was going so well for him."

# PART THREE

Sam was well aware of Lily's view that chasing a ball around a patch of grass and knocking the shit out of each other to get hold of it was an odd way to make a living.

# 13

By borrowing his mother's car or getting lifts from Lily, Sam had managed to stay clear of a station or a train since the incident, as he preferred to call it. Suicide was a word lodged in his thoughts, ticking away like grit in a tyre, but he couldn't bear to say it. Nor could he spend the rest of his life avoiding rail travel.

The journey to Bath was a nightmare. He looked at his sports apps, read his phone messages over and over and idly watched the scenery go flashing by, but every time the arrival at the next station was announced the palms of his hands sweated and he imagined his father waiting on the platform. How fast would the train have been going when it hit him? What would a body smashed by a train look like? His mother hadn't talked about identifying the body and he hadn't wanted to ask. It made him feel sick to think of it. As the train slowed down he looked at the passengers waiting to get on. Had any of them considered ending it all, or were they all happily going about their business? Mum had offered to help him with the deposit to buy a car and he promised himself that he would find one as soon as possible. He had rarely felt greater motivation to get something done.

Sam was desperate to put this chapter of his life behind him but it was difficult. When the word got out that his father had committed suicide, he felt the stigma of it being an unnatural death and the efforts of those around him trying to avoid saying the wrong thing. He hadn't been in Bath for long and, although he was sharing a house with two other academy players, he had yet to make any close friends so he avoided talking about the subject as a kind of self-protection.

He was excited to be starting his rugby career but couldn't shake off the unhappiness that had overwhelmed him. He was also finding it hard to cope with being separated from Lily who bore the brunt of his bottled up emotions during some testing phone conversations. When she moved to Cardiff, she enjoyed the excitement of starting university life and the hectic social scene that went with it. It was her style to throw herself enthusiastically into everything. To Sam, Freshers Week seemed to be one long party (apparently all the students on her course were cool) while his fitness regime was rigorous in the extreme. He wanted her to enjoy herself but perhaps not quite as much as her calls and texts suggested, so it cheered him up when she proposed a visit to Cardiff.

"You could come and see me now you've got your car. Surely you're not running around on a pitch or in the gym all of the time."

He ignored the sarcastic edge to the invitation. "That would be great."

"Let's do it then."

*

Sam was late and not in the best of moods when he arrived at Lily's accommodation, an old house converted into units for six students with a common room where they hung out. He had texted her after he parked the car and she was waiting for him in a small entrance hall cluttered with umbrellas, boots and wellies which were too mucky to be allowed further into the building.

"The traffic was a nightmare. It's only about fifty miles but it took me an hour longer than I thought."

"Hi Lily, lovely to see you," she said.

"Sorry."

"This way."

He followed her to a room on the first floor at the front of the building.

"Well you're here now. Do I get a hug?"

He dropped his bag, wrapped his arms around her and kissed her, gently at first but then more urgently. She smelt of shower soap.

"Not now Sam. It's late and I'm hungry… Don't look so stroppy. You should have got here on time."

It wasn't his fault he was stuck on the motorway but it wasn't worth arguing the point. "Like the room."

"Yeah, it's OK. It's convenient for shops and pubs and not far from the hospital." She gave him a reassuring smile. "Bed's a bit small for two but we'll survive."

She took him to a pub, one of several she had visited during Freshers Week. It was packed with students and they had to wait by the bar until a table was free. Lily looked around to see if there was anyone she knew and then checked her phone for texts. Sam felt out of place but concentrated on attracting the attention of one of the bar staff.

"Students aren't short of money then."

"Half of them spend most of what they've got for the first year by Christmas."

"You're too organised for that. Anyway, it's my treat tonight."

"Big spender now then."

"No, but at least I have a salary."

"Sounds very grown up."

A table finally became available and they shuffled through the crowded bar area to the far corner of the room trying not to spill their drinks on the way. Pictures of Welsh rugby players were hanging on the walls and menus with dragons printed on the front were in a rack next to a tin bucket containing cutlery and red paper napkins.

Lily grinned. "Thought you might appreciate the décor here."

"No mistaking where we are."

"The burgers are good and they do a great fish pie."

A quick glance at the menu was all Sam needed. A double cheeseburger and chips would be a real treat, a break from the diet he was trying to follow during training. So would a second pint of beer. He took in his surroundings while Lily checked her phone again. Their table was more private than being at the bar where they had to speak loudly into each other's ears to be heard. The waiter soon arrived to take their order. Moving customers through quickly was the system here, Sam thought.

"How's it been?" Lily asked after sending a couple of texts.

"Tough. Really tough."

Lily sighed. "Sam, I'm sorry you've had to go through this terrible experience. It must be horrendous trying to deal with it. I want to help but I feel a bit out of my depth to be honest. You need to see an expert, a counsellor, like someone who's qualified to deal with this sort of stuff."

"I don't want to see a counsellor."

"Why not?"

"I just don't."

"That's stupid."

"I don't really want to talk about it anymore."

"OK by me. I was hoping we'd get on to other things at some stage."

"What sort of things?"

"Us. Our future. How we're managing being apart. Bath. You might even ask me about my course," she added sharply.

"I'm sorry. My head's full of crap. I've not been thinking straight."

She looked at his sad face across the table and made him look back at her to be sure he was paying attention.

"*Please* Sam, somehow you have to find a way to move on."

"It's easy to say that. Doing it's a different thing. I'll always know that my Dad killed himself. That'll never go away."

They sat in silence for what seemed like an age. Sam rubbed the joint at the base of his thumb which had taken a knock during training and watched Lily looking vaguely around the room. She waved to a girl who was about to sit down at a nearby table.

"She's on my course… Look Sam, we can't go on like this. Tell me, what's the most important thing in your life… apart from me."

Lily's attempt to lighten the mood brought a flat response. "Rugby, I suppose."

"Only suppose. Surely it's been your dream to play for England ever since you started playing the stupid game."

The waiter conveniently arrived with their food and drinks and there was another lapse in the conversation. Sam was well aware of Lily's view that chasing a ball around a patch of grass and knocking the shit out of each other to get hold of it was an odd way to make a living but he thought she might have been a little less critical in the circumstances.

"It's still my dream," he said decisively.

"Get on with it then and make a success of it. It's what your Dad wanted you to do and what made him proud of you. As I said, you've got to move on."

She was right but it wasn't that easy even though he knew that his anxiety was becoming hard for her to bear.

Lily changed tack. "When you're training does it help you to clear your head of all the bad vibes?

He nodded. "Yeah, it does. I enjoy the physical stuff and I can focus for hours on my skills without getting bored."

"So, what do you do when you're not in a gym or on a pitch?"

He could see where this was going and hesitated before answering. "Not a lot if I'm honest."

"There's got to be other things. You'll go nuts."

"Well, I watch TV, play video games and talk to the coaches and senior players about how I can improve my game."

Lily looked at him, wide eyed with disapproval. "Is that it? Have you read a book since you went to Bath?"

"Yes, I have," he replied indignantly.

"What?"

"A history of the British Lions."

"So, that's not exposed you to anything new."

"Dad gave it to me."

The conversation stalled again and Sam tried to take the initiative for once. "OK then. What do you do?" As soon as the words came out, he wished he hadn't asked.

"I'm on a demanding course so there's always going to be assignments and background reading to do and there's like a society for every conceivable thing."

She spoke with enthusiasm and self-confidence, perhaps a little too pleased with herself, Sam thought.

"I've joined the Film Society and the Climbing Club. There are loads of people to meet who are doing different things."

She stressed the word different. There was no mistaking the implication that Sam was in a dull environment with boring people.

"The Students' Union is buzzing too. I've been to a gig there by an awesome local band and there's a comedy night coming up soon."

"OK Lily, I've got the message."

"Bath's a great city. There must be lots going on. You've got to get off your arse and find it. God knows what you'll be like if you get injured."

# 14

The weekend in Cardiff had not gone well but one positive thing Sam took from it was Lily's uncompromising advice to get on and make a success of his rugby. It was a stark reminder that it was now his job, not merely a game. He returned to Bath determined to apply himself and 'be the best player he could be', a cliché he had heard expressed by dozens of coaches over the years.

He approached his training with an almost unhealthy intensity in the hope that it would help to block out his worries about what Lily might be doing, what was going on at home and the constant intrusion of thoughts about his father. He practised hundreds of box kicks every week, was invariably last off the pitch and spent hours improving his passing skills to make sure that he was just as strong off his left hand as his right. He followed dietary advice to the letter, hardly ever drank alcohol and approached his fitness with the dedication of an Olympic athlete. He earned the training name Boxer for having an attitude to work like the horse in *Animal Farm*. The smart arse who gave it to him was called Prof for having been to university. He was one of the senior pros who had a reputation for giving more than enough advice to the younger players but Sam found him helpful in small doses. He wanted to learn and thought that Prof's years of experience were worth listening to.

Sam's obsessiveness drew more than the average dressing room banter, but he didn't mind. The team camaraderie helped him to find his feet and he and Prof weren't the only ones to be given nicknames. Single syllable surnames usually had a 'y' added, so Jonesy, Doddsy and Hunty became firmly fixed in everyone's mind, and Jim Treadwell, who had the misfortune to have a cauliflower ear sticking out at right angles, was christened Wing Nut.

They were all proud of Farleigh House, a grand old Gothic Revival country mansion reborn as Bath Rugby's elite training facility. The old chapel had been converted into a gym equipped with every kind of machine designed to cause pain and exhaustion. Former outbuildings housed a rehab unit, changing rooms, medical centre and meeting spaces. Offices and kitchen and dining facilities were in the main house. The aim was to have the whole Bath Rugby community – players, coaches, medics, analysts, estate workers, catering staff and the admin team – working together in one place. There was even a striking sculpture, a whorl of stainless steel on a plinth, stationed in the courtyard which players had to pass numerous times during their working day. It was rumoured to have cost sixty thousand pounds. Sam wondered if the novelty of training in such opulent surroundings would wear off in time and Farleigh would become just a place of work. He was at his most content out in the fresh air, training on the pitches beyond the ha-ha in front of the House, even on the wet days when driving rain tested the resolve of the toughest of individuals. Hunty, a gritty back row forward who grew up in the north-west wondered what all the fuss was about. They were wimps. Somerset only had piddling little showers compared with Cumbria.

Sam began to establish a reputation for being a well-motivated young player with considerable potential. The Academy Manager was pleased with his progress but suggested that he should learn to relax a little and be patient. His time would come. If he continued his present development there was a good chance that he would be offered a full contract in due course, but he had to remember that there were only about five hundred full-time professionals in the English system and many of those were from overseas.

*

The downside of Sam's rugby progress was that he and Lily began to drift away from each other. It was a gradual process. As the months passed, they became busily engaged in different worlds and spent little time together. Lily rarely came to Bath. She preferred to go climbing at weekends with new friends from all over the UK and abroad who shared a love of the Welsh mountains. To be fair, she had always been honest about finding rugby boring, so it wasn't a surprise to him. He remembered her telling him how proud she was of his achievements and how much she admired the modest way he dealt with the adulation he received from the West Park students when he won his England caps. Then, they were bound together by their local friends, the rhythm of school life, their hopes for the future and the excitement of a first serious relationship. They had discovered so much together, but things were different now. When they did meet, invariably in Cardiff, it was awkward. Sam avoided talking about rugby. Living in a city steeped in rugby history had made no difference to Lily's view of the game.

"Not all Welsh people are rugby fanatics you know, apart from when they're playing England."

She dutifully asked how things were going in Bath but the conversation soon dried up, and there was little else that Sam was doing to engage her interest. On the other hand, Lily was bursting with news of her social life and everything from medical matters to the rock faces around Tryfan. She made him feel inadequate. Even their sex had lost its magic and become part of a routine to be got through during the visit. It was in bed after an unsatisfactory session when Sam did everything too fast that it all unravelled.

She sat up and looked down at him before delivering the killer question. "You must have had lots of offers from would be WAGs. Have you slept with any of them?"

"No, on both counts," he answered, too quickly to be convincing.

"I don't believe you. You lot must be like bulls waiting to get at the cows in the next field."

He couldn't argue with that. Lily was spot on. There was enough testosterone in the squad to double the population of the city. He was a hopeless liar and his face was telling the truth even if his words weren't. Lily knew him too well for him to dig a deeper hole.

"I had too much to drink at a party and I hadn't seen you for ages."

"So, that makes it OK then."

"No, but…"

Lily interrupted. "What if I'd said, I just had a fuck after a party?"

Her aggressive tone surprised him. "Well, did you?"

"No, it was after a difficult climb with my instructor."

Sam was stunned. Her response was calm and matter of fact, as if the admission was of little significance and she'd planned to tell him. "Just to get this straight. Is your instructor the same person as the one you fucked?"

"I'm not sure what difference it makes, but yes."

"You'll be climbing with him again, I suppose."

"Yes, I will. Most weekends."

*

They didn't argue after the revelations. There was no point. Exhaustion had set in and neither of them had anything left to say. Sam was desperate to get away. He dressed, packed his bag and left as quickly as he could.

"So that's it then," he said lamely.

Lily turned away as he closed the door.

It was after midnight and his head was spinning, not an ideal time to drive home. He wasn't sure whether to be angry or miserable and frightened himself when he lost concentration at a roundabout. He couldn't get Lily out of his mind. Had she deliberately set out to finish it all? It felt like it. Brutal. She seemed to want him to know about her climbing instructor. He'd made a mistake and admitted it. Sex on offer and he couldn't resist. But neither could she. Who cheated first? They hadn't got on to that, but what did it matter? It was all over and that was that. He'd seen it coming, but it had been a long relationship and one he would never forget.

Sam's anger subsided once he had got over the initial shock and come to terms with the fact that their lives had inevitably moved in different directions. He rang his mother a couple of days later. She was still the only person he felt able to talk to about Lily. He told her that she had found someone else. It wasn't quite the full story, but it would do.

"Oh, Sam. I'm so sorry. Why don't you come home for a couple of days? It'll do you good to get out of the rugby bubble and see some of your old friends."

"But they're Lily's old friends too."

"You'll have to face them at some point. Anyway, they probably know already. It'll be out via WhatsApp or whatever."

Sam wasn't sure that he wanted or needed to see them. His circumstances were different now and so were Mum's. He hadn't been home much since Mike had moved in and still hadn't got used to the idea of another man being in the house. Someone more important than him.

"I want you to meet Mike's daughters."

"I'm not sure I'm ready for two stepsisters."

"We're not planning to get married, Sam," she responded defensively. "They only come here when it's Mike's turn to have them for the weekend."

He couldn't help thinking that his mother was making a new life for herself without him, just like Lily. "But you're living together so you're like their step mum, aren't you?"

Jill sidestepped the question. "I bumped into Mrs Woods in town the other day. She asked after you. I think she has a bit of a soft spot for you, you know. Charlie's enjoying being in London and loves her course."

"Look Mum don't take it the wrong way but I'd rather not come home just now. I want to concentrate on my rugby and, if I'm honest, I'd prefer to be with my new mates than the old ones."

# 15

After the break up, it felt good to be back at the Club. He missed Lily but Sam gradually got used to being without her. The hint that he should have more interests outside rugby went largely unheeded. He was determined to win the respect of his coaches and team-mates by giving a hundred percent to everything he did on and off the pitch.

Prof and Sam were recovering in the changing room after a session which Prof had found particularly demanding and Sam had taken in his stride.

"You're loving it, aren't you? Rugby life."

"Yeah, I am."

"It gets harder."

"Aren't you still enjoying it then?"

"I suppose I am but not always during a session like that." He managed a strained smile. "There's a lot of pain and tough times but overall, the game's been good to me. Being in a rugby family is special. A lot of the guys I know who've retired have found it hard to adjust to life without it."

Sam remembered the conversation and appreciated the increasing interest Prof was taking in his development. His big chance came in his second season when he was picked on the bench for an Anglo-Welsh Cup fixture, a key opportunity for an academy player. The Director of Rugby gave him the good news in a cool and understated tone. "We think you're ready Sam so give it your best shot."

Sam struggled to contain his excitement in the lead up to the match. He slept badly and worried about letting himself down. His dreams were full of misdirected kicks and poor passes. The backs coach was a stickler for counting errors. Should he be adventurous or play safe? It depended on the situation of the game when, and if, he got on. It would be a pain in the arse if he didn't. He wanted at least fifteen to twenty minutes. Being on the bench was frustrating. You had to be mentally ready to cover for an injury at any moment but later in the game as time ran out you wondered whether there would be any chance to make an impact.

Prof who was on his way back from injury was also picked for the match day squad which, as usual for the Anglo-Welsh competition, provided the opportunity to try out new talent mixed with some more experienced players. Sam was pleased to have Prof's reassuring presence in the team. He was a powerful second row, with remarkable upper body strength, huge hands and surprising mobility for a man of his size. Quiet and thoughtful off the pitch he was fearless on it and relished the opportunity to compete against the best players in his position.

"Just relax Sam and take it as it comes. You'll be fine."

"It's easy for you. You've been doing this for decades."

"Piss off…Look, you're bound to get some game time. The point of picking you is to give you a taste of the next step up and for the coaches to see how you react."

In the event he went on at a critical time in the match. The result was in the balance. Bath were five points in the lead with fifteen minutes to go but they were under pressure in their own half with a scrum against them in their twenty two.

"I need a lot more energy at the base Sam. Just play your natural game and enjoy it."

It was exactly what Sam needed to hear from the coach. They must believe in me to put me on now. And what was the point of devoting so many hours to training if you didn't enjoy the match days? As he jogged across the field to join his teammates, he breathed in slowly to check his adrenalin rush. He had to be in control at this critical scrum.

The opposition scrum half tried to elbow him aside to put the ball in but Sam stood his ground and kept the pressure on. The strike wasn't clean and the Bath pack eased forward forcing the No.8 to pick up and deal with untidy ball. He was a big man but Sam drove into him with every ounce of weight he had and dislodged the ball. Knock on, scrum down, Bath put in. There were roars of 'YES' from the forwards and a slap on the back from the blind side winger who rushed over to congratulate him.

Now the put in. Concentrate. Listen to the referee. Get it right for the hooker. Don't rush. A good strike, a stable scrum, a burst from his No.8. A solid ruck. Good protection from the forwards. Now for the box kick. He'd done this thousands of times in practice. Up it went, high, hanging and absolutely on the money. The opposition winger caught it but was swarmed over by the chasers and bundled into touch. Now Bath had a lineout on halfway and the pressure was back on the opposition. Lineout cleanly won, the ball driven into midfield and an infringement at the ruck. Penalty to Bath forty metres out, straight in front of the posts. The fly half calmly drilled it through the middle. Three points. It was enough to secure a win.

The coach gave Sam an approving tap on the shoulder at the end of the match. "Nothing flashy but the basics done really well, Sam. That exit when you first went on was crucial."

The Director of Rugby began to take more interest in him. He was on the radar for the England U20 squad and was told that it was possible for a twenty-year-old to get a full contract. "If you're good enough you're old enough."

Sam's motivation grew even stronger when he made the first team squad for a Premiership match. Admittedly, one of the scrum halves higher than him in the pecking order was having problems with his Achilles tendon. In the cruel world of professional sport, one person's injury gave someone else his opportunity.

"Sorry about the Achilles, Will. Hope it repairs quickly."

"Gives you a chance though, doesn't it?"

Will's wry smile, shaped by the cynicism of experience, made Sam feel uncomfortable. They spent a lot of time together in training but his expression made it clear that they were rivals not friends. "At least when you're injured you've got an excuse for not playing. It's when you're not being picked that it really hurts."

Sam hadn't thought of that. He had so much to learn. It brought home to him the fragility of life as a professional sportsman. He remembered Lily questioning what he would be like if he had a bad injury and he began to worry about it. What would he do if he couldn't play? He'd been lucky so far, no serious injuries and a maximum lay-off of three weeks. He had found that difficult enough so how would he cope with something worse. It was his nightmare scenario. Small niggles gained a status out of all proportion to how serious they really were and he became one of the Club's most regular visitors to the massage tables and the spa.

"I hear you've become a physio addict, Sam." The Director of Rugby was in an unusually good mood and said it with a smile on his face. "Despite that I've decided to offer you a full time contract."

Sam looked at him in disbelief. "That's amazing Boss. I don't know what to say."

"I assume you're willing to accept."

Sam grinned. "Thanks Boss. It's what I've always wanted. It's the best day of my life." He was elated but a sad thought spoilt the moment. He wished Dad was around to hear the news. He would have been so chuffed…

They shook hands firmly and Sam sensed that their relationship had already moved to another level. It gave him the confidence to believe that he was respected within the Club and his morale was sky high as a result. He didn't rest on his laurels in training and continued to put everything into it as he believed all good professionals should but not everyone was as keen as Sam and some found his enthusiasm wearing.

Doddsy who joined the Academy at the same time as Sam had become a good mate but was one of his sternest critics. He was a winger with a devastating side step and electric pace who believed in conserving energy and his hamstrings for eye catching moments when he could show off his bursts of speed and agility. Sam's all-consuming approach to training was not in his DNA. He was the subject of constant bollockings from the backs coach who was frustrated by his laziness but knew he had the potential to win matches at the highest level. Doddsy famously brought a practice to a laughter induced standstill after shouting, "For chrissake calm down Sam, you're like a fucking springer spaniel."

The following week Sam tripped over another player during a routine kick and chase session and fell awkwardly onto his shoulder. He clutched it and knew immediately that there was a problem – intense pain and the joint out of place.

"Fuck. It's gone."

He gritted his teeth and supported his left arm as Doddsy helped him to his feet and walked with him to the medical centre. "Maybe now you'll learn not to do everything at a hundred fucking miles an hour. It was an accident waiting to happen."

Sam could have done without Doddsy's analysis but he wasn't known for his subtlety. Further bad news came with the physio's immediate assessment. The dislocation would almost certainly need surgery and there would be a significant rehab period before he was ready to play again.

# 16

"You have a Bankart Lesion. To put it in simple terms your upper arm bone has been forced out of the cavity of the shoulder blade and the supporting ligaments have been torn which means the shoulder is unstable… and no doubt rather uncomfortable," the surgeon added with an unhelpful smile. "My job is to re-attach the ligaments so that the shoulder regains its stability. The procedure has the advantage of allowing patients to resume normal daily activities while the repair is healing, but you won't be playing rugby for a while."

"How long?"

"Three months before you return to full training if all goes well. Surgical treatment provides a good chance of avoiding recurrent instability, but there are no guarantees. On the plus side, you should be able to start exercises the day after the operation – with strict instructions from the physiotherapist," he said firmly. "Flexion, rotation that sort of stuff. No lifting anything heavy, and, for a short while, you may want to use a sling for support between exercise sessions, and at night while sleeping. Actually, you probably won't sleep very well. Driving could be as early as two weeks after surgery, if the shoulder can be used comfortably, and light, low-risk activities, such as swimming and jogging at eight to ten weeks."

It was all briskly explained with the minimum of fuss. The surgeon had seen it all before, but for Sam it was deadly serious. He listened carefully with a mixture of determination and fear. Being sidelined would be a nightmare.

And it was, even though the operation went smoothly and he was quickly into the routine of rehabilitation. The physios tried their best to keep him positive, but he felt like a spare part being away from the team training and match preparation, an observer rather than a participant.

"I didn't become a professional to watch from the stands. I hate this."

"Everyone feels the same Sam but injuries are part of the game. There's no pro I've worked with that hasn't had to get through months of rehab during his career. It's a fact of life. And, if I'm being honest, you're not great company at the moment."

"Thanks, that's just what I want to hear."

It already seemed light years since his brief taste of the big time. Would the Director of Rugby put up with his absence or was he already seeking cover for his position? What would his next tackle feel like? Would the shoulder be strong enough? And how would he cope on the artificial pitches that were becoming more popular but seemed to cause more injury problems?

At times, Sam thought that enduring rehab was the worst experience he'd had in his life, until he remembered his father and felt guilty for putting an injury on that high a level. He began to realise how much training and playing had helped him to keep the demons at bay. Being in rehab gave him too much time to think and the pain of his loss resurfaced. So did his memories of Lily and her comments about his lack of interests outside the game. He was bored without rugby and depressed about other things. He knew his mother was disappointed not to see more of him. She thought it would do him good to get away from Bath and see some of his old school friends, but he couldn't face the inevitable questions about how his rugby was going and why he and Lily had broken up. And Mike was now the man of the house. That's what Mum used to call me when I was living with her, he thought. He'd lost his Dad. Mum and Lily had found new loves in their lives. He couldn't play. The world was against him.

The Director of Rugby finally took him aside after a Monday morning squad meeting. "You're not handling the situation very well, Sam. If you're going to be a successful professional, you must learn to cope with setbacks, and I can assure you there'll be plenty more. We judge you by your performance on the pitch, but we find out a lot at times like this. You've become negative and self-absorbed and you're so bloody miserable that everyone's beginning to steer clear of you in case it's catching. Even the physios are finding you difficult and they're used to hacked off rehabs.

"I'm sorry boss but…"

"No buts Sam. I'd like you to go home for a week, to give yourself and everyone else a break and have a think about the future. The guys tell me your Mum's a nurse and her partner's an orthopaedic surgeon so you'll be in good hands, and I'm sure there's a local gym you can use for a few days to keep up your rehab exercises. In fact, it's your head that needs more attention than your shoulder."

*

Sam's room was the same as he left it when he first moved to Bath. Jill still regarded it as his space even though it was rarely used. The last time was at Christmas. There was a brightly coloured envelope on his chest of drawers. It was a present from Mike's daughters, Rose and Grace. They had spent Christmas with their mother, and Sam had returned to Bath before they came to stay at home. When he met them the previous summer, he had to admit that he had found it enjoyable to be doted on by two pretty teenage girls, and now they had given him tickets for an Ed Sheeran concert. His depressing songs were not exactly what he needed in his present mood, but it was a kind gesture, no doubt funded by Mike.

Jill fluttered about trying too hard to make everything just right but only succeeded in putting Sam on edge.

"Relax Mum. I'm not one of your patients."

"Sorry." She slipped away to the kitchen before saying anything that might be misconstrued.

There was tension over dinner when Mike broached the subject of Sam's injury. He was aware that Mike was a respected surgeon (Mum was always banging on about it) but his attitude to rugby was cynical and the last thing that Sam wanted was a lecture on the high incidence of injuries in the game.

"It's no surprise to me that you've started your serious injury count but at least you've been fixed up by one of the best guys in the country and you're getting good rehab."

There was no need for the dig about his injury count but it was pleasing to hear confirmation that his operation was done by a top surgeon.

"I'm finding it hard." Sam took a long time to respond and paused again to consider whether he wanted to drop his guard and say more. "I've been sent home to clear my head."

There was a lengthy silence during which Sam noticed his mother's warning look at Mike. "I think that's a good idea. It helps to have a change of environment. Patients tend to get better quicker when they go home."

"It wasn't quite like that, Mum. The Director of Rugby was pissed off with me. Said I wasn't handling the situation well. It was a warning shot about my attitude."

The Club performance psychologist and most of the coaches encouraged players to be open about their vulnerabilities, but Sam found it difficult and tended to bottle things up. Having Mike there didn't help but it felt good to get it off his chest and he guessed that his mother would be supportive.

"So, we must all be positive and help you to make the best use of the week." She flashed her most encouraging smile.

"I could do my exercise in the gym at school. Do you think they'd mind?"

"Of course not, they'd be thrilled to have you back. I bet the PE staff would be all over you. They might even ask you to speak to the students about being a professional sportsman."

"I could see Mrs Woods too. She always encouraged me. She knows me as well as anyone."

Sam was conscious that his mother might have taken the comment the wrong way but her response was more understanding than he expected. "It's good to have someone outside the family whose opinions you respect. Why don't you ring the school in the morning to see what's possible?"

The school secretary could not have been more helpful. She remembered Sam well. He and Lily had been a couple of the school's better known students. "Two of our young celebs," she called them.

"We're not together anymore, Miss Carter."

"Sorry about that, Sam but there'll be plenty more fish in the sea for a good looking sportsman like you. I'm sure Mrs Woods would be pleased to see you."

*

Although he was looking forward to it, Sam felt nervous about meeting Mrs Woods. He had asked himself why he wanted to see her and hadn't come up with a conclusive answer. Perhaps it was just because he liked her. She had always seemed to approve of him and had the knack of motivating him. She had given the same advice as many of the other staff, but somehow it had sounded more convincing coming from her. Maybe she could help him get his head together. He didn't like the expression. It made him sound like some sort of freak and had hurt when the boss mentioned it.

They had agreed to meet at a local café after Mrs Woods finished work. Sam made sure he was there early. He wanted to be in position when she arrived. It was embarrassing but he didn't like the idea of having to look around the room for her if she was there first. He had lost confidence in dealing with what should have been quite simple situations.

Now he had too much time to kill. He bought himself a diet coke and found a suitable table from which he had a clear view of the entrance. He wasn't used to sitting in places on his own and wished he had brought his *Rugby World* magazine to read while he was waiting. He looked around aimlessly hoping that someone or something of interest would catch his eye. The complicated espresso machine stood out but nothing else. The smell of coffee and cakes was overwhelming. He gulped some coke, sat back in his seat and stretched his arms. The minutes ticked by too slowly and he began to wonder whether this meeting was a good idea after all, but he couldn't back out now. Constant glances at his watch didn't help… At last the door opened and Mrs Woods appeared. She was smartly dressed, as usual. Fashionable but right for her age Lily used to say. He stood up as she approached the table and held out his hand. They had never shaken hands before but it seemed the right thing to do.

"Hi, Mrs Woods."

"Hi, Sam. I hear you spoke well to the PE students today."

Classic Mrs W, he thought. A positive comment straight away. "Thanks Miss. I felt nervous at first but once I got going and they asked me some questions I enjoyed it."

"You can call me Clare if you like, Sam."

"Thanks Miss…er Clare. Could I get you a drink?"

"I'd love a coffee."

"Anything else? They do great cakes here."

"No thanks. Philip's taking me out to dinner tonight. Mustn't over indulge now."

Sam went to the counter and brought back an americano and another diet coke for himself. Buying a drink for his teacher, even just a coffee, felt like a big deal.

"Thanks Sam, she said warmly. "It's not every day you have the chance to have coffee with a former student."

He smiled. "It's good to see you, Miss." Using her first name didn't feel right. He wasn't ready for such familiarity and hoped she wouldn't suggest it again.

"It's a privilege for a teacher to meet past pupils, and to hear how they're getting on." Clare paused, but Sam sipped awkwardly at his coke and didn't respond.

"So, how are you getting on? I was sorry to hear that you've been injured. It must be frustrating."

"Worse than I ever expected," he confessed. "You think you're invincible until the first serious injury comes along. I'm having to learn that it's part of the life of a rugby professional. It's tough."

"But you're in good hands aren't you. I mean the medical back-up's the best, isn't it?"

"Yes, but it's still means weeks away from playing."

"What do you do when you're not doing the rehab?"

"Not enough Miss, if I'm honest."

"That can't be good for you, Sam. You're an intelligent guy and you need other interests apart from work, especially in your job."

"I know. And I'm not seeing Lily anymore… I expect you knew that Miss."

"Yes, I did hear it on the grapevine. I'm sorry."

"She found someone else."

"It's hard to keep relationships going from a distance."

"Yeah, it is. She's having the time of her life at uni and the rugby kind of got in the way in the end. She was never a great fan," he said wearily.

"You seem a bit gloomy, Sam. I'm not sure how I can help."

"Just talking helps – with someone outside rugby who's not my mother." He noticed the look of concern on her face. "Don't worry, Miss. She thinks it's a good idea for me to talk to you."

He lost his nerve as he said it. Maybe this wasn't such a good idea. How needy I must seem. Dumping my problems on an unsuspecting teacher who hasn't seen me since the funeral. What must she think of me? Probably what the Director of Rugby thought – negative and self-absorbed. Those words were burned on his memory. But wasn't sympathy what he really wanted? An understanding response to his anxieties from someone away from work. Or was he simply not up to the life he'd chosen? His dreams of fame on a rugby pitch were already fading. That was the problem. He needed to change the subject.

"How's Charlie?"

"She's fine thanks. She's in her second year at Imperial and enjoying her course."

"What's she reading?"

"Biomedical Engineering."

"I'm not totally sure what that is, Miss."

Clare smiled. "I've learnt a lot more about it in the last couple of years, as you can imagine. It's to do with using modern engineering skills to design equipment and devices such as artificial internal organs, replacements for body parts and machines for diagnosing medical problems."

"I could be needing her expertise at some stage then."

They both laughed and Sam was pleased to discover that his sense of humour hadn't totally disappeared. He must remember this feeling when he was in one of his moods.

Clare indulged in a moment of parental pride. "She's become a real academic and is keen to do research if all goes well with her first degree."

"I'm sure it will, Miss. She was scarily clever at school. The best at everything."

"I've got a confession to make, Sam." She paused. Sam wasn't sure what was coming next, but she certainly had his attention. "I've never quite forgiven myself for not getting you and Charlie together that summer after you left Oakwood. She was very keen to see you."

He grinned. "I was cross with my Mum. I thought it was her fault."

"I was much more to blame."

"We met at a party a while back."

"She said you had."

"I doubt if Charlie's interested, but I'd like to see her again one day."

"Really?"

"Yes."

"Do you ever get up to London?"

"Not a lot, Miss."

"Charlie knows it well now. Maybe she could show you around."

"Is she seeing someone?"

"No-one in particular. Would you like me to put you in touch? I could give her your details."

"Thanks Miss. That would be great."

# 17

They were having one of their occasional lunches together in a small Italian restaurant not far from St Paul's and a few minutes' walk from Adi's office in the City. His crazy hours meant that more often than not he ate at his desk in front of the screen which dominated his working life. He was earning good money but his lifestyle had resulted in tired eyes, a sallow complexion and an expanding waistline. Charlie thought that the beautiful man who made other girls look twice when they were together was beginning to lose his looks. Adi's bank balance might be healthy but he wasn't.

"I'd always hoped you'd come and live with me now I've got my own flat."

"It's kind of you to offer Adi but I don't want to."

"Why not? You won't have to pay for your accommodation. Think how much you'll save."

"I'm happy as I am with my room in Hall and being near the Department. I don't want to commute from your place and waste hours sitting on the bloody tube."

"Your work's taken over your life."

"You're one to talk. All you do is obsess about the markets and bonuses."

"They pay the bills."

"If you're suggesting that I don't pay my way, then you can piss off. I don't need smart meals and a flash car."

It was a deliberately low blow but to Charlie's surprise Adi ignored it and pressed on.

"I'd like there to be a bit more to our relationship."

"As far as I'm concerned, we have a perfect arrangement now."

"Perfect for you maybe, but not for me."

"So, what more do you want?"

"More time together, not just a meal out and a fuck every now and again."

"Sorry if that's not enough for you Adi but I'm happy as we are. I don't want to be tied down to one person."

"So, who else is there?"

There wasn't anyone at present but fortunately there was a convenient example she could use. "A guy I knew at school wants me to get in touch… He's a professional rugby player," she added, bigging Sam up to add weight to her argument. Adi's only reaction was to shrug his shoulders.

"There's another thing. If I was living with you, I wouldn't get anywhere near enough work done."

"You're clever enough to do OK without working all hours."

"I don't want to do OK. I want to get a first and prove I'm good enough to do a PhD. I'm not ready for the complications of a serious relationship… To be honest, I'm not sure I ever will be."

"So, you'll be studying for years."

"I hope so. That's my aim."

"What is this passion for academia. I don't get it."

"I'm learning about stuff that will change people's lives. It's exciting, at least it is to me." She paused. "I want to do something that's worthwhile."

It was another unkind blow. Charlie wasn't proud of it but it was time to get this whole issue out in the open. Apart from in the bedroom their passions in life were incompatible. She had no respect for the world in which Adi worked although she did have to admit that she was selfish enough to enjoy the benefits it brought.

"So, it's the status quo or you'll bugger off."

She opened her palms to suggest that he take it or leave it. "Let's just carry on with no strings attached and a good time when we're together."

He looked at her with the eager eyes which had so often turned her on. "OK, but I'm not giving up," he said firmly. "Do you want another drink?"

"Please. Same again."

*

Charlie was irritated by Adi's casual reaction to her mention of Sam and it strengthened her resolve to get in touch with him. In truth she had already made up her mind even though it felt weird wanting to contact someone Mum approved of. She remembered how much she had wanted to see him again all those years ago and how annoyed she was when it didn't happen. She had also enjoyed his company at that party. There was something endearingly vulnerable about him and, unlike Adi, he didn't seem to realise how attractive he was: the strong face, kind eyes and his attentive way of listening to her. He was just the right height with a perfect build. Clothes looked good on him. She wondered how his six pack had developed now that he was a professional athlete. It would be fun to find out. Charlie had noticed with competitive satisfaction that Sam's girlfriend was stressed by the amount of time they spent together. Now she was no longer around the way was clear.

Most telling of all was her memory of hearing the news of Sam's father's suicide. It still made her shiver to think of it. Her parents were occasionally irritating (whose weren't?) but the thought of one of them jumping in front of a train was too horrific to contemplate. Her life had been full of privilege and free of tragedy. Sam's traumatic experience had a powerful effect on her. How did anyone recover from such a thing? He had said that he would like to see her again, so why not? She scrolled through her contacts to find the latest addition and after a few seconds a text was on its way.

*Hi Sam. Mum says you'd like a trip to London. Call me if you're interested.*

*

After his week away the coaching staff noticed an improvement in Sam's morale, and so did his mates who had begun to lose patience with him. It wasn't as if he was the only one with an injury. At any given time, the rehab team had about ten of the squad under their care and there were usually one or two of them who had been out for almost a year.

His time at home had been better than Sam expected. It felt as if he'd been suspended from school when the boss told him to take a break, but now he realised that it had been beneficial for him to get away. Most important, he had some good conversations with his mother, the best since Mike came on the scene. She helped to bring some perspective to his relationship with Lily.

"You both had strong ambitions which were bound to put pressure on you. I know it hurt when you broke up but you're glad that you had Lily in your life, aren't you?"

"Definitely. No regrets."

"There'll be someone else, you'll see."

It was a heavy hint but Sam didn't want to go there. Perhaps in the future it might be easier, but this wasn't the time, especially with other things stressing him. His mother was desperate for his approval of Mike but he couldn't bring himself to show it. It was selfish not to be pleased for her but he still hadn't come to terms with the fact that she was settled with a new partner, especially one he didn't like.

It was a major boost to Sam's morale when Matt, his regular physio confirmed that he was on track with his recovery and could look forward confidently to full training, and the prospect of playing again next season.

"There's no point in rushing you back for the last couple of games, Sam. Better to be cautious than risk playing too early. You'll be raring to go come pre-season and probably as fit as you've ever been. Sometimes a break turns out to be a good thing."

Sam gave him a wry smile. Matt had been really supportive. A highly regarded physio and someone he could talk to. "It doesn't feel like that when you're in here every day."

"That's why physios spend half their time counselling players as well as supervising their exercises." Matt paused while he adjusted the weights on the cable shoulder press. "Can I be honest with you Sam?"

"Sounds ominous."

"You've not been easy to deal with, you know."

"Yeah, I do. Sorry."

"You're going to get more injuries. So, I'm wondering how you're going to react next time."

"Not like I have this time…I hope."

"It's not easy but it's part of the game, I'm afraid."

Sam stopped exercising so he could speak more coherently. "I thought about it a lot when I was away. I know everyone thinks I'm a bit of a nutter at training but pushing myself and practising hard helps me to keep thoughts about my Dad at the back of my mind. Doing fuck all except rehab isn't good for me."

"Everyone struggles in rehab and you've had other stuff to deal with at the same time."

"I think it's made me more cynical."

"How do you mean?"

"We talk about Club culture and the team ethic, but isn't every player out for himself? If you aren't in the team do you *really* want everyone to play well?"

"Maybe, as long as they're not in your position."

They both laughed. "Don't get me wrong. I still love it and want to do well but this injury has been a dose of reality."

"Good. That's been useful then."

*

Charlie's text pinged in as Sam was walking back to the canteen to get a cup of coffee. He was drinking too much of it but it had become a habit during rehab. This was awesome news, an unexpected bonus – a quick text in response was needed.

He wasn't ready to call her. He had to collect his thoughts first.

*Hi Charlie. Good to hear from you. Will call tonight. OK?*

*Fine before 8* came back within five minutes.

Sam had limited experience of London, apart from Twickenham which didn't really count. He had seen some of the main sights on a school trip to Parliament but, as a family, they had never been to a show or done much visiting of galleries or museums. Dad wasn't particularly interested and Mum never pushed it so the capital was exciting new territory as far as he was concerned. Chris Kenny, a guy Sam knew from his school rugby days who played for Harlequins raved about living in London and had offered him an open invitation to stay at his flat in Teddington.

"We could have a good crack with a few of the lads if you ever want to come up. Just let us know."

He'd never taken up the offer but now he had the opportunity to meet Charlie as well. Perfect. Things were looking up.

"Hi Charlie. It's Sam."

"Hi. How are you?"

"Getting back to fitness after my op. Did you know about that?"

"Yes, Mum mentioned it. Shoulder wasn't it?"

"Yeah. Good news today though. I'm on track for next season."

"So, you want to come up to London."

Sam wanted to make it more personal than just going up to London. "I'd like to see you again. Could we have lunch somewhere? My treat."

"Sounds good. What do you want to see, apart from me?"

"I don't know London very well. You choose a place to meet."

"How about 12 o'clock at Eros, next Wednesday."

"That's fine."

"Sorry Sam but I've got to go. I've arranged to go out with a friend for a drink."

"OK. See you next week."

"Bye."

An efficient call, Sam thought. Perhaps the friend was a convenience to keep it short and to the point. He wondered if she would choose an expensive restaurant. Too bad if she did. He had made the offer and would have to accept the consequences.

Chris Kenny was pleased to hear from him and seemed unconcerned about the short notice or Sam's worries that he was taking advantage of his hospitality just to see Charlie.

"No problem. We'll have a drink at my local when you get back. Good luck mate. Hope it goes well."

Once that was settled Sam began to fuss about his travel arrangements. He would drive to Teddington and leave the car there. He didn't fancy taking it all the way into central London and he might want to have a couple of drinks now he was on his summer break. He could take a taxi but that would cost a fortune and a bus would take too long. It would be best to go by train, but rail journeys still haunted him. He'd done a few trips in recent months but still found them stressful.

For fuck's sake, grow up, he mouthed to himself. Someone my age and a professional sportsman who worries about going on a train. It's pathetic. I've got to get over this phobia. He had avoided talking about it to anyone. It was far too embarrassing. He would just have to grit his teeth and get on with it.

# 18

The tube was as difficult as the overland, and more claustrophobic. Sam stood well away from the rails and avoided looking at the dark gap a few metres in front of him. He concentrated on the group of passengers close by and when the rush of air down the platform indicated that a train was about to arrive, he faced the wall and plotted an imaginary route on the Transport for London map. He turned round when he heard the doors open and walked purposefully towards the haven of the nearest carriage.

He emerged from Piccadilly Circus into bright sunshine via the wrong exit having plunged towards the nearest one in his desire to get out, but Eros wasn't far away across the busy junction. Hordes of tourists meandered about, almost all of them armed with a camera of some sort or other. Hundreds of photographs would be taken before Charlie arrived. Sam was there way ahead of time, but it didn't matter. More people-watching would help him to relax and while away the next half hour. He took a photo of the sculpture and worked his way into a space on the top step next to two French girls who were speaking too fast for his GCSE to be of any use. He picked up the odd word about the beautiful weather, but it was their fragrant smell that he would remember. After fifteen minutes (he didn't want her to know that he'd arrived *that* early) he texted Charlie to confirm exactly where he was and was disappointed that she didn't reply. Perhaps he was expecting too much.

Just before midday he caught a glimpse of a tall, long legged girl walking through the crowd down below him on the pavement. Was that her? She moved away too quickly to be sure. A pity if it wasn't, she looked cool in a short skirt and close fitting T-shirt. The warm weather was being used to full advantage. Awesome legs, he whispered to himself and looked at his watch – again. It was just after twelve.

A few minutes later a tap on the shoulder startled him. He turned to his left to be confronted by a pair of red Converse sneakers and a small ankle tattoo of a butterfly inches from his nose. He stood up clumsily trying to create some space without stepping on the French girl beside him. It was Charlie alright, but she had changed since he last saw her. Piercing blue eyes accentuated by smoky make up, a row of hoops in her upper ear and a nose stud made the strong statement he had seen before but her hair was darker, nearly black and cut aggressively short above the ears. The gelled spikes on top added to the impression of someone keen to make an impact.

"You look different," Sam said lamely.

"Thanks for the stunning compliment. You don't. Just bigger."

"Good different."

"That's better."

"I've put on weight during rehab. Deliberately," he added quickly so she didn't get the wrong impression. "You walked past."

"Of course. Just checking you out."

"At least you came back."

"Yes, you should take that as a compliment."

"I'm glad you did."

"Should I take that as a compliment?"

"Definitely."

She flashed a smile. "So, I don't need to be back in the department until three. We could have a wander around before lunch, or after."

"Let's walk first."

"So where do you want to go?"

"I don't know London very well. You choose."

"Trafalgar Square's not far. There's always a buzz there and we might catch a good busker near the Gallery."

"The National Gallery?"

"Yes, and there's the National Portrait Gallery next door. When you live in London it's easy to assume that everyone knows all about it, but there must be thousands round the country who've never even been. All they know is what they've seen on TV… I've never been to Manchester," she added randomly.

Sam was grateful that Charlie replied without seeming superior. "Neither have I. Not to the city centre anyway, but I've been to the AJ Bell Stadium in Salford." Charlie looked puzzled. "Sorry, it's the Sale Sharks rugby ground."

"I expect you've done a few rugby grounds."

He smiled. "Yup, lots. I'm an expert on them."

"I'd have thought they must all look the same, but I guess they don't to you professionals."

"There are definitely some that you enjoy playing at more than others."

"Let's go," she said pointing in the direction of Haymarket as she picked her way down the steps. She moved quickly despite the crowds and Sam had to lengthen his stride to catch up. He manoeuvred himself next to her once he had found some space.

"How come you're away from Bath?"

"We do have holidays you know," he replied, louder than he intended. "The main season's over. It's only the play-offs left and we're not in those. I've got to clock in with my physio but that's it until pre-season training starts in July."

"I'm sorry you've had problems with an injury."

"Yeah, it was frustrating. I got a bit down about it. We all live for the matches so it's difficult when you're injured."

"I looked you up on the Club website." She looked round at him and grinned. "I liked your picture in the Bath shirt. Do you wear sports kit all the time?"

"At work, yes, but I do occasionally get out of uniform."

"It must be boring doing rugby as a job."

It was a challenging remark which put Sam on the defensive and brought back uncomfortable memories of conversations he'd had with Lily. "Don't all jobs have their boring times?"

"I suppose so, but most of them have a point to them. I mean, what's the use of rugby?"

Sam paused to collect his thoughts as they neared the junction with Pall Mall.

He remembered Charlie's reputation at school for being outspoken and upsetting other pupils. Now he was being tested by the adult version – beautiful but assertive. No doubt she'd throw some more verbal grenades while they were together, but it wouldn't be dull.

"Like all sports it provides pleasure for the supporters and creates lots of jobs. We're in the entertainment business." He sounded like an advertising executive, even to himself.

"On inflated salaries."

"I wish. I'm definitely *not* on an inflated salary."

"The top players must be doing well."

"I'm hoping to be in that bracket one day. They do OK but it's nothing like in tennis, football, or golf. And it's a short career with a high risk of injury."

"Sounds like a dumb choice to me."

"It has its negatives but it's what I've always wanted to do."

To Sam's relief she shrugged her shoulders and left it at that. She had fired a shot or two, made her point and wanted to move on. Their arrival at Trafalgar Square provided the opportunity.

"What's that phallic symbol all about?" Sam asked.

"Er, Nelson's Column," Charlie suggested, struggling to keep a straight face.

"I don't mean that. The one over there." He pointed at an elongated thumb aiming skywards from a giant fist.

Charlie burst out laughing. "You've got to loosen up a bit." She reached out, gently squeezed his upper arm and waited until he broke into a smile. "It's the Fourth Plinth Sculpture Commission. They have a new one every couple of years."

"Is it supposed to look like a skinny penis?"

"The sculptor meant it to be a thumbs up sign for London. I like his sense of humour," she said, in a way which suggested that Sam needed to get one.

He kept quiet while they ambled across the square past two chalk-dusted pavement artists and sat down on the wall in front of the gallery. A silver painted man with a top hat and cane stood stock still offering photo opportunities in the hope of donations. Small children were intrigued by this weird figure but squealed and ran away when he moved. It was mostly adults who were having their pictures taken. What a desperate way to earn a living, Sam thought. A guitarist was packing up his kit to make way for the next busker, a pretty girl with a saxophone and a backing amp. Sam assumed that they must be good to get a gig in Trafalgar Square, but wondered, who decides?

"Probably students at one of the music colleges," Charlie said before he asked. "It helps them to pay their way through uni."

"How do you manage?"

"Mum and Dad saved up for it while Sophie and I were growing up and Grandma left us some money to help with the fees. I also do some restaurant and bar work."

"London's expensive."

"Yeah, but not too bad when you know your way around. Students are good at finding the cheaper places."

The saxophonist began playing her first piece and soon stopped their conversation. Milling tourists paused to listen and watch. She was a natural performer whose instrument seemed to be an extension of her body. Sam couldn't take his eyes off her.

"I'm not a big fan of jazz, but she's a class act."

"Are you talking about the music or the way she looks."

"Both."

"We haven't got time to watch the whole of her set if we're going to get lunch."

"I'd like to listen for a bit longer if that's OK." It was the first time that Sam had taken the initiative and it felt good. He sat still and took it all in. He could see why people got excited about London. It must be good to be a student with all this at your disposal, even if you were a bit short of cash.

"There's a pizza place not far from here, if you're happy with that."

"Fine by me," he replied with his eyes still firmly fixed on the busker. "As long as you're happy."

A tune later Sam stood up to applaud. For a hopeful moment he thought he'd caught her eye, but there were many other fans whom she milked with easy smiles and elaborate bows.

"Ready now?" Charlie asked.

"She's so cool."

"Well, you clearly think so."

"I do." And you're not used to someone else being the centre of attention, he said to himself.

*

"Do I make you nervous?"

"Let's just say that you don't feel as intimidating as you used to."

Charlie paused and shook her head. "I don't like the thought that I'm intimidating."

"You were famous for it at Primary School. We were all in

awe of you. It didn't help that you were taller than everyone else and so bloody good at everything."

"Do you wish you hadn't come?"

"No, it's been OK. I've seen a phallic sculpture and fallen in love with a busker," he said with a grin.

Charlie smiled back and stuck up her middle finger.

"I'm glad your Mum gave you my details. She told me she still felt guilty about not getting us together after we left Oakwood."

"It's weird but true. She's gutted if she thinks she's let someone down. Can't let go. And you were one of her favourites."

"Teachers aren't supposed to have favourites."

"I know, but you were a project. Apparently, you still are. She always has a few on the go before you get too conceited."

"Your Mum's a star as far as I'm concerned. She was a great teacher. Made me feel that I wasn't stupid, even though rugby mattered to me more than academic work. If it hadn't been for her and Lily my results would have been crap. She made me understand how a good teacher can make a difference. It's like that with coaches too. Some are worth listening to and others make you want to join another Club." He hesitated, unsure whether to say what was on his mind. "And she came to my Dad's funeral. It meant a lot."

"She was pleased that you visited the school and wanted to see her. You've had a tough time and she wants to help."

"She helped to fix up the chance for me to speak to the PE students."

"Did you enjoy that?"

"It was great. I got a real buzz from it."

"She doesn't approve of my boyfriend," Charlie announced.

The sudden revelation took Sam by surprise. "Er, why not?"

"He's a bit pleased with himself and he's working in the city. Making money is what matters to him, and Mum, well both my parents, think there are better ways of contributing to society."

I'm not on strong ground playing rugby for a living then, he thought. "Has he got a name?"

"Adi."

"Is it serious?"

"He was my first proper boyfriend and he's very beautiful but we're drifting apart. I was at school and he was already at uni when we started going out. Lots of street cred for that… He takes me out for nice meals. God, that sounds awful."

"Yeah, it does. Sorry you're having to slum it with a pizza."

"Mum says you and Lily were a bit like a married couple at school."

"People used to give us stick but we didn't care. We grew apart when she went to uni. She got hooked on her course, met new people, and she wasn't really interested in rugby. It does dominate my life."

"It's your job. It has to."

"But I'm not contributing much to society."

"Not a lot, but we're all keen on sport, and it's not quite as bad as being in the money markets or an estate agent."

"Are you still running?"

"Yes, but not seriously. Dad calmed down when I told him I didn't want to be an Olympic athlete but I still keep fit. I'm doing a half-marathon for charity in the autumn."

"Which charity?"

"Breast cancer research."

"I'll sponsor you."

She'll find that hard to refuse, he thought, and maybe it'll help me to keep in touch. He had already made up his mind that he wanted more of her company.

"Are you sure?"

"Yeah, as long as I can see what you look like in pink."

She grinned. "That's cool, thanks. I'll send you a picture."

"I'm going to Spain with a couple of mates next week and then I'll be at home for a while before pre-season starts. Will you be around?"

"I'll be in London most of the time and then I'm going to France," she replied, shaking her head.

"Do your parents still have their place there?"

"Oh, yes. They're total Francophiles. As soon as the holidays arrive, they're off. They'll probably end up there for good."

"Even with Brexit?"

"They're firm Remainers, like all sensible people, and willing to take the risk."

"What about your plans for the future?"

"I want a First class degree and the chance to do a PhD. Beyond that, I'll wait and see." She glanced at her watch (it had a huge dial and a red strap to match her shoes) grabbed her bag and stood up. "Look, I must go, Sam. Thanks for lunch."

He stood up too and raised his hand to catch the eye of a waiter. "What do I do to make a contribution when you've done your half-marathon?"

"You really did mean it."

"Yeah, I don't say things I don't mean."

"I'll send you details of my fundraising page when I sort it out."

She put her hand on his shoulder and gave him the lightest of kisses on the cheek.

"Look, is there any chance of seeing you again?"

"I'd like that. Let me know when you're in town."

He watched her walk confidently out of the restaurant. Other diners noticed her too. She moved like a model on a catwalk.

# 19

Charlie generally enjoyed her Saturday evenings in Borough Market, but Adi and his friends were already the worse for wear when she arrived, and it wasn't long before they were getting on her nerves.

"Are you going to carry on drinking with these piss artists all evening, or are we going to get something to eat?"

"Don't be a drag. Harry's celebrating his bonus and he's buying. He's been at it since last night," he slurred.

"He can show off till Monday for all I care. I'm bored. And that sweaty arsehole with all his shirt buttons undone needs to keep his hands to himself."

"He doesn't mean any harm."

"If he comes near me again, I'll do him some harm. We either eat or I'm off."

"OK," Adi sighed after a pregnant pause. His brain was

working more slowly than usual. "We'll go to the Gourmet Burger place round the corner."

He downed the rest of his Peroni (almost a pint in one go) and suffered jeers and a shout of, "Hope he's up to it Charlie. I'm on call if he's not," as they walked out of the pub.

"I can't believe you really like these people."

"They're good mates."

"They need to grow up and, by the way, too much drinking and sitting in an office all day is making you fat."

"That's a bit harsh."

"Just the truth, Adi. It's about time you heard it. You need to start taking some exercise."

Charlie looked sideways at him while he walked unsteadily beside her struggling to keep his stomach under control. She had never seen him so drunk or looking less attractive. Lunch with Sam was a totally different experience. She had enjoyed his company and confirmed her view that it was time to move on from the Adi chapter of her life.

Things got worse when he bumped into a girl on the way into the restaurant and then clumsily weaved his way through to a table at the far end. Soon after he sat down, he had to go to the Gents and leave Charlie to order. She was fuming by the time he returned ten minutes later looking green and guilty.

"I'm not feeling great."

"How long have you been drinking?"

"Since lunchtime." He belched and Charlie smelt his breath from across the table.

"That's disgusting."

He belched again and made an unsuccessful attempt to catch it in his hand. Two rich smelling naked cheeseburgers arrived with baskets of fries and a generous bowl of salad to share.

"I don't think I can manage this," Adi said, pushing his plate aside. "Or the red wine."

"You'll have to sit there and watch me then."

Charlie concentrated on her food and left Adi to suffer in silence. He sipped his water with exaggerated care and tried to avoid looking at the oozing cheese and juicy meat.

"Mmm, delicious," Charlie said, to draw his attention to them. She gave him one of her penetrating stares. "D'you know what, you've changed since you started work."

"How d'you mean?"

"You're surrounded by greedy arseholes whose only concern is to make as much money as possible as quickly as they can. It's rubbing off on you."

"There's nothing wrong with wanting the good things in life."

"And what you think they are?"

"A flat in London, a villa by a golf course in Portugal and a boat."

"So, no expensive car then."

"Of course, that's taken as read." He grinned inanely.

"In vino veritas," she mumbled, and shook her head.

"What d'you say?"

"Nothing...I won't be staying at yours tonight, by the way."

"Why not?" he said loudly and drew disapproving looks from the occupants of the nearby tables.

"I'd have thought it was obvious. You're an embarrassment. Last week I had lunch with a guy who knows how to behave."

"What you mean is that he does as he's told."

Charlie looked at him with utter contempt and carefully placed her knife and fork next to her half-finished burger.

"You can carry on pissing it up with your friends. I'm off. I need a walk to clear my head of you before I go home."

She finished her last drop of wine, grabbed her bag from under the table and stood up. "Don't forget to pay the bill."

*

Outside, the market area was humming with the sound of social activity and seemed happy with itself in the fading light. Charlie walked briskly along Borough High Street and onto London Bridge. The cool breeze coming off the river was refreshing after the stifling atmosphere of the pub and restaurant and she slowed down to enjoy it. HMS Belfast looked imposing compared with the smaller fry working their way up and down the river. Further downstream Tower Bridge stood proudly, confident in its role as one of London's iconic landmarks. Reflections from the riverside lights flickered on the surface of the water.

Charlie began to relax. That's definitely it. Enough is enough. Now's the time to make the break. She glowed with the satisfaction of finally making a decision she had been considering for ages. She smiled. It was Sam who had given her the impetus. Who'd have thought it?

She liked him and was impressed that his offer to sponsor her half-marathon was not an idle promise. It was thoughtful of him to remind her to send the details before she left. A new relationship with a little more depth to it would be an improvement on the partnership of convenience she had with Adi. Sam's passion for rugby was all-consuming but what was wrong with that? He was making the best use of his talent. Just what she was trying to do and it didn't prevent him from being an attractive guy – seriously fit, actually…

These pleasing thoughts were rudely disturbed by the noise of a white van speeding north across the river. "What an idiot," she mouthed to herself. One of a group of people coming towards her, no doubt heading for the Market, shouted his disapproval more aggressively – "What the fuck's he on?" – and turned to stick up two fingers at the culprit. His friends shrugged their shoulders and looked skywards in collective agreement that there were always a few nutters around on a Saturday night.

Charlie's irritation turned to fear when the van performed a screeching U-turn and accelerated towards her and other pedestrians making their way across the bridge. A drunken show off was bad enough but this driver was fucking crazy.

She froze, rooted to the spot, unable to make her legs work. Screams of terror signalled the impending disaster as the van mounted the pavement and mowed them down leaving broken bodies in its wake.

# 20

Sam's holiday in Spain was only a partial success. Doddsy and Hunty had rented a two bedroomed apartment and offered him the sofa bed at a reduced price.

"It's fine just to crash out and we won't be sleeping much anyway," Hunty explained.

He was a popular member of the squad, a northern warrior as hard as nails and utterly committed on the pitch but also a regular instigator of evenings out, card games on the team bus and sweepstakes to add extra interest to their matches or other sporting events in the calendar. Unlike some of his colleagues Hunty was always highly organised in going about his professional and social life so Sam was easily persuaded, but he and Doddsy turned into different people on holiday.

Ibiza was a place to get drunk and laid, and they went at both with total dedication. Sam had never been a big drinker, but it was difficult to avoid when you were with two guys who were determined to get hammered every evening. He regretted being involved on the first night and having an appalling hangover after throwing down shots he didn't even like in order to keep up appearances. It was difficult being the odd one out who had to tag along with what the others had agreed or be Norman-no-mates for the day.

In the more sober moments, they met some fit looking girls but most of them turned out to be less available than the way they dressed and behaved suggested. Some of those who were up for it were so over the top that Sam worried what he might catch. His heart wasn't in it but Doddsy and Hunty had fewer scruples and gave him stick when he declined an offer to join them back at the apartment with two drunken girls, one of whom had to rush out of the bar and puke up in the street after accepting their challenge to neck a bottle of lager and two vodka shots against the clock.

Doddsy pointed to the gay bar across the road. "You might find someone you fancy in there," he taunted.

"Fuck off Doddsy. And don't expect any sympathy from me when your bollocks start to itch."

He slept on the beach that night and dreamt of Charlie. Images of those awesome legs and her stunning eyes had been constantly in his head since he saw her in London. No other girl had affected him like this since his breakup with Lily, and the ones he met in Ibiza weren't in the same league.

But the trip wasn't all bad. For Sam, the best moments were when they were together at breakfast with sore heads and big appetites talking about the game they loved, the Bath Club and their hopes for the future. They made each other laugh too, with that edgy banter which strengthens the bond between those who work and play together. There's nothing like it they agreed. Retired players who came back to the Club all said how much they missed the dressing room spirit. Adjusting to a 'normal' life had been difficult. He found it reassuring that Doddsy and Hunty's major worries were similar to his: selection, injuries, contractual arrangements, and clubs bringing overseas internationals into their squads as marquee players. "On massive fucking salaries," Hunty added bitterly. It wasn't only Sam who suffered sleepless nights over his chosen profession.

*

Back home after the holiday these and other problems were put into perspective when the story broke about the London Bridge terrorist attack. Sam found it impossible to understand what went on in the minds of people who were prepared to commit acts of mindless brutality in the name of their god. It was horrendous to imagine the effect of such carnage on those involved. An unexpected email from Mrs Woods made the incident of shocking personal relevance.

> *Dear All,*
>
> *Forgive this brief email but I thought you should know that Charlie was caught up in the incident on London Bridge and is in intensive care with serious injuries after being hit by the terrorists' van. Please keep her in your thoughts.*
>
> *Clare.*

It was devastating news. Once again tragedy had struck close to home. Sam had never felt genuine hatred before but now he could taste it. He wanted to lash out at somebody, something – anything to release his anger.

"Look at this Mum." Sam handed her his phone. He was glad he was at home with her. There had been some tricky moments since Mike's arrival but she was the best person with whom to discuss a situation like this.

"Oh my god, Sam. I can't believe it."

"Bastards. What's the point?"

Jill shook her head. "No point. They achieve nothing other than gaining publicity and ruining people's lives, but I suppose that's what terrorists want."

Sam feared the worst. "You've seen the results of traffic accidents at work, Mum. How bad do you think it is? They say that the van was travelling fast." He paused, not really wanting to say what he was thinking. "Three of the people it hit were killed."

"There's no point in pretending Sam. "I'm afraid that Charlie's likely to be very badly injured."

"What sort of injuries?"

"Speculation isn't helpful. I know it's difficult, but I think it's best to wait for further news."

"I need to know what to expect when I go to see her."

"You'll have to speak to Clare Woods about that."

"I know that," he replied angrily. "You don't think I was going to march into the hospital without checking first."

"No, but…" Jill stopped. "Look, Sam, we're both upset, and it won't do us any good if we get irritated with each other. Charlie's in intensive care and her family is having to come to terms with what's happened. Heaven knows how they're feeling at the moment. And the injuries are not the only thing they're dealing with. There'll be significant mental trauma associated with being the victims of a terrorist attack – for all the family."

Jill gave him back his phone and they fell silent, locked in their own thoughts. "Do you want a coffee?"

He nodded and looked again at Mrs Woods's email. The more times he read it the worse it sounded. Would Charlie survive? She must. She had to. He pressed the reply button and tried to think of the right words to respond to Mrs Woods. The fewer the better. Then there would be less chance of getting it wrong.

*Hi Mrs Woods*
*So sorry to hear the terrible news about Charlie. Thinking of you all.*
*Sam.*

Jill returned with the coffees and a plate of shortbread biscuits, always the answer in times of crisis. "Are you OK?"

"I've just sent an email to Mrs Woods. I said *Hi Mrs Woods*. Do you think that's too casual?"

"No. She's got more important things to worry about. She'll be grateful to hear from you."

"I can't help thinking about Charlie's injuries and whether she'll get through this. It puts my problem into perspective. It's embarrassing to think how I whinged about my shoulder."

\*

It was a week before Sam heard further news. Another round robin email from Mrs Woods confirmed that Charlie was out of danger but facing a lengthy period of recovery. His sense of relief was overwhelming but he continued to worry about how serious her injuries were.

"I don't like the sound of 'lengthy period of recovery', Mum. What does that mean."

"What it says, but I can't say how long when I don't know what's wrong with her."

"Should I get in touch with Mrs Woods again or is it too soon to visit?"

"You can ask but don't be upset if Charlie doesn't want to see you. Some patients long for company but others find it a strain having to answer the same questions over and over again. It's tiring. You may find that Mrs Woods is protecting her but I'm sure she'll be honest with you if you contact her."

"I think I'll risk it."

"Well, if you do go, be ready for a shock. She won't be the same girl you took out to lunch." Jill paused. "You're really keen on her, aren't you?"

"Yeah, I am," he admitted and then picked up his phone to text Mrs Woods.

There was no immediate response. Although Sam didn't expect one, he was frustrated after a couple of days had passed and he still hadn't had a reply.

"Clare Woods has enough on her plate without having to worry about answering dozens of texts and emails."

"But I have to be back in Bath in a couple of days."

"Then you'll have to travel from there if you want to see her, won't you." Jill responded tetchily. "I imagine they'll let you out for a few hours."

*

Sam slipped on the shiny floor and almost fell over after he had made his way through the main entrance. He thought how dumb it would be to injure himself visiting someone in hospital. He had never liked hospitals even though his mother had encouraged him to regard them as positive and inspirational places. She found it intensely irritating that the media concentrated on bad news stories about the NHS and rarely reported on the thousands of patients all over the country who received good service every day. Ever since his shoulder operation Sam had associated them with frustration and discomfort even though he was provided with the best possible care through the Club's private medical arrangements.

Finding the right ward was more difficult than he expected. The hospital was vast, a cavernous hive of activity with long corridors and confusing blue signposts. He was nervous and failed to concentrate hard enough when the assistant at reception gave him directions and he ended up outside the gynaecology department. A helpful cleaner put him straight.

"Thanks. I'm not quite ready to be a dad yet."

"Let me know when you are, love," she replied with a grin.

He wondered how many people worked in the whole complex and marvelled at the huge responsibility given to the person in charge of running it. He thought that the Bath Director of Rugby had a big job – it was certainly well paid – but it was like comparing a minnow with a whale.

Clare Woods was waiting outside the ward. "Sorry I'm late Mrs Woods. I took a wrong corridor."

"Don't worry, Sam. It's easily done." She paused and gave him a tired smile. "We're getting to know the place rather too well."

"Thanks for letting me visit."

"That's OK. It's good of you to come all the way from Bath. I'm sorry it's taken a while to get you here, but Charlie's had a really tough time."

"Are you sure she's happy to see me?"

"Yes, she'll enjoy seeing a new face. She's had enough of us sitting by her bed hour after hour. Go ahead. She's in the third bay on the left. I'm going for a coffee at the canteen."

Sam had prepared himself for the worst after noting his mother's warning but he was still shocked when he saw her. She seemed diminished, lying in an unflattering hospital gown, looking vacantly at the ceiling with her arms by her sides. The left one was in a cast from wrist to elbow and the right was bound almost to the shoulder in soft bandages. A patch on her head had been shaved and covered with a dressing which stood out brightly against her dark hair. Her nose stud and earrings were missing. She'll be really pissed off about that, he thought. A sheet and light blanket covering her legs were supported by a frame. Sam wondered what damage had been done down there.

She turned her head slowly towards him. "Don't tell me. I look as if I've been run over by a bus."

He smiled. Charlie's sense of humour was intact but her voice was weak and her eyes looked tired although they retained a spark of defiance. "Yeah, you do. Most of the bits I can see of you are bandaged." He hesitated. "Your Mum didn't say anything about your injuries."

"Will you sit down so you're not towering over me."

"Sorry." He fetched a plastic chair from near the entrance to the bay and positioned it as close as he could to Charlie's bed. He caught a distinctive smell of antiseptic as he sat down.

"Mum and Dad wanted to wait until I was out of intensive care and we knew all the details. Then I decided I'd prefer to tell people myself once I'd got my head together about it all. I hated the idea of a bulletin going out on social media."

Sam could understand that and nodded in agreement.

"So, a broken arm, broken ribs, a fractured skull and concussion from hitting my head on the pavement, plus scrapes, cuts and bruises everywhere. That's just the top half."

"So, what's going on under there?" He glanced nervously towards the end of the bed.

"A broken leg which they say should heal well, and a missing one."

Charlie spoke in such a matter of fact way that Sam took a while to process the information. "You mean…"

"It was so minced that there was no way of saving it. The consultant told me after the surgery."

"Shit," he said under his breath as he stared at the blanket imagining the space underneath it.

Charlie knew what he was thinking but not wanting to ask. Other visitors had reacted in the same way. "It's the left one – just below the knee," she said quietly. "At least my ankle tattoo survived. I paid good money for it. And you won't have to sponsor my half marathon, not this year anyway."

The humour seemed too slick, almost rehearsed, but she had found a way of telling her story. Sam respected her for that and for putting on a brave face. Yet again he was reminded of how minor his shoulder operation had been compared with what she was going through.

"You seem like…calm."

"Actually, I'm knackered, and I need to conserve my energy. I'm angry too but getting agitated isn't good for me.

I'll never forgive the bastards responsible but at least they're dead and I won't have to live through a trial, although I suppose there'll be an enquiry."

There was an edge to her voice. Not surprising, Sam thought. What must be going through her mind while trapped in bed wondering how the future will pan out. Survival was one thing: the quality of it another.

"I'm bloody lucky to be alive and, thank god, I didn't get slashed with a twelve inch ceramic knife like the victims in the Market. There were a lot of horrendous wounds, you know." She paused to let Sam take it all in. "There's always someone worse off than you are. I think it's important to remember that."

Sam looked at her, full of admiration, more convinced than ever that Charlie was someone special and that he wanted to be close to her to assist with her recovery.

"My study of prosthetics is going to take on a whole new meaning. I'll be able to be my own research project."

More dark humour to shore up the wall of resistance, just like soldiers at the front line. "To be honest Charlie, I'm struggling to know what to say, other than I think you're amazing."

"That'll do. Flattery's always welcome. I need it. I'm not a pretty sight, Sam. It's hard lying here like a broken doll."

"But you'll get better, and I know what you really look like."

"Not now I've lost half of one of my best assets. It'll be cold at the end of the bed with only one leg to warm it up."

Sam's throat tightened and he had to cough to clear it.

"Crazy things go through my mind, like which shoes shall I wear? Should I always wear trousers from now on. How bad will my limp be? Will people stare at me?"

"I want to help but I need you to tell me how… That is if you want me to."

"Just being here and letting me ramble on is helping. I guess there'll be other things you can do later. There'll be a lot of scars, not least in my head."

Sam was encouraged by Charlie's reference to the future but was careful not to push too hard. "We could keep in touch if you like, and you can let me know if and when you're happy for me to visit again."

She slowly lifted her arm and reached to touch his hand. "Thanks Sam. That would be good."

# 21

Pre-season training was going well and Sam felt positive about life. He was fitter and stronger than he had ever been, his shoulder felt comfortable and, perhaps most important of all, he was on his way to see Charlie again. It was frustrating to be so far away from her but they had kept in touch with occasional calls and regular texts. He learnt that Charlie preferred WhatsApps to phone conversations. They were easier to control. Hers were short and sharp (very much her style) but some of them were surprisingly revealing. They gave him an insight into her mood and how she was progressing but they didn't always make comfortable reading.

*It's difficult to do much strapped up like an Egyptian fucking mummy* was a case in point. On the other hand, *my target's to be back at uni in Jan* was positive proof of her determination to have a good recovery and easier for Sam to find the right words in response. *I'm learning to love my stump* caused his stomach to turn. *Phantom pain's weird* prompted detailed research on google and *My physio's SO fit* made him jealous. His collection grew (he kept them all and regularly scrolled through them) but he couldn't help wondering how Adi was feeling about the situation and how many other friends were in touch with her.

It was a pleasant surprise to see Charlie sitting up in a wheelchair waiting for him outside the ward although seeing her stump resting on a board in front of her was a stark reminder of the challenge she was facing. It was over a month since his first visit and it was encouraging to see the change. Her eyes were brighter and her face had more colour compared with the depressing grey pallor it had the last time. She was free of bandages on her right arm, the plaster cast on her left had been removed and hair was growing well over her bald patch. She greeted him with a broad smile and raised her arms to encourage a hug.

"Hi Sam. It's good to see you."

Hugging someone in a wheelchair was a new experience and he found it awkward to put his arms around her from a standing position with a protruding right leg and a stump in the way but, somehow, they managed a clumsy hold.

"I'm going to need more practice at that," he said apologetically, and sat down next to her on the seat she had been saving for him.

"I'm not going to be in a wheelchair for ever."

"How much longer?"

"I'll need one for a while yet but I've started using crutches now my arms are free and my ribs have calmed down. They were so painful, almost the worst thing. It hurt just to breathe. My bloody broken leg held up my walking aid assessment but it can bear weight now and my stump's in good shape. I'll be using the inflatable walking aid in a couple of days and taking my first steps. I can't wait to start."

"It's good to hear you sounding so positive."

"The hospital counsellor has helped a lot. She introduced me to a guy who lost his leg in a motorcycle accident when he was about my age. He hated trying on the prosthesis and thought he could never wear one until he saw a little girl walking with two little pink drainpipes." Charlie smiled. "He said it was embarrassing. A grown man feeling sorry for himself and there she was bravely dealing with the problem."

"How's he doing now?"

"Fifteen years on he's married with two children and running a successful business. He volunteers to support other amputees whenever he can. I think it's his way of paying back that little girl."

"Are you seeing him again?"

"We're in touch and he says we can meet whenever I feel the need. He's kind of on standby." She paused. "Something else he said really hit home. He told me that a below the knee amputation was nothing to be frightened of. I suppose you have the confidence to say that when you've come through something worse but he thinks I'll be fine once everything else has healed and I can get on with learning how to walk again."

"That sounds encouraging," Sam said brightly but he wondered if it might be an over optimistic assessment. "Do you fancy a coffee?"

"I'd rather go outside and get some fresh air. There's a courtyard area on the ground floor where we can sit."

"Let's go." Sam grabbed the handles at the back of the chair. "Do I need a licence to drive this thing?"

"No speeding like a boy racer."

"You'd be surprised. I'm actually quite a cautious driver."

"Funny, but that doesn't actually surprise me."

Sam steered Charlie via shiny corridors and a spacious lift to the oasis as she affectionally called it.

"I've spent a lot of time here since being allowed to get out of bed. I'm not sure why but it's never that busy."

He reversed her into a gap next to a bench situated in front of a colourful flower bed and sat down as close to her as he could. Sam had no interest in gardens (outside spaces were for playing games as far as he was concerned) but even he was impressed with the care that had been taken to make this an attractive haven protected from the hassle of day to day life in the hospital.

"I'm sorry I've been talking so much Sam but it's easy to become obsessed with yourself when you're in recovery and you've got nothing else to think about."

Sam knew exactly what she meant. "You've been through an horrendous experience."

"Like I don't want to be drowned in sympathy but it does help to let things out."

"Carry on then."

Charlie looked down at her legs. She seemed to be struggling for words, a rare experience for her, Sam thought. "The van didn't hit me head on. I wouldn't be sitting here talking to you if it had. Others weren't so lucky so I have a responsibility to make full use of my escape. Like I'm duty bound to be positive."

"That's easier said than done."

They fell silent. Sam looked around the garden area and the towering structure above him. Eight floors he counted, thousands of yellow bricks holding together acres of glass behind which dramas were playing out day after day. His and Charlie's wasn't the only one.

"You're a good listener, Sam. I noticed that about you when we had lunch. You'll have to be careful not to let me take advantage of you."

"I wouldn't mind."

"You could live to regret saying that." She paused to adjust her position and relieve the pressure on her right buttock. "And you're surprisingly sensitive considering you're a rugby player."

"We're not all psychopaths, you know."

"You don't get that impression when you watch the New Zealand team doing the Haka."

Charlie's knowledge impressed him but Sam blundered into a clumsy response. "So, you know something about rugby then."

"Don't be so patronising. I know stuff about a lot of sports."

"Sorry, that came out the wrong way. I like the idea that you have an interest in what I do, even though you think it's a dumb way to earn a living."

She grinned. "Maybe I was a bit harsh when I said that… Could I ask you something?"

"This sounds dangerous." Sam nodded and steeled himself for an awkward question.

"Have you had any serious girlfriends since Lily?"

"Not really."

"What do you mean, not really? Surely you have or you haven't."

He shrugged his shoulders to make light of it. "Just a few casual dates. Nothing serious."

"Why not?"

"It just hasn't happened."

"But you're good looking and my Mum likes you so you must have some other plus points. What's gone wrong?"

"You don't hold back, do you?"

"Not if I can help it. You can't find out what you need to know if you don't ask."

"So, what do you need to know?"

"Were you in love with Lily?"

This was getting complicated and for a moment Sam wished he hadn't encouraged her. He shuffled awkwardly in his seat. "Yes, I was," he admitted, gently nodding his head.

"What's it like?"

Sam managed a wry smile. "Great until it goes wrong."

"How did that feel?"

"It hurt."

"Are you over her?"

"It took a while. It didn't end well."

"Mum thought she was a lovely girl."

"She was. She is. Look Charlie, Lily's with someone else now. She's not part of my life anymore," Sam insisted but Charlie pressed on with what was beginning to feel like an interrogation.

"Surely the first girl you loved will always be part of your life."

"Well, I won't forget her if that's what you mean. Look, this is getting a bit weird Charlie. What's it all about?"

"Tell me, why were you so keen to visit me? Who in his right mind would be interested in a beaten up girl with half a leg missing?"

"I would."

"I don't want you here out of sympathy."

So that's it, Sam thought. He was stunned, unsure what to say. Why was he so confident on a pitch but riddled with doubt off it? There's always someone worse off than you, she said. Was that why he was here? No, it wasn't. She's beautiful, clever, she excites me. I want to be more than a hospital visitor.

"I'm not," he protested.

"So, what would your friends think if they saw me?"

"They'd be jealous and I'd be proud to be with you," Sam replied firmly.

It was Charlie's turn to search for the right words. She paused and reached out to touch Sam's cheek with her hand. The sensation took his breath away.

"That's the kindest thing you could have said. I can't bear the idea of people feeling sorry for me. You said the right things about Lily too. You didn't pretend she meant nothing when she clearly meant a lot."

They sat quietly until Sam plucked up the courage to address another tricky subject. "Can I ask something now?"

She laughed. "It would be hard for me to say no wouldn't it."

"I guess it would… Is Adi still part of your life?"

Charlie's hesitation said a lot. "I was with him on the night this happened." She nodded at her stump as if to emphasise the point. "I haven't seen or heard from him since."

"I can't believe he would just blank you."

She hesitated again and looked distinctly uncomfortable. "It's not quite as simple as that. He was drunk, we had a row and I walked out on him, unfortunately across the fucking bridge. I didn't actually tell him but I'd decided that was it… We're finished."

"So, does he know?"

"He must have realised. We were drifting apart. I'd refused to move in with him and he wanted more from our relationship than I did."

"He should still have got in touch with you to see if you were OK."

"Well, he hasn't."

"My turn for the killer question. Were you ever in love with him?"

"No, I wasn't," she answered quickly. "If I'm honest, he'd become a bit of a convenience."

"I'm not going to ask what that means."

"Please don't. It's messy and I'm not proud of it."

Sam saw a glimpse of vulnerability and liked her more for it.

"Can we move on now?"

He smiled and took hold of her hand. "When the time's right, will you come to Bath and give me the chance to show you off to my mates?"

She leant forward and kissed him. "Yes, I think I could handle that."

# 22

Sam had grown to appreciate Prof's advice and their occasional pizza evenings together so he was pleased that he had suggested an outing on the evening of his return from visiting Charlie. Prof was someone with whom he could have a serious conversation about things other than rugby, a mentor, like an older brother who was well aware of Sam's hopes for his relationship with Charlie to develop further. He took them to a small family run Italian restaurant hidden away down a side street in Bath. "More friendly than those big bloody outlets and much better pizzas too," he announced.

Sam was happy to go with the flow. He wondered whether he would become more particular about where he ate as he got older but had to admit that the restaurant was stylishly decorated and felt like the kind of place he would like to take Charlie.

"So, how is she?"

"Pretty good considering the battering she's taken."

"Do you want a beer."

"Why not," Sam replied with a grin.

"You're looking pleased with yourself. You must have something to celebrate."

"Yeah, things have moved on with Charlie. I think I'm now entitled to call her my girlfriend."

"Only think."

"Just being cautious, as usual, but she did agree to come to Bath to meet the lads."

"That's a big step, especially your mates. They're a challenge."

"Like you, do you mean?"

"Nothing like. I'm not in your age bracket for a start."

"True, old man. You're a proper grown up."

"Piss off. One day you might become a senior pro."

"I hope so."

"We'll see. The game doesn't get any easier."

"Anyway, it's not going to happen any time soon. She's got to learn to walk again for starters."

The waitress brought their drinks and they took a couple of minutes to order their pizzas.

"It's hard to imagine how tough that must be."

"We talked for a couple of hours, a lot of serious stuff. It's daunting but I want to help as best I can. She said I was a good listener," he added, feeling slightly embarrassed to have blown his own trumpet.

"That's quite a compliment. There's not enough of them about."

"She was having a meal with a guy on the night it happened. He got pissed and she walked out. They'd been going out since she was at school, like me and Lily, so you'd think he might have sent some sort of message."

"Yeah, but, look Sam, I'm not making excuses for him… what's his name?"

"Adi."

"If he's got any sort of conscience he'll be thinking, if I hadn't fucked up, Charlie wouldn't have left the restaurant at the wrong time."

The pizzas arrived and there was a break in the conversation while they concentrated on wheeling their slicers. Sam was relieved to have something to occupy him while he collected his thoughts. He hadn't considered how Adi might be feeling. Prof had a way of making people see another point of view. Sam had been pissed on occasion and made mistakes too. Who hadn't? He was lucky that the consequences weren't so dire.

"Charlie asked me a lot of questions about Lily and she's talked to her mother about us. We were both in her A Level Biology set."

Prof's eyes widened. "So, Charlie's mother already knows you."

"I saw her on most school days for two years. She was good to me, got the best out of me. I went to see her when I was injured and she helped to get Charlie and me together."

"An ally in the camp, heh. I thought daughters stayed clear of anyone their mother approved of."

Sam shook his head. "Don't worry. Charlie's totally capable of making her own decisions."

"Does she know about your father?"

"Yeah, she does. Mrs Woods came to his funeral, but we haven't talked much about him."

The waitress came over to ask if they wanted another drink. Sam noticed her brightly coloured trainers and wondered whether they would be Charlie's footwear of choice from now on.

"Knowing someone with real problems helps me to keep mine in proportion."

"That's not easy in our job. It's too much of a bubble. Living with Rachel keeps me sane. She refuses to let me drone on about work. Let's leave all that at Farleigh House, she says. Concentrate on me and the girls when you're at home."

"How did you know that it was serious with Rachel?"

"Lots of things: sense of humour, easy conversation, looks, good sex, the usual stuff. But there was one moment that clinched it. I was watching her playing with her two year old nephew and I thought, if I'm going to have kids, I'd like her to be their mother."

"Kids. That's too scary a thought but I suppose you are a decade older than me."

Prof raised two fingers and looked Sam in the eye. "Anyway, what is it about Charlie that's got you so hooked? You hardly know her."

Sam hesitated. "That's kind of true but I met her at a party a while ago and there's something I haven't told you. We were at Primary School together."

Prof laughed. "Don't tell me, you've been in love with her ever since."

"Bollocks. But she was the prettiest girl in the class, good at everything. She beat me in the fifty metre dash on Sports Day."

"A wounding experience from which you're still recovering."

Sam shook his head. "I knew I shouldn't have told you that. So, when we had lunch in London, after two hours with her I knew I wanted more."

"How do you feel about her now, after the incident? Any different?"

"I haven't been able to get her out of my mind since."

Prof sat back in his chair. His frown put Sam on his guard. "You're not doing the sympathy bit are you? Something to distract you from your own problems."

It was Sam's turn to sit back and frown. "That's harsh. It's nothing like that."

Prof looked across the table and quietly responded. "Knowing someone with real problems helps to put mine in proportion is what you said, just a few minutes ago."

"What's wrong with that?"

"Nothing, as long as it's not the *reason* for wanting to see her."

Sam was rattled. It had upset him when Charlie asked why he was so keen to visit her and now Prof was exploring the same territory. I must be sending out the wrong vibes, he thought.

"It isn't," he said louder than he intended.

"Good. It's the last thing Charlie needs."

"Why are you giving me so much grief Prof? I don't deserve this."

"Just saying. You've been thrown together in unusual circumstances to say the least."

Sam sighed. "Mum has the same problem but I know what I'm doing."

"I'll shut up then. As long as you're both clear about what you want from the relationship."

"I'm clear. Charlie's the best thing that's happened to me since Lily. I'm not sure what she wants yet but I intend to find out."

There was an awkward silence.

"You're not pissed off with me, are you?"

"No, I needed it. You make me think." Sam smiled. "By the way, Charlie was taller than me at Primary School, and she had longer legs."

# 23

Charlie had found her mother's visits to the hospital more demanding as time moved on. She was always pleased to see her but once the medical update, the quality of the food and routine matters from home had been covered they both struggled to find fresh things of interest to spark further conversation. Hearing from Adi was a welcome injection of something different and Clare had barely settled into her seat in the visitors' room before she blurted out the news.

"Adi wants to come and see you, darling."

Charlie wasn't sure whether to be pleased or not. "It's weird he got in touch with you first."

"Not really. He couldn't just turn up here, and the thought of calling or texting you was obviously too much for him after what happened."

Fair point, Charlie admitted to herself. "It can't have been easy getting in touch with you either."

"No. I was quite impressed that he did."

"What did you say?"

"That it was your decision not mine."

Charlie thought for a moment. "I should see him. It's taken too long but he wasn't to know that a bunch of terrorists were about to have their fifteen minutes of fame."

"I said I'd let him know when I'd spoken to you. What do you want me to do?"

"It's OK Mum. I'll text him with a date."

*

Charlie asked Adi to meet her in the ground floor courtyard thinking that it would be quieter there for what might be an awkward conversation. She wasn't sure what to expect or what she was going to say but when he arrived she noticed that he had lost weight.

"You're looking trim again."

"I haven't had a drink since that evening. There's not been a day when I haven't thought about what an arsehole I was. I'm so sorry. If only I could turn the clock back."

His voice was weak and subdued, Charlie thought. This wasn't the confident Adi she knew. "You look better for it… Have you stopped eating as well?" What a dumb question. She immediately regretted it. Intended to lighten the conversation, it fell flat.

"No, but I'm eating better and taking regular exercise," he replied with an earnest look on his face.

OMG, she thought. Where do I go from here? Grasp the situation. No more platitudes. Help him out. "I shouldn't have behaved like a drama queen, Adi. I'm sorry."

Charlie had to stop herself smiling at the look of surprise on Adi's face. "I can't believe you're apologising to me after what happened."

"I know you got pissed, we've all done that and regretted it, but it wasn't you who ran me over with a van."

"But if I hadn't…"

"Stop there Adi. But ifs aren't helpful. Eg. But if only I'd gone the other way and not across the bridge."

"Aren't you angry?"

"Very – with the terrorists and Muslim fanatics."

"Not with me?"

"I was at first but I've had enough time in here to think it all through." She took a deep breath. "This is hard, Adi. I wasn't straight with you when you asked me to move in. I'd already decided we should stop seeing each other and should have told you. I really wish I had. Then, when you got pissed with your mates, instead of being honest with you, I just got angry and went off on one like a temperamental teenager."

"So, it's over."

"Yes, it is."

"I knew it was but I just didn't want to believe it… I'm glad I've seen you again."

"Me too. We've had a lot of good times together. I'm sad it ended so badly."

*

*Adi's been to see me* ☒ It was another of Charlie's trademark texts but the smiley face threw him. Sam felt guilty for feeling a tinge of jealousy. She had said it was over with Adi. Maybe… No – ditch that thought. Grow up and remember

Prof's advice. Charlie wasn't proud of the way it ended so she'd be pleased to have the chance to clear the air. Yes, that explains the smiley face. Now he was cross with himself. This was the kind of over-analysis which depressed him during the dark times after his father's suicide and his shoulder injury. For god's sake, just ring her and talk. He got straight to the point.

"It was good that Adi came to see you."

"Yes, it was. I was upset that it took him so long to get in touch but I'm pleased he did. He's not had a drink since that night."

"Good for him."

"I'm over him, just like you are with Lily, but I can't pretend he didn't happen. He's the first guy I slept with… He taught me a lot," she added.

I could have done without that bit, Sam thought.

"Parting amicably made me feel much better."

"Good."

"Now, I've got some other news. I'm going home next week if everything continues to go well."

"That's amazing."

"I'm making progress with my prosthesis and enjoying the practice sessions. I can even do stairs now. I can't tell you how good it feels to be standing up and actually walking rather than sitting in a wheelchair or shambling about on crutches with my stump hanging down.

"It must be hard work."

"It's early days and it hurts but we're working out the right level of pain medication and I should notice small improvements each day. It helps that I'm young and pretty fit. Overweight and older people find the process really difficult."

Sam was encouraged. She was buzzing. This was the Charlie he'd met in London.

"How are you going to manage at home?"

"My parents have organised everything for me. Grab rails, a shower seat, slopes for wheelchair access – all that sort of stuff. I'll also be under the care of the nearest specialist centre and other support services I can access when I need them."

"It's all sounds great."

"The next thing is for me to get back on my course. I'll be really pissed off if they make me miss a year."

"Surely they won't do that."

"I've asked them to send me some work for when I get home but you never know with these academics. They can be very inflexible."

"Won't you be one of them one day?"

She laughed. "I hope I will. I'll be a breath of fresh air for my students."

"The trendy lecturer."

"With one leg."

"One and a half."

She laughed again. "Do you know what, it's so good to be talking about the future. Not so long ago I was afraid that I didn't have one."

"Will I be part of it?" he asked cautiously.

"I'm not planning on binning you just yet."

He punched the air as if he'd scored a try and almost dropped his phone. "So, when can I come and see you again?"

"Let's wait until I'm home. You can come and take me out. It's about time we had a normal date."

What a thought. A normal date. Sam went to training the next day in a lively mood fuelled by the desire to make

Charlie proud of him. Having someone special to play for was a powerful incentive.

During the off season, the Director of Rugby had signed a scrum half from Australia with several international caps, a decision guaranteed to annoy the other scrum halves already in the squad, including Sam. Admittedly, one of them had left at the end of last season to try his luck elsewhere but no one had expected this quality of replacement. It suggested a lack of confidence in the others. Getting a decent amount of game time would be more competitive than ever. It was another stark reminder of his lack of job security. If an injury didn't get you, loss of form would. The owner wanted success from his investment so if your face didn't fit, you'd be moved on. It was the same for coaches as well as the players.

Fortunately for Sam, after a good pre-season, he emerged as number two in the pecking order after Oz – not the team's most creative nickname. He was clearly a talented and experienced player and it was difficult to argue against his right to be first choice so Sam knuckled down to learn as much as possible from his new rival and ensure that he became a regular in the first team squad. From there he could bide his time and wait for further opportunities. A twenty minute cameo off the bench in the opening game of the season showed him at his best and prompted a compliment from the local press scribe whose usual preference was for critical rather than positive remarks. A couple of weeks later he was on the bench for a Friday night game in London which gave him the perfect opportunity to see Charlie at the weekend.

Jill was pleased to hear that Sam was coming home but under no illusion as to what was the main attraction.

"We'll be seeing more of you then, now that Charlie's at home."

Sam smiled to himself and resisted rising to the bait. He had gradually come to terms with the fact that Mike was around. It was easier now he had a new relationship of his own to think about. "I guess so, Mum. I hope that's alright."

"Of course, it is. How is she?"

"I'll know better when I've seen her but she's pleased to be out of hospital and learning how to walk again."

\*

Charlie had described it as a normal date but for Sam it was anything but. Collecting her from home felt like a big deal even though Mrs Woods had been responsible for bringing them together. And he hadn't seen Mr Woods since Sports Day at Oakwood. Sam phoned to check the disabled access at the pub they were going to but when he spoke to Charlie, she made it clear that she didn't want to use her wheelchair. It was a chance to walk in public and she wanted to test herself. She insisted that she'd have no problem getting into his car but Sam wasn't so sure. Looking after her was a big responsibility.

He was nervous as he approached the front door but a warm welcome from Mr and Mrs Woods gave him confidence.

"Lovely to see you again Sam. It's been a long time."

"We're so grateful for the support you've given Charlie. It's meant a lot, and so has your mother's."

It was news to Sam that she had been in touch with Mrs Woods. He was glad that she had but felt guilty that he didn't know. He needed to call her more.

Sophie appeared and gave him an unexpected hug and a kiss on the cheek. "Thanks from me too," she said. Her face was a picture, framed by immaculately groomed hair hanging loosely down to her shoulders. It smelt of expensive shampoo. She was as tall as Charlie and looked stylish in ankle boots, tight jeans and a short sleeved shirt. God, she's changed since showing me what was in her backpack, he thought.

Charlie came slowly into the hall on crutches. It was good to see her standing up. Her ear hoops and nose stud were back in place, announcing her return to the person she was, *before London Bridge,* a phrase which had become part of the family vocabulary since she came out of intensive care. They were gestures of defiance as much as fashion items. Her hair was short, spiky and gelled but a little longer than before to cover the scars from her head injuries. Her makeup was just as it was when they met in London. It spoke of new beginnings, about life getting back to normal, and perhaps a fresh start for them too. He hoped so. When Charlie leant forward to kiss him in front of everyone his cheeks reddened. It was a huge moment, a welcome into the Woods family as well as their home.

Philip insisted on them all having a drink together before Charlie and Sam went out and helped to make the conversation easy for Sam by bringing up the previous night's victory.

"Well done last night, Sam. Away wins are hard to come by in the Premiership. You must be chuffed."

"Really chuffed. I only played for half an hour but I was pretty pleased with my performance."

"You're doing incredibly well to be playing at this level and you're still young."

"So far so good," Sam replied with a smile. It was enjoyable to receive compliments from your girlfriend's father.

Charlie insisted that she didn't want people crowding round fussing over her when it was time to leave. Sam was taking her out and it was his job to help. Anyway, it wouldn't be long before she could manage on her own.

"Sorry about the tracksuit bottoms but they're comfortable and I'm not quite ready for skinny jeans."

"No worries. You look good in anything."

Sam opened the passenger door. Charlie handed him her crutches and leant on the car while he put them in the back seat.

"I'll need the seat right back. If you help to guide my new leg in, I can do the rest." She backed herself in and noticed him hesitate. "Don't worry, it won't bite. You'll get used to it."

He raised it gently over the sill and placed it carefully next to her other leg. It was an intimate experience. Although it wasn't a real limb, he felt a strong sense of it being part of her.

"Thanks Sam. That wasn't too bad was it?"

"I'll get better with practice."

Their entry into the pub was more of a performance. Charlie's walking was fine from the car to the entrance but neither of them was prepared for the elaborate clearing of space by well-meaning customers when Sam opened the door. The bar was crowded and it felt as if heaven and earth were being moved to enable them to go through into the restaurant area.

"God, it was like entering stage left for Act II Scene I," Charlie commented once they were sitting at their table. "I hope I won't always create a stir like that when I go somewhere."

They laughed but the experience made them realise than being stared at was something that Charlie would have to get used to. "You as well when we're together," she added.

Things settled down after the initial drama. They ate well, talked happily and Charlie made Sam's evening by holding out the promise of good times ahead.

"Thanks for a lovely meal, Sam." She smiled and then adopted a more serious expression.

"How do you feel about getting into bed with someone who has to take off her leg before her clothes?"

He thought for a moment. "You could do it the other way round if you wanted."

Charlie grinned. "I suppose I could. Would you prefer that?"

"I'm not sure. Either sounds good."

"We could try both."

Sam smiled uncomfortably. "It's up to you."

*

"Did you have a good time?"

"It was brilliant to be out having a social life again. There were times when I wondered whether it would ever happen."

"How was Sam?"

"He was fine. You were right, Mum. I'm pleased you got us together. He's a lovely guy, good looking and kind, and he wants to please me. I think he's the one."

"What do you mean?"

"The one I'm going to sleep with."

# 24

Charlie had planned it all. Sam arrived in time for coffee the morning after a Friday night home match which conveniently coincided with a weekend when her parents were away for her mother's birthday treat and Sophie was going to a party and staying with her boyfriend. She found it frustrating having to wait for an opportunity after the easy freedom of student life and ready access to Adi's place when the mood took them. Her parents would probably have been happy about having Sam to stay, but this was new territory for them both and Charlie wanted him to herself.

The feeling was mutual. At this stage, the idea of sleeping with Charlie with her parents in the house was too creepy to contemplate. Sam sipped his coffee from the SUPERMAN mug which she had carefully selected from the large collection in the tea and coffee cupboard and flashed a flirtatious smile before sitting down opposite him at the kitchen table. Charlie had told him that chats by the side of a hospital bed, texts and telephone conversations and a night out at the pub were all very well but this was the weekend when they would find out where their relationship was really going. No pressure then. He prepared himself for some serious conversation but hadn't expected the tough questions to kick off so quickly.

In true Charlie fashion she had done her research. "My counsellor says it's perfectly possible for an amputee to have an active and adventurous sex life, especially if you're still young, fit and flexible but we have to be open with each other if this is going to work."

She paused, a break clearly intended to ensure that she had his full attention, and fixed him with those eyes. "Can I trust you to be honest with me?"

"I'll do my best."

"Surely, it's a yes or no. You're either honest or you're not."

A black and white way of looking at the issue, Sam thought, but not the right time to explore it further. "OK. Try me out with something."

Charlie took a deep breath before she replied, a sign of vulnerability which, Sam guiltily admitted to himself, was something of a relief. "I find it hard to look at myself in the mirror and I'm frightened you won't like what you see."

"I'm sure I will," he responded with a little too much emphasis.

"How do you know?"

"I just do. You look great."

"But you haven't seen me naked yet. I've got to know if it turns you off…You will tell me, won't you?"

"I couldn't hide something like that. You'd know without me saying anything."

"I suppose the lack of an erection would be a clue."

It hadn't taken long for her to recover her composure. "It probably would but it's unlikely," he boasted.

"You might regret saying that." She grinned. "My counsellor said that it's important to keep a sense of humour. Laughter helps to overcome the awkward moments. Apparently, having sex in the shower is really tricky."

"Yeah, I can see why that might be a bit of a challenge."

"Let's go for a walk. I'm sorry but I'm not ready to leap into bed yet." She smiled. "Actually, I won't be doing much leaping, but you know what I mean."

It was an abrupt change of subject and a suggestion that took Sam by surprise. It was frustrating but he understood Charlie's caution and would have to be patient. "So, is that OK with the medics?"

"I'm not suggesting a 5k trek. Just a steady stroll. I have to practise every day, you know. It'll be good to get out somewhere different and have you to hang onto."

"Does your leg hurt?"

"Yes, but I'll get through it. I'm on strong pain killers at the moment but they don't want me to take them for too long unless it's absolutely necessary."

"We'll go to the reservoir. There are level paths round it and plenty of seats for a break if you need one." He was careful to say if rather than when.

"Perfect."

It wasn't quite perfect, not for Sam anyway. The last time he had been at the reservoir was with Lily, not long after Dad… It was ideal for Charlie's exercise but there were disconcerting moments along the way when he could hear Lily's voice in his head.

"I like this place," Charlie said.

"I used to come here with Mum to feed the ducks when I was a kid." He didn't mention occasions with Lily – an unnecessary complication. He was now with Charlie and had the chance to create new memories. Walking slowly with her made him appreciate the calm beauty of his surroundings and when she needed a rest, they sat down on a bench to look at the autumn colours of the trees across the water.

"Sit on my good side. The one with a whole leg. I'm happier that way round. I want you on that side when we're in bed too," she added.

"Is that another recommendation from the counsellor?"

"No but touching and hugging is. I need lots of it. I've forgotten what it feels like."

"I think I can manage that." He put his arms around her and kissed her. Charlie's response was eager and arousing. It made him hungry for more.

She slid her hand onto his lap and smiled. "Plenty going on here then."

"I told you."

*

Charlie was tired when they got home. She had walked further than usual and the effort had taken a lot out of her. "I need a rest. My stump's hurting. Let's watch a movie."

"OK."

"Have you seen *Silver Linings Playbook*?"

"No, I haven't."

"I've got it saved. It's a great film and had lots of Oscar

nominations, including one for Jennifer Lawrence. Trust me. You'll love it."

Sam did and it enhanced his enjoyment to be curled up with Charlie on the sofa following the advice of the counsellor whom he was beginning to regard as an ally. Charlie had taken off her prosthesis before they settled down. Once he had reassured her that it hadn't phased him, she also removed the liner so he saw the naked stump for the first time and watched her apply moisturiser before putting on a clean one.

"It's to prevent dry skin. I usually do it before I go to bed but today's been a bit different."

Charlie had made a ragu for their evening meal. "My own version…and we've got fresh pasta."

Sam wasn't sure that he'd be able to tell the difference but he nodded his approval to show that he was impressed. "Do you like cooking?"

"Yes, I do. Actually, we all do. Sophie and I were learning to bake cakes and biscuits when we were toddlers. What about you?"

"I'm brilliant at bacon butties."

"Great, you can do breakfast." She reached for the small rucksack in which she kept all the usual girlie crap (her words) and her other bits and pieces. "I need to have a shower. Could you pass me my crutches and carry my prosthesis upstairs for me?"

Sam followed her closely while she negotiated the stairs. "You don't need to creep up behind me like a wicket-keeper. I can do this without the crutches when my prosthesis is on."

Getting the balance right between offering too much help and too little was going to be important.

Crossing the threshold into Charlie's bedroom was unnerving. Ever since she had planned their weekend together Sam had tried to imagine what it looked like and dreaming about what might happen there had regularly disturbed his sleep. The bright red wall struck him first and then the bed, a king size double, topped with fat pillows and a thick duvet.

Charlie saw his eyes widen. "Plenty of room for both of us."

It seemed a large bed for a single person to have but he was more than happy to take advantage of it.

"I love red," Charlie confirmed.

Sam nodded. "I can tell. I remember your Converse sneakers, and the butterfly tattoo."

A laptop and angle poise lamp looked business-like on a tidy desk. The notice board above it was covered with randomly pinned pictures and large font inspirational mottos like those in the changing room at the Club. *Fall down seven times, get up eight* was in a prominent position across the top of the board. White fitted wardrobes with full length mirrors in the doors dominated another wall. It would be hard to avoid getting a view of yourself in one of those. He was excited at the thought of returning here later but not totally at ease. It felt strange being upstairs in his former teacher's house.

"I'll leave you to it."

"There are beers in the fridge. Help yourself. I won't be long."

He found a bottle of Becks in amongst the impressive range on the bottom rack. It took a while to find an opener in the myriad of kitchen drawers but it was worth the search.

He was unsettled and thirsty. He took a deep draft from the bottle and then wondered whether he ought to be using a glass. Surely everyone drinks out of the bottle these days. Maybe not, but I'm on my own with Charlie and she does. He flicked his way through his texts and emails. Nothing of great interest there so he switched on Sky Sports to check the results. No big surprises apart from Man Utd losing at home. Must be tough when you're the team everyone wants to beat. Charlie's taking an age. Sam was useless at waiting at the best of times but this was purgatory.

It took his breath away when she walked into the room wearing denim shorts, black tights, a close fitting red scooped neck jumper and, most intriguing of all, the famous Converse sneakers.

"I thought I'd introduce you to the new me. How do I look?"

"Amazing." He didn't know what else to say so he repeated himself. "Really amazing."

She blew him a frivolous kiss. "Thanks. You sound as if you mean it."

"Well I do," he responded emphatically, rather offended that she might have thought otherwise.

She moved on. "This prosthesis is pretty basic but there are lots of different styles available these days. You can even wear heels if you use wedges and you're willing to endure the discomfort."

"I guess you'll try everything out in the end."

"Definitely," she replied. "I'd better get supper ready."

"Do you need some help?"

"No thanks. I'm fine."

"I'll take a shower then, if that's alright."

"Of course it is. Relax."

He would try but it was hard.

Charlie's ragu was delicious, served with sliced tomatoes, a green salad and large quantities of tagliatelle. Next came an apple crumble which Sam riskily described as being almost as good as his mother's. They chatted about this and that: cooking, France, the demands of professional sport, having parents who were teachers, hospitals and Charlie's academic aspirations. She was still waiting for final confirmation that she could return to Imperial for the Easter term but things were looking positive. The university's Disability Advisory Service had been extremely helpful and there would be suitable accommodation for her in one of the Halls.

Charlie was great company and it was brilliant to have her to himself but at the back of Sam's mind was the distracting thought that they would soon be going to bed. But how soon? Much to his relief, Charlie broached the subject but he hadn't bargained for the instructions that followed.

"You'll have to be patient. It'll be like losing my virginity again. I've got to work everything out. Positions, balance, angles. I'm going to take off the prosthetic first and I think I'll leave the liner on to protect my stump in case it gets bumped. I'll feel safer that way."

"Now you're making me nervous."

"And maybe we shouldn't fuck straight away. I need to feel confidence in my body first…and you."

"Charlie. Please can we just go upstairs and get on with it."

She looked across the table and burst out laughing. "Sorry."

"Look, there are scars on my body as well. You don't mind, do you?"

Sam tried to reassure her. "Stop worrying. You look great."

Charlie encouraged him to explore. "I want you to touch every part of me to remind me what it feels like to be wanted."

She gave him plenty of advice while he searched for the places that gave her most pleasure until she grasped his hand and pressed it between her legs. His fingers worked patiently and it wasn't long before she was moaning and shuddering in his arms.

She kissed him. "God, that was good. Better than doing it myself."

"So, you've not been totally starved then."

"Of course not. I needed to check it was still working." She grinned and stopped any further response by touching his lips with her fingertips. "Your turn."

A few gentle strokes were enough.

"I hope you last longer than that when you're inside me."

# 25

Sam was having the time of his life.

"As good as it gets," he told Prof.

"Enjoy it while it lasts," he replied gloomily.

Prof's unusually downbeat response was the result of an ankle injury which was taking longer to heal than expected. In contrast, Sam was fit, playing well and enjoying his rugby as much as he had ever done. His first Premiership start was under his belt. He enjoyed gaining experience playing off the bench but it was nothing like the thrill of going on first and helping to shape the game rather than finishing it. Oz, his main rival, was a fine player who turned out to be a helpful mentor but he was as hard as nails and incredibly competitive.

"My contract's for two seasons. Then I'm back to sun and surfing in Sydney. You won't be getting a regular first team place before then," he boasted.

"I'm going to push you Oz, so maybe you should stop coaching me."

"It'll take a lot more than coaching to be better than me."

"We'll see."

"You gonna introduce me to your girlfriend at the weekend?"

"Will she be safe."

"Not if she's as fit as you say she is."

Sam grinned. Oz was short and made up for his lack of height by being prodigiously strong and on maximum volume for much of the time, but underneath the brash exterior was a dry sense of humour and a quirky way of looking at life. He thought that Charlie would enjoy meeting him.

"I'll chance it. We're going to the pub with a few of the lads on Saturday night. Doddsy and Hunty will be there and Prof might drop in for a while. Do you want to join us?"

"I'd better if that's the company you're forcing on her."

*

Winning the match put everyone in a good mood. The bar was crowded and Sam was amused to see his teammates form a protective circle around Charlie. They seemed to be taking pride in looking after her.

Doddsy who was well known for speaking his mind, not always with exactly the right words, took Sam aside. "She may have half a leg missing but she's fucking gorgeous."

"Thanks," Sam replied with a grin. A Doddsy compliment was one to savour.

"I admire her," he continued in an uncharacteristically serious voice. "How bad was it? You know, at first."

"Really bad. She's lucky to be alive."

"Fuck me. Tough girl then."

"Yeah, she is."

Doddsy nodded. "Respect."

It wasn't long before Oz had manoeuvred himself close to Charlie and engaged her in an animated conversation.

"Look out for him, Charlie," Hunty warned. "He's a wild one from the outback. Even funnel spiders steer clear of him."

"No worries," she replied in an impressive Australian accent loud enough for everyone to hear. "I've got a steel toecap in my prosthesis."

There was laughter all round including people by the bar who weren't in their group.

"I don't have a clue what she sees in you Sam but I'm taking her back to Sydney with me if I get half a chance."

\*

Charlie was the subject of much of the non-rugby chat at Monday training.

"She's gone down well Sam. You're a lucky guy," Prof said as soon as they met in the changing room.

Sam felt that his status at the Club had gone up a notch. The praise gave his confidence a boost and reinforced his desire to be with Charlie. When he was on a pitch and fully engaged in an important session, he was able to concentrate on rugby but his mind wandered during the dull post-match debrief sessions (he thought some of the coaches must have had a sense of humour bypass) and the repetitive grind of gym work left him vulnerable to detailed analysis of how their relationship was going and sadness that Dad hadn't been able to meet her.

Being in the first team squad was a huge commitment so he wasn't able to see Charlie as much as he would have liked. Lurking in the dark corners were the difficult questions. Would they drift apart like he had with Lily? He was dedicated to his rugby and committed to having as long a career as possible – at least ten more years, all being well. Charlie was determined to do a PhD at Imperial after her first degree. She was confident of getting a post-graduate place and hopeful of gaining funding. Her parents would support her if she didn't. Should he change clubs to be nearer London? Perhaps they could share a flat. But he was used to being at Bath, and would another Club employ him?

He was getting ahead of himself. It was brilliant being with Charlie but it did make life much more complicated.

*

Clare raised her glass of prosecco.

"It's so lovely to be doing this again. At one stage I thought it would never happen."

"Is that why you booked such a smart place?" Charlie asked. It was definitely one of those restaurants which was in Mum's 'special occasions' bracket.

"It's months since we've been out together and I wanted to celebrate. It's another step on our way back to normal life. I think that's worth pushing out the boat a little, don't you?… Would you have preferred Pizza Express?"

"No, Mum," she grinned. "This will do fine."

Charlie was buzzing with the excitement of being back on her course. "I'll be at the front line of this as a patient and an academic. How cool is that?"

"I'd prefer it without the patient bit but it all sounds incredible."

"It really is. There's a new device being developed that mimics natural foot motion through a motor-powered ankle. It means you can look around rather than having to concentrate on your feet. There are sports prosthetics systems that mean amputees can ski and the first sentient hand prostheses are being developed. There's so much innovation and the future's full of possibilities. Things are going to get better and better during my lifetime."

"I'm thrilled for you, Charlie. To hear you like this was an impossible dream a few months ago."

"Maybe I could come and talk to your A level students."

"Would you do that?"

"Yes, of course."

"Charlie, that's brilliant. I thought about asking you but I wasn't sure you'd be willing."

"It's fine Mum. I'd enjoy it."

"Let's do it in the summer term. It'll be a refreshing break from the grind of exam revision. Now, how's Sam?"

"OK. He's in a good place at the moment. The rugby's going well. He's a regular in the first team squad."

"Does he talk to you about his Dad?"

"Hardly ever. He keeps that tucked well away."

"I'm not sure that's good for him…So, how are you getting on together?"

"Fine, but he's a strange mix. So aggressive on the pitch but so gentle and attentive off it. He's almost too caring if that makes any sense."

Clare nodded. "Too smothering?"

"He'd do anything for me but it's a pressure. God, that

sounds selfish but I don't mean it to. We're good together and I'm fond of him in a way that never happened with Adi."

"I'm glad things worked out with him."

"Me too. I feel better now I've seen him."

"Sam needs to allow you more space."

"Yes, he does."

"How was Bath?"

"Good. I enjoyed the match. It was fun meeting his mates – real characters. He can stay with me when he has a game in London but I don't want to trawl around the country every weekend to watch him."

"Have you had this conversation with Sam?"

"Not yet. I'm not looking forward to it."

# 26

Sam jogged slowly across the pitch after the warm-up and breathed deeply to slow down his heart rate. He was too hyped up and he knew it. The pre-match routine felt so much more significant than when he was on the bench. This was one of the biggest matches of his career and he had warmed up as if his life depended on it.

Oz put a friendly arm round his shoulder before they went into the dressing room. He had pulled out at the last minute with a niggling hamstring and Sam found himself with an unexpected opportunity to start his first European game. In just a few minutes he would have to be at his best with a calm head on his shoulders.

"Settle down mate. I'm sorry to drop you in it but you'll cock up if you get too excited."

"Thanks Oz. Any other last minute advice?"

"Yeah, simple. I want you to play the arse off their scrum

half. He's an old rival from back home. He's a good player but not as quick as he used to be and his service ain't as fast as it was. Hassle him and make sure you get under his fucking skin. He's got a short temper."

At last, the whistle blew. The Bath forwards caught the kick off safely and drove efficiently to the edge of the twenty two. Sam dragged the ball back from the ruck and lifted a towering box kick which gave the maximum time for the chasers to put pressure on the receiver. He caught the ball safely but was driven into touch near the halfway line. Bath had the throw at the lineout and the success was celebrated with slaps on the back for the tackler and roars of approval from the crowd and players. Everyone was up for this match and a smooth exit was just the start they needed.

"Great kick, Sam," rang out in an unmistakably Australian accent.

Oz had joined the bench to watch the match and hearing his support meant a lot more to Sam than anyone else's at that moment. It gave a timely boost to his confidence. He was in the game and had started well.

Sam knew that French packs tended to be big but being only a few feet away from them gave him a close up view of some freakish giants of the game. Shit, they must recruit by the kilogram, he thought. Half of these could be competing in the *World's Strongest Man*. The game plan was to play at a high tempo and move these heavyweights around the park as much as possible to test their fitness. The last thing Bath wanted was to be caught up in an arm wrestle with massive opponents who relished close quarter battles. Saying it was one thing, doing it another.

The hooker's throw was slightly too long and put huge pressure on the jumper. He just managed to gather the ball but a powerful drive from the opposition forwards moved him and his lifters backwards. Momentum was lost and untidy ball emerged from the ruck with no time for Sam to deliver it safely to his fly half. He took responsibility and ran forward into a gap which quickly closed. Trunk like arms held him up and marched him downfield as if he was a practice bag. The whistle blew. Scrum down. Opposition ball.

"That'll teach yer to make a fucking break," shouted their scrum half, loud enough for the world to hear.

Another Aussie voice – this time less acceptable. First blood to his opposite number. Sam kept his cool and said nothing. Mustn't give him the pleasure of drawing a response. He edged close to him and stood on his foot to distract him while he was getting in position to put in the ball. The resulting flare up led to them both receiving a warning from the referee. "No penalty this time but I don't want any more of it or the yellow cards will be out." Oz was right, this guy was easy to wind up. The contest was on and Sam was loving it.

Half time arrived with the score at nine all, three penalties each. Sam's body told him that it had been the most physical forty minutes of rugby he had ever played. A heavy shower had drenched an already damp pitch and played into the opposition's hands. It was difficult to play open rugby and there were few opportunities for Sam to make the darting breaks which were such a strength of his game. The coach made it clear that there would need to be an improvement in the whole team's physicality if they were going to win the match. Sam had already taken a battering but he ran out for the second half with a rush of adrenaline and a promise to himself that he would give it everything.

A few minutes into the half Sam was confronted in open play by a rampaging Fijian with thighs like concrete bollards. He stood his ground and drove into him as hard as he could. The collision made the crowd gasp and the players stop as if a pause button had been pressed. The shrill blast on the referee's whistle rattled the ears of the players in the immediate vicinity and signalled to everyone in the ground that all was not well. He raised his arms to summon the medical team but they were already on their way. Experience told them that this one was serious.

Sam was conscious but couldn't feel anything. It was as if someone had switched off his power supply. His numbness and an eerie silence around the stadium were frightening. The doctor spoke to him calmly and told him to keep still. It felt as if he had been lying in the middle of the pitch for hours but it was little more than ten minutes before he was on a stretcher carefully strapped to ensure he remained absolutely still and ready to be driven off the pitch on a medical wagon. The player he had tried to tackle limped over to speak to him as he was moved away. Sam could see the distress on his face and responded with a weak smile of forgiveness. It wasn't his fault that he'd got his head in the wrong place.

# PART FOUR

Look what she'd been through.
Nothing he had to face could compare with that.

# 27

During many hours staring at the ceiling Sam had created an imaginary map of what lay beyond the mask of flimsy square panels peering down at him. Pipes, ducts, wiring, light fittings, insulation, vents – a hidden web of working parts breathing life into the wards below. He had rarely examined anything so closely but then he had never spent so long stuck in one place. Being still was alien to him. He found it painfully frustrating – and there was too much thinking time.

After being stretchered from the pitch Sam was taken to hospital where he had an operation to stabilise his spine. His cervical vertebrae had been knocked out of alignment and he was extremely lucky not to have been paralysed. He would be in hospital for at least couple of weeks and then there would have to be a long period of rehabilitation. And no, at this stage the surgeon would definitely not be drawn on when or if he might be able to play again.

Sam was horrified to learn that 'if' was on the agenda but he was also concerned that he would have lost his confidence after such a serious injury. If he could play again, would he still have the guts to make that tackle? He hated the thought of becoming a weak link who had a reputation for being off the pace when the going got tough. Someone would take his place while he was injured and it would be hard to get it back. He had struggled through dark moments during his last recovery and he doubted if he could stand an even longer period of rehab.

An experienced player in the Club with a long term Achilles tendon problem had told him that there were days when he simply couldn't face it anymore. "It was tough love from my dad that kept me going." The advice was well meant but it was a painful reminder that Sam's Dad wasn't around to provide similar support.

Harry, one of the props in the squad, had gone through six operations by the time he was twenty seven. Sam had already had two and dreaded the thought of descending into a similar injury abyss. His career had begun to take off but it would be next season at the earliest before the fans would see him playing again. He would be a sad figure watching from the stands on match days, sidelined yet again and grafting at the rehab work away from the buzz of the build-up to the weekly contest. A man apart, always on his own with the physios. And who was going to give him the tough love he needed? His mother was proud of what he had achieved but had reservations about his playing professional rugby and, although she wouldn't admit it, would probably be relieved if he gave it up. Charlie would support him and give gritty advice when required but she was busy with her own challenges. Look what she'd been through.

Nothing he had to face could compare with that. Sometimes being with her was overwhelming. He had become addicted to her. When they were together in bed and he could feel the warmth of her against him, bad memories and the pressures of life faded away. He could sleep, and when he woke up his first thought was of her and not his next match or the mistakes he made in the last one.

*

Charlie feared the worst when Prof first rang to tell her the news but his next call was more reassuring and she was able to visit Sam a few days after the operation. It was not a role reversal either of them wanted but she managed to make him smile. Colliding head on with a giant Fijian was a dumb thing to do but at least he had avoided paralysis and she was relieved to know that his tackle was still in working order.

"You'd be no bloody use to me without it."

"It could be a while."

"I'll try to keep control of myself."

She smiled and bent forward to kiss him. The taste and smell of her were a soothing antidote to the antiseptic atmosphere of the hospital.

"How's your Mum taking it?"

"She was by my bed when I woke up but pretty calm. She's used to seeing patients and as soon as she knew I was out of danger her professionalism took over and I'd got myself an extra personal nurse."

"Lots of advice then."

"Oh yes. Probably too much. I'm worried I won't play again and she's worried that I will."

"So, when will you know?"

"First, the surgeon wants to get me back on my feet and ready to start a full rehab programme. Then there'll be another scan before we look further ahead."

"What are you going to do if you have to stop playing?"

Just like Charlie, straight to the point, and too soon. "I don't want to think about that at the moment. I'm concentrating on recovering and getting back next season."

"You said on the phone that you wanted me to help you face the future. It's crazy to pretend that everything will turn out well. You have to be prepared for the worst."

It was too much. At this stage he would have appreciated her looking on the bright side rather than highlighting his fears. "Charlie, I know I do but I can't cope with that at the moment. Didn't you have doubts and fears when you were on your back in hospital."

"You know I did but I didn't pretend it was all going to be fine. There is a world outside rugby you know."

The expression on Sam's face told Charlie that she had gone too far.

"It's my career, Charlie. I thought you understood that."

"I do," she insisted.

"Is there another world for you, outside your academic bubble?" He looked away in a vain attempt to hide the tears that were welling up. "Not everyone is as strong as you."

*

Charlie left the ward angry with herself for the way she had handled the situation. After the kindness and patience he's shown to me all I managed was to give him a lecture, she thought. Fuck. He deserves better. As she approached the main exit she caught sight of Prof on the way in and tucked herself behind some other visitors hoping to avoid him. The last thing she wanted was to get involved in another conversation about Sam but he had spotted her and came straight over.

"Hi, Charlie. Do you fancy a coffee before I go up to see him? He could do with a break before his next visitor."

"Sorry, but I ought to be getting back to London."

"It won't take long. I'd like to hear how you think he's doing."

She hesitated. "OK, I suppose a few minutes won't hurt."

"You seem a bit stressed. What's happened?"

"He's not in a good place."

"Then we really do need to talk."

Charlie had recovered her composure by the time Prof had brought two flat whites to a table in the hospital café. She was pleased he had persuaded her to stay for a while. Sam liked him and she was disappointed not to have spoken more to him in the pub in Bath but he had left by the time she had escaped from Oz.

"What's your real name? All this laddish nickname stuff is a bit weird. It was you that called Sam Boxer, wasn't it?"

He nodded. "Guilty as charged but the guys don't use it much. He's usually Sam except when he's doing extra training."

"It seems a bit childish to me."

"Sebastian, but I prefer Seb."

"Somehow I didn't have you down as a Sebastian."

"My father thought Sebastian Coe was one of the UK's greatest ever runners so I got stuck with his name. I heard him speak at a dinner once. He said going to a tough Secondary Modern school, being small and having a posh name had made him learn to run fast."

Charlie smiled. "Right, Seb it is from now on." She sipped her coffee. "That's good… So how did you get into this game, Seb?" She stressed his name to confirm her decision.

"I was spotted playing for England Students and offered a professional contract."

"Which uni?"

"Bristol."

"What were you reading?"

"Philosophy but I didn't finish it, much to the annoyance of my parents. I was too impatient, wanted the money and thought I could always return to full time study if things didn't work out. Fortunately, they did but it won't be long before I have to start my second career."

"Sam calls you the old man, the senior pro."

"Well, I am well into my thirties with a wife and two kids so it's a fair description."

"He says he has conversations with you that he wished he'd been able to have with his father."

"We got to know each other when he was dealing with the suicide and I think he found it easier to talk about it to me than his contemporaries… being much older."

"He did."

"And then it was losing Lily and his shoulder injury."

"Agony aunt's going to be your next career then."

He smiled but then changed the mood. "We're dodging the main issue, Charlie."

His challenge caught her unawares and she stared studiously at her coffee…

The pause said it all. "You're right. It didn't turn out the way I wanted."

"A new experience for you then."

"That's harsh."

Prof pressed on. "Maybe, but you're tough enough to take it. You're also attractive, clever and strong willed – one hell of a combination. People are in awe of you."

Charlie was rattled. She wasn't used to being on the receiving end of straight talking like this. "I tried to make him face up to reality. Clearly, I pushed him too hard."

She sounded too casual and didn't come across in the way she intended.

"Not everyone is as resilient as you. Sam's a tough guy on a pitch but he's vulnerable off it."

"That's what my mother says."

"Take note then. Rugby and you are his whole life, and he's frightened of losing both."

They had moved into deeply sensitive territory. Prof hesitated and Charlie sensed what was coming.

"He's in love with you, you know."

"He's never told me."

"He hasn't told me, directly, but it's bloody obvious. Surely you must realise that. And if he can't play rugby anymore, he'll be relying on you to help him get over it."

"This is unfair. It's too much pressure," she responded impatiently. "What about you and all the medics and sports psychologists. Aren't they going to give him the support he needs?"

"Yes, but we'll never be able to provide what you can. You understand more than any of us what it takes to get through something really challenging."

She was upset. "I know he's fragile and, yes, I do care but I'm still struggling to deal with my own problems."

"I understand that Charlie but, whether you like it or not, you have an important part to play in his recovery. He needs you." He let the words sink in.

"Would you like another coffee?"

"I'd prefer a hot chocolate if that's alright."

Charlie was relieved that Prof had chosen the right moment to create a break. If she became more involved with Sam where would it lead? He had helped her when she was at her lowest point and she had chosen to sleep with him. No regrets there. He deserved her support but how demanding would he be? Could she handle the commitment if things went wrong? Prof was still in the queue so she took the opportunity to visit the Ladies but returned to the table no more in control than when she left it.

The hot chocolate was waiting for her. "Tell me, Seb. Would you have tried to get in touch to discuss all this if we hadn't bumped into each other?"

"I'm not sure I would but it's been a happy coincidence."

She shook her head. "I don't think I'm ready for what you're asking me to do. Is he really that vulnerable?"

"I think he is. When he lost his father, he was on the edge of serious depression and I don't want to watch a repeat performance."

"So, there's pressure on you too."

Prof nodded. "Yes, there is."

"You know how I feel then."

"Yes, I do, so I hope you'll forgive me for enlisting all the help I can get."

"You could have been gentler about it but at least you've been honest."

"Do you love him?"

"That's not a fair question and you know it." She paused. "I'm fond of him. Will that do?"

"I guess it'll have to. Shall I tell him we've met?"

"Up to you. I don't mind. My main concern is whether or not he can carry on playing."

God, I fucking well hope so, she said to herself...

# 28

It was a surprisingly small room. A desk, two chairs and a curtained couch filled it. The desk was home to a computer with a larger than average screen and, next to it, a silver framed picture of a woman who Sam assumed was the consultant's wife. A mistress? Of course not. Strange, the things that crossed your mind when you were nervous. The shelf above the desk housed a small collection of books and journals sitting at awkward angles. Sam would have had them upright and kept tidy by a bookend – maybe a skull or a rock found on a beach. He preferred the look of books on a shelf to reading them. Perhaps because the consultant had a national reputation Sam had expected more impressive surroundings but although he was the best, he was an unassuming man, not the sort who expected a luxurious consulting room in which to do his work. It was the operating theatre and his skills as a surgeon that really mattered.

Ken Jones greeted him with a smile and a firm shake of the hand. No clues there then. No gloomy expression to give the game away. Sam had told his mother not to join him for the appointment, and Charlie was tied up in London. Would it have been better if either of them had been with him? Not really. Charlie had made it clear that she thought he had to face the situation on his own. In the end, it was his problem and he would have to deal with it. He had prepared for the appointment as if he was getting ready for a match. Working out what the opposition would do in various situations on the field and planning how they would respond was a major part of team training. The coaches constantly banged on about processes and Sam had instinctively gone through the process of considering how he would react to whatever Mr Jones had to say. It didn't help. He sat down feeling as tense as he had ever been in his life.

"I hear from the medical team at the Club that you've been working extremely hard at the rehab since you came out of hospital."

He smiled and nodded in agreement. "They gave me lots of encouragement and I've worked my arse off for the last two months."

"Good, it's paying off. The op went well and the scan shows that your vertebrae have stabilised. You're making a sound recovery but that's not the same as being ready for professional rugby."

"I wasn't expecting to be ready yet. I know it will take a long time."

"I'm afraid it's not as simple as that. Look Sam, I don't want to be overdramatic but there's every chance you'll be in a wheelchair for the rest of your life if you have another similar collision. I'm sorry, but you're going to have to give up the game. It would be too big a risk to carry on playing."

Sam's chest tightened and an invisible weight pressed down on his shoulders. He had thought about the worst case scenario but having it confirmed by the surgeon was still a shock. Being sentenced must feel like this. He tried to think of something to say but the words wouldn't come. Mr Jones waited patiently to allow the news to sink in. It was a long time before Sam broke the silence. He was looking down at the floor as he spoke, quietly, as if he was talking to himself.

"So, all that hard work has been a waste of time."

"Definitely not. It's helped your recovery and ensured that you'll be able to carry on with life pretty much as normal."

"But not rugby."

"No, that would be dangerous."

"Isn't that my risk to take?" He knew it was a futile comment as soon as it came out.

"Not just yours, Sam. There are lots of other people involved: family, friends, teammates, coaches, the management at the Club. The welfare of players is paramount and it would be madness to ignore expert medical opinion."

He knew all this but couldn't help himself from putting up some sort of resistance to the inevitable. "But rugby's my job."

"I know it's tough but you're a young man with your life ahead of you and plenty of time to find a new direction. There's much to look forward to."

It sounded simple but Sam didn't believe a word of it.

He told Prof first. A text – *It's bad news* – was all it took.

The response was quick. *I'll pick you up from yours at 6.30 we're going out.*

Then Mum, and finally Charlie. No need for further announcements at the moment. The word would get out soon enough. It might even be in the papers – a couple of column inches for all the wrong reasons. He felt drained and his limbs seemed to have slowed down. He hoped his energy would return once he had come to terms with this dramatic change in his circumstances. Life-changing – a well-worn cliché but spot on in his case. This was huge.

*

At first, Prof had planned to take Sam to one of the players' regular haunts but thought better of it. The news was dire and he wouldn't be ready to face questions from his mates so soon after hearing it. Instead, he decided on a pub restaurant out of town.

"I've not been here before. Looks good."

"Rachel likes it. Let's have a drink at the bar first. It's on me tonight. No argument."

Sam appreciated Prof's effort to sound upbeat. "So, I can go for it then."

"No expense spared. Beer?"

"Nothing to stop me now. I can drink every night," he said blankly.

"Yes, I suppose you can if you like. But I guess you'll want to stay fit."

"What for?"

"That's a lame attitude. Pride, your health, because you're used to being a professional athlete. Lots of reasons."

"The main motivation has gone."

"It's only been a few hours since you heard. You're bound

to be shattered. Give it time and you'll find a way to move on and make plans."

"I've got no plan. Rugby was the present and the future – until today."

They needed a pause to help them take stock. Prof took the initiative. "Let's go to our table. I'll get you another beer or do you want some wine?"

"Red would be good."

After Prof had ordered the drinks they moved to a table in a quiet corner where it was possible to have a private conversation without worrying about nearby diners hearing every detail.

Prof noticed Sam's look of surprise when a bottle of red arrived. "I fancy a glass with my steak and you look as if you need the rest."

Sam sipped his wine in silence while Prof waited patiently for him to speak. It took a while but Sam eventually opened up.

"I always loved rugby as a kid but after I'd played for England Under 16s I was totally besotted with becoming a professional and getting an academy contract. It was all I wanted."

"You got reasonable A Levels, too."

"Not bad, thanks to Lily and my teachers but they should have been better."

"Good enough to go to university."

"You sound like my mother. Truth is, I don't really want to go. Anyway, you gave up your course for rugby."

"True, but I might go back once I retire."

Sam pressed on. "I've got used to the way of life. Everything planned out and organised, not having to think.

Told when to turn up, when to eat, what to eat, when to sleep, how to play. Nothing to think about except the next game. And you're hanging out with your mates every day."

"Now you can do other things."

"But there's nothing else I want to do."

"Surely you must have considered what you were going to do after playing."

"Not really. To be honest I don't believe many young players do."

"Maybe you're right but it's dumb not to have some sort of exit plan."

"I thought I had it sussed. A decade or more playing at the top level and then some kind of coaching role when I have more experience to offer the players. Now I'm fucked. Redundant. No more buzz from playing in front of a full house at the Rec."

"You'll find something. It'll be better when you get things into perspective."

"For chrissake, don't you think I've been trying to do that ever since I woke up after the op? It's easy for you. You've had a full career."

The discussion was getting out of hand and Sam was relieved that the waiter arrived to take their order. Just in time, he thought. He didn't want to argue with someone who had been so good to him.

"Sorry Prof," he said after the waiter left. "Can we enjoy the meal and talk about something else?"

Prof nodded. "We can try."

# 29

Sam felt lonely. Everyone around him at the Club had a purpose in life but he was no longer a contributor, more a hanger on destined to leave sooner or later. He found it disconcerting to be asked when his rented flat would become available but, on the whole, his teammates were sensitive to the situation, realising the possibility that one day they might be in his shoes.

Even in the current depressing circumstances Sam found it hard not to smile when he went into the Director of Rugby's office. It was a shrine to his sport decked out with photographs, shirts and caps in the way a teenager might cover his bedroom walls. A laptop and two trays designated PENDING and TOO DIFFICULT were positioned on a functional desk which was too big for the space and looked as if it had been imported against its will from a grander office. Behind the desk was an expensive looking executive chair from which the Boss conducted his meetings. Sam respected him. He was a tough but fair man who could give a bollocking that made you never want to stray again or show a fatherly warmth to young players when the situation required it.

"How are you doing?"

"Not too bad thanks, Boss."

"I'm sorry things have turned out this way, Sam. I was really worried when it happened. I know it's easy for me to say but the outcome could have been a lot worse."

"I know you're right but I'm struggling to see the positives at the moment."

"Totally understandable but when you next see someone in a wheelchair just remember that it could have been you."

Sam nodded. "When you put it like that…"

"OK. Let's look at some practicalities." He shifted forward in his seat to grab Sam's full attention. "Have you spoken to anyone at the Rugby Players Association?"

"Not yet."

"You must get on it. There's counselling available and lots of expert advice. While you're here you can use all the Club facilities and carry on your rehab with the medical team. We can also link you with one or two of our local schools to continue your coaching qualifications."

"Thanks Boss."

"Now, don't laugh. I was speaking to a referee yesterday who asked if you would be interested in taking up the whistle. They like ex-players, especially scrum halves. They're famous for chipping away at refs and become good gamekeepers when they take up the job." He smiled but drew a blank answer.

"I can't imagine doing it at the moment but I'll think about it."

"Look Sam. You've been a committed professional and to lose that so young is a nightmare but everybody has to give up at some stage. I know it's not the same but if you're passionate about the game, rugby can continue to be part of your life until you pop your clogs. There are only a few hundred full time pros but thousands of volunteers contribute every week to the sport."

Sam thought carefully before he answered. "You're right Boss. There's plenty I could do and I hope I will but I think I need a break from the game first."

"Fair enough. Just remember, the Club will give you all the support it can and I'll be there if you need me."

The following evening Prof and Rachel invited him for a meal at their place. Eating in a family house was a welcome change. He tried hard not to allow his gloom to spoil the evening but discussion of his plans for the future was inevitable. He needed to get away from Bath, he wanted to, but where would he go? His mother had encouraged him to come home until he was back on his feet. He had no immediate financial worries but it would be helpful for a while. On the other hand, it wasn't fair on her. She had her own life to lead, and he didn't like the idea of having to return to the family home after being used to the independence of having a salary and living in his own place. Tensions were inevitable.

It was Prof who mentioned the elephant in the room. "What about Charlie? What does she think about this?"

"I'm seeing her at the weekend to talk it all through. Neither of us wanted to discuss it on the phone. Better to be together for something so important."

*

He took a walk around Farleigh House and grounds in the morning before he left for London. Charlie had questioned why he had such an attachment to a mere training facility. "What's all the fuss about? It's only a workplace." He explained that it was much more than that. Accommodation was provided for some young players, usually when they first arrived at the Club, although Sam did admit that it was probably wise to get away from the place after work. He tried his best but doubted if she would ever fully understand the emotional ups and downs and the bonds of friendship that were part of life at Farleigh.

He bumped into the scrum coach, Tony Baker, in front of the old house.

"Taking it all in, Sam."

"Yeah. I'll be leaving soon and I doubt if I'll come back here again after I go."

"I've been meaning to catch up with you. Have you got a moment?"

"Sure."

They walked around the ha-ha and out towards the pitches. Sam liked Tony and was always happy to spend time with him. He had been through all the peaks and troughs of the professional game and the advice he gave to players was as uncompromising as his coaching methods. He was one of the Club's larger than life characters, as hard as nails but totally devoted to his wife and children. He was often the target for some cruel jokes but Sam enjoyed seeing him gain his revenge by extending the session and making it more painful for the comedians in the pack. He would always remember Tony's legendary response when asked what he thought was the secret of a successful marriage. "Knowing I'm bloody lucky to have anyone prepared to sleep with me."

"I'm sorry about what's happened Sam. It's a player's fucking nightmare."

"I thought I'd prepared myself but I'm struggling."

"It'll take time but you'll learn to manage it."

"I'm not sure I will. I find it hard to put things behind me."

They reached the posts at the far end of the pitch and stood quietly under the crossbar looking back at the grand buildings where both of them spent so much of their time. It was eerily calm with no one else in sight but soon the pitch would be fully occupied and ringing with the sounds of sweating players and vociferous coaches.

"You should be proud of what you've achieved."

"But it could have been so much better."

"Remember what you've done," he boomed. "They can't take away those age group caps and your first team games for the Club. Most people get nowhere near your level."

"It gives you a taste for more."

"It's not going to happen. That's a fact so get on and make a success of something else. You've got your life ahead of you. It's different for an old fart like me."

"Wouldn't you be gutted if you lost your job?"

"I would because I need the money."

"But you'd miss the work."

"Not particularly."

This was a surprise. Tony was one of the most highly respected scrum coaches on the circuit. The idea that he might not enjoy it was a revelation. "Surely, you wouldn't do anything different."

"It would be great to do something different but the

options are limited at my stage in life. I've no bloody qualifications and there's fuck all chance of finding something else which matches my current salary."

Sam could hardly believe what he was hearing. "You'd never know watching you work."

"Bluff and bullshit hide a lot. I like the people, the crack and the environment and this is a luxury set-up so I count myself lucky and just get on with it."

"I counted myself lucky too, but now it's all over."

"Get things in proportion. Rugby's not all it's cracked up to be. I'm a scrum guru. Big fucking deal. That makes me a top man at getting nine hundred kgs of meat to bend down and grind the shit out of another nine hundred kgs wearing different shirts. I'm looking up their arses half the time. What sort of job is that? Coaching scrummaging is fucking dull, and my livelihood depends on it."

Sam wasn't sure what to think. Who was supposed to be doing the mentoring?

"So, what's the message, Tony?"

"A lesson in life Sam. There are a lot of people in this world doing jobs they don't enjoy. You're the exception rather than the rule. You're suffering at the moment, I know that, but my advice is to remember the good times you've had in rugby, crack on and find something new."

*

"Sounds like good advice to me, Sam."

They were in Charlie's single bed. "A tight fit, but it's good to have three feet at the end of it," she remarked when she welcomed him in.

The room was larger than average to ensure easy wheelchair access and the disabled shower unit was excellent. She had stamped her personality on the place. It smelt of her and many of the personal touches she had in her bedroom at home (sadly, not the bed) had been successfully introduced to give it an air of permanence. Sam basked in the warmth and security of Charlie's body next to him. Her head was tucked neatly in the crook of his arm and the palm of her free hand was resting on the flat of his stomach tantalisingly close to his penis.

"It was sad."

"Clearly, rugby has lost its appeal but you shouldn't dismiss everything Tony said. He was telling you not to end up like him. He feels trapped but you've got options, and time."

"I don't believe I'm the exception to the rule. Everyone I know well likes what they do. Your parents, mates at the Club, my Mum and Mike, you…and me, until it all went wrong."

"That's a very limited evidential base," Charlie whispered in his ear before nibbling the lobe and sliding her hand lower.

"You bloody scientists."

"Ooh, it's stirring. Let's do it again. You were in a bit of a hurry last time. How about in the shower?"

"Are you serious?"

"I want to give the seat a try and it might as well be with you."

Another flippant and slightly unnerving comment but Sam was too aroused to let it put him off. "Is it strong enough?"

"We'll be in a heap on the floor if it isn't."

Charlie was almost wrapped in a towel sitting on the desk chair casually running her fingers through her hair.

"The seat held out."

"So did you." She turned towards him and flashed a congratulatory smile. "SBGO is good," she said mysteriously.

"Another bit of scientific spiel?"

"No."

"What then?

"Sex Before Going Out."

# 30

They were on their way to the underground and Charlie still hadn't told him the plan for the evening.

"Come on. Where are we going?"

"Borough Market."

"Why there? I'd have thought you'd want to steer clear of the place."

"We all have to find ways of dealing with our demons and this is one of mine. I thought I'd show you. Two fingers to the terrorists. Life's got to go on."

It wasn't the subtlest of hints.

Sam was never at ease on a train. He would get through it but there were other things on his mind which were stressing him out. Being with Charlie, particularly in bed, was as exciting as ever but too many perfunctory texts and strained calls had undermined his confidence. It was clear that she was fully back into the swing of university life. So, where did he fit in? Now his rugby career was over he would have more time to see her but did she want that? People watching, reading adverts and looking at Charlie's reflection in the darkened window across the carriage occupied the time until they arrived at London Bridge. He felt better when they emerged from the station and the mood lightened when Sam commented that Charlie's walking had come on in leaps and bounds. She refused to believe that he had used the expression on purpose but she didn't mind either way. Joking about disability was all part of the rehab process, as was revisiting Borough Market.

"This is the bar I was in with Adi on the night. It was one of his favourite haunts. Trouble was, he'd been there all day and was pissed. Let's have a drink here."

The place was too big for his liking and packed with Friday night start-the-weekenders, not a culture he was used to. Another sign of change. He was usually working at weekends during the season. They weaved their way to the bar and Sam noticed how skilfully Charlie negotiated the press of people. It was remarkable how well she had adapted to the demands of her disability. She insisted on buying the first drink.

"And I'm treating you to the meal tonight."

It was clear that there was to be no argument. "Thanks. You must be feeling flush."

"I have to admit that Mum transferred some cash so I could take you out."

"So, I'm still a project."

Her eyes held him and she grinned. "We both are."

Sam was hooked like a salmon on a fly and, as if by magic, a couple vacated two stools at the end of the bar where Charlie was ordering the drinks. She gave Sam her bag, grabbed his hand and, with a little support to help her balance, deftly manoeuvred herself on to the perch.

"You've done that before."

"Yeah. It takes a bit of practice but I'm getting quite good at it."

"Another hurdle overcome."

"I'm learning to work on the things I can do and to stop worrying about those I can't."

Another hint but gently expressed this time and more effective as a result. Sam agreed, but it was easier said than done.

"Where next?" he asked after they had finished their second drink.

"A gourmet burger round the corner."

"Don't tell me…"

She nodded. "Yes, you're getting the full tour."

Sam wondered if there were any other pit stops on Charlie's rite of passage. Where the hell might they end up next? He wanted her advice but it was unsettling to have it delivered this way. He found out after he'd finished his burger and chips and half a bottle of red wine.

"Must be good to have a drink on a Friday night."

"Being with you is what makes it good."

She laughed. "That's too smooth but I'll take it. You do say some charming things at times." She paused. "That sounds a bit patronising, doesn't it?"

"Yeah, it does."

"Sorry." She pressed the buttons on the card machine with a flourish. "Now it's time to walk over the bridge to get some fresh air."

He shook his head in disbelief. "So, the grand tour hasn't finished."

"You may think I'm mad but it's the most important thing. Having a drink and a bite to eat is the easy part."

"Haven't you done it before?"

"Three times. On my own, with my parents, and then my sister, but never in the evening."

Sam left the restaurant wondering whether it was a compliment or a challenge to be the first person outside the family to cross the bridge with her. He decided it was both. They were near the middle when Charlie stopped to lean on the parapet, looked downstream towards HMS Belfast and took a deep breath.

"At first I couldn't face the thought of coming here but I forced myself to do it after my counsellor talked to me about that shooting on Utoya Island in Norway. A few weeks after the massacre they organised a trip for survivors and relatives to go back as part of the grieving process. Hundreds went. There was a guy about the same age as me who played dead and survived after the killer had aimed at his head and hit him in the shoulder. He said he needed to return to the island so he could remember what had happened, face it and try to get on with his life."

Sam had a vague recollection of the attack being talked about by his Head of Year in a school assembly. "Weren't they all about our age."

She nodded. "It was a summer youth camp. Over seventy were murdered."

"Carnage. It's hard to get your head around it."

"She explained that it might help me to go back to the scene of the crime, so I risked it. All I had was a ghastly image of a white van coming straight at me – then nothing.

I needed to understand what happened so I had a narrative and could move on."

"Has it helped?"

"Yes, but I still see that fucking van in my dreams."

"It's pathetic to compare it with your experience but I have nightmares about that tackle. I used to sleep well but I'm crap at it now."

She put her arm round his waist and pressed herself against him. "So, you have some idea of what I'm talking about."

He nodded.

"After the first visit I wanted to come back again as a mark of respect for those that didn't make it and an act of defiance against the shit who tried to kill me. Fuck you. I'm a survivor not a victim and still have my life ahead of me. You didn't win."

She paused to calm herself. "It made me realise I was lucky. It's tough for someone else to tell you that. You have to work it out for yourself."

Sam stared thoughtfully at the river and the myriad of lights along the banks. The current was running fast and the water looked forbidding under the darkening sky. You wouldn't last long in there, he thought. Charlie had been through a harrowing experience. Her strength and determination were an example to everyone but beyond the reach of most people, including him. It was daunting. She had nearly died in a deadly attack. By any rational comparison Sam's problems were less significant than hers but he had yet to get them in perspective. He felt inadequate. He had told himself a hundred times to get a grip. Charlie in her own inimitable style had given him an insight into her way but it was almost too much for him.

"Will you go and watch Bath play."

It was an unwelcome question but it snapped him out of his introspection. "I couldn't face it."

"Why hide from the sport that you love?"

"Because I can't play anymore." He was rattled. "It would be torture seeing my mates doing what I want to do. I don't want to watch any fucking games at the moment let alone my old team."

"Doesn't everyone have to face up to the fact that they'll have to stop playing at some stage."

"Yes, but not at the age of twenty two."

Nothing was said for a while. The water and boats below received further detailed examination until Charlie took hold of Sam's arm and encouraged him to walk to the north side of the bridge. On the way to the station they looked briefly at the Monument. Needless to say, Charlie was able to tell him its height and the fact that there was a panoramic camera system at the top. How did she know so much stuff? It was like having walking Wikipedia next to him.

"So, what's your plan."

"I don't have one, other than moving back home. I'm not keen on the idea but I can't hack staying in Bath."

*

Charlie's lunch with Mum did not start well. She had arranged it to follow the weekend with Sam and although Charlie had agreed she thought the timing was so blatant that she couldn't let it pass without a comment.

"Strange coincidence that you chose this week but I suppose you were keen to check that your investment was worthwhile."

"Ouch, that's unkind Charlie. You didn't have to come."

"You know me. Anything for a free meal."

"God, you're in a mood. What's going on?"

She shook her head. "He's struggling."

"So, he needs your help."

"He's depressed and it's hard," she replied making no effort to hide her irritation. "I know you all think I'm strong and I've made a good recovery but there have been some dark times. It's taken a lot of willpower and I don't think people realise how difficult it was. Don't worry about Charlie. She'll pull through seems to be everyone's attitude and it pisses me off."

"You've never said this to me before."

"Well I have now," she replied sharply.

"I'm so sorry Charlie. I didn't realise."

"I didn't want to upset you and Dad so I've tried to keep things to myself."

"I feel terrible. It's awful to think you couldn't share the problems with me…us. Dad would be upset too."

"I've had a counsellor. And Mum, children never share everything with their parents. You must know that. Nor parents with their children. That's the way it is."

Clare poked at her salad and sipped some fizzy water. "Being a parent is bloody difficult. Wait until you do it."

"I'm not sure I want to. The idea scares me to death. I don't think I'd be much good at it and I might get a daughter like me."

They both laughed, a welcome release of tension.

"It may be difficult but I do still love being a mother."

"You're not perfect, but you'll do. I'm far from being a perfect daughter but we've both got what we've got, haven't we? Neither of us chose…You know Mum, being responsible for Sam is daunting. He's relying on me too much and I'm not sure I'm up to it."

"So, what did you do over the weekend?"

"Some things I don't need to talk about but the main outdoor events were a visit to Borough Road and a walk across London Bridge. I had this stupid idea that if I showed him how I was trying to face my demons it might help him with his but I think he found the whole thing rather intimidating."

"Don't be too hard on yourself, darling. It's early days. He'll come round. Remember how you were at first."

"At first, I was so full of drugs that I didn't know what the hell was going on."

"True, but once you were out of danger you had to face up to the future."

"Sam's not doing that. He's moving back home but it's just to get away from Bath, not for any positive reason." She paused and looked inquisitively at her mother. "Which do you think is worse, losing a leg or a job?"

"God, what a question that is." She paused to think. "Do you remember doing your First World War history and reading about those poor victims of shell shock who had no visible signs of injury. Some were even charged with cowardice and desertion. They received little sympathy until their symptoms were properly understood."

Charlie nodded and smiled. "Point taken Mum."

She was thankful that the conversation moved on to more mundane matters. The problem of Brexit for people with properties in France. How were things going at school? Was Dad still considering going for promotion or had he settled for the comfortable life at Chelston Grammar?

"And what about you Mum? Do you fancy being a Head?"

"I have thought about it but I enjoy the classroom too much. Heads seem to spend most of their time dealing with government initiatives, staff issues and looking for more funding. They don't get the fun of working with the students. And I'm not sure we'd have as much time in France if either of us was running a school. That would be sad after all the hard work we put in to renovate the barn."

"I've not been for over a year and I'm missing it."

"Then you must go. Dad and I have been invited to a wedding in Portugal during the holidays so there's a week free when you can have it to yourself. You could take some friends... Or a friend."

Charlie couldn't help laughing. "Mum, you're completely outrageous."

"Well, the offer's there if you want to go down."

# 31

Sam had never been a fan of heavy nights out with the lads and didn't want a farewell dinner. Getting hammered wouldn't solve his problems. He was missing the discipline of being a professional athlete and felt guilty that he had been drinking too much since his playing days were over. He would have preferred to slip away quietly but Doddsy insisted.

"We can't let you bugger off without doing something. Nothing flashy, just a meal and a few bevvies in the back room at the pub."

"You might have told me that you'd already organised it."

"It'll be an insult to me and the lads if you don't let us get you pissed on your last night in Bath."

"OK Doddsy. I didn't want any fuss but it's good of you to get the guys together."

"There'll be ten of us at the last count. It'll be a good crack."

It was meant to be a positive send-off. Sam appreciated their generosity but he felt sad to be reminded of what he was about to lose. Prof was spot on when he proposed a toast to "our reluctant guest." What Sam hadn't expected was the presentation of a tankard engraved *To BOXER from the lads at Bath.* It brought a lump to his throat when Prof handed it over and shook his hand.

"SPEECH," rang out.

"I'm not sure what to say," Sam slurred.

"Sit down then."

"No. Let's hear his words of wisdom."

"Wisdom from him, fuck off."

"Give him a chance."

"Yeah, don't let him get away without saying anything."

"So let him get on with it. I need a piss."

"Me too."

A loud combined "SHUSH" from Doddsy and Hunty gave Sam an opening.

"Go for it, Sam."

He didn't feel in full control of his mouth and had to concentrate hard to get the words out. "Thanks to all of you for this." He waved the tankard in the air. "It means a lot. I'm disappointed that I've had to stop playing early in my career but I'll remember the good times I've had with you guys." He sat down.

"For fuck's sake. Is that it?"

"At least I can go for a piss now."

"No Oscar this year Sam."

"Let's go to the bar."

Sam was relieved to escape. Against his better judgement he said yes to a whisky and fell into a depressing conversation with Joey who had just heard that his contract was not being renewed for next season.

"At least you've got a good reason for leaving. They've just decided that I'm not fucking talented enough."

The idea that he was considered to have a 'good' reason for leaving wasn't what Sam wanted to hear.

And that was it. His dream was over and all he had to show for it the next morning was a pint pot and a hangover. Later than intended, he chucked the last few bits and pieces into his car and headed for home. But wasn't Bath his home? He was driving away from his team-mates to a place where he had lost touch with most of the people he knew. And there was no plan. It was frightening.

\*

Sam had accepted the fact that Mike was now part of his mother's life. They were happy together and Mike was good to her but Sam was uptight at the thought of living with them. He had to admit that he found Mike less difficult than when he first moved in but he was pleased that he was going to be away at a medical conference in Edinburgh during the first week. He would have Mum to himself.

The evening didn't go well. The whiskies after the previous night's dinner were not a good idea. Sam was knackered and still hung over. All he wanted to do was go to bed.

"How was the journey?"

"OK."

"It's wonderful to have you home. I've scrubbed up your room and bought new bed linen. Should have changed it long ago," Jill gushed.

"Good."

"Mike's sorry he's not here. He's looking forward to seeing you and so are the girls. They're coming for Sunday lunch in a couple of weeks. I'm working tomorrow but I've got a couple of days off after that so we'll have plenty of time together."

"That's nice."

"Steak for dinner."

"Sounds good."

Sam picked his way through the meal and couldn't find the energy to engage in any sort of meaningful conversation or show his appreciation. An explosion was inevitable when he made no effort to help clear away the dishes.

"What the hell's going on Sam. It's like having a surly teenager back in the house. I hope you'll be in a better mood when you've had a good night's sleep."

"I don't sleep well these days," was all he could manage.

*

Sam felt ashamed of himself when he woke up the next morning. Mum deserved better. He got up to pee and looked out of the window on the way to the bathroom. Her car had gone. He had missed the chance to apologise before she went to work. He glanced at his watch. Shit, it was past ten o'clock but he still felt tired. Might as well go back to bed to shake this off. There's nothing else on.

When Jill arrived home, Sam was ready with a glass of wine. "Sorry about last night Mum. It was the worst hangover I've ever had. Give me a hug."

She wrapped her arms around him and spoke quietly. "Don't do that to me again, Sam. It was hurtful."

Sam held on tightly as if to prove that he still loved her. Her calm response had made him feel even more guilty.

"So, what have you been doing today," she asked as they separated.

He hesitated. "I went to the pub." He was embarrassed by his answer but it was only half the story. He didn't tell her that he had been in bed all morning.

Mum's look said it all. "Did you see anyone you know?"

"I went to a place out of town so I wouldn't. I don't want to see anyone just yet. I'm better off on my own."

"Oh thanks."

"I'm all over the place Mum. I'll try harder, I promise."

They sat down at the kitchen table and Jill sipped her drink. Sam pointed at his diet coke. "That's what I had at the pub too."

"You should stick to it."

He managed a smile. "I haven't got any immediate financial problems so you don't need to worry about that."

"Well, I wasn't going to ask you to pay rent."

He ignored the signal that there were more important issues on her mind and ploughed on. "I get an insurance pay-out and I have a few months' salary from the Club before they terminate my contract." Terminate my contract – he hated the phrase. There was a horrible finality about it.

"I was looking at the Rugby Players Association website. It's good. Have you been in touch with them yet?"

"No."

"Don't you think it would be a good idea?"

"Give me a break. I've only been home for twenty four hours," he replied sharply.

"I thought you might have done it before coming home."

"There's nothing I want from them at the moment. They won't be able to wave a magic wand and sort my life out."

"There's good advice from people who understand what you're going through. The Lift the Weight programme seems excellent."

It was no surprise to Sam that Mum had done some research. He would have been upset if she'd shown no interest but he could do without her putting pressure on him. He could feel his temperature rising.

"Just let me deal with it."

"You can't expect me to sit back and do nothing when you're so obviously depressed. I want to help. What can I do?"

"Just leave me alone for chrissake."

*

Sam made himself go for a walk around the reservoir the next day. He was up late again, still finding it difficult to shake off the tiredness that was affecting him. The fresh air would do him good. Everyone said that you had to seek advice: talk with a trained professional about what you were experiencing, try counselling, don't be afraid to take medication, antidepressants aren't addictive. But surely, a grown man should be able to cope with his own problems. It was an embarrassment not to. He had been warned as a young academy player that all rugby professionals have to find a 'normal' job at some stage. At least he had reasonable

A Levels but what sort of job did he want? He didn't have a clue. He'd never considered preparing for life after rugby. Too young, too invincible, too narrow minded. What the fuck was he going to do that would make it worth getting up in the morning?

He sat on the bench where he had been with Charlie on his last visit. He was helping her then. Somebody to worry about apart from himself. She was a strong character, almost too resilient to be true, but the road to recovery had been hard, even for her. He believed he had played his part in her rehabilitation. Could she do the same for him? It wasn't fair to put pressure on someone else. He'd made that mistake with Lily, but Charlie was different. She would see him through. He couldn't wait to see her and longed for her to feel the same way. At a time when nothing seemed to matter, he still wanted Charlie. There was no person on earth he would rather be with.

# 32

Since returning home Sam had found it increasingly difficult to concentrate and he began to worry about doing everyday tasks. He regretted his offer to do the weekly shop when on the way to Sainsbury's he almost ran into the car in front of him at a set of lights and then needed several goes to reverse into a parking space. Finding his way around the aisles was like negotiating a maze and at the checkout he forgot his mother's credit card number, punched in the wrong one and had to use his. He put these difficulties down to tiredness but a panic attack following an unusually vivid dream proved to be a much more frightening experience.

He was lying naked on top of his duvet and could hear someone talking ⸗ the skills coach relentlessly putting him through his passing drills. Strange sleep patterns were a regular problem but this was more intense than usual. His arms burned, beads of sweat dampened his forehead and his heart began to race. He couldn't move. The edge of the bed was a precipice. He might die getting up.

The alarm on his phone rescued him. He set it regularly even though these days he rarely responded other than to switch it off. He sat bolt upright, still sweating but chilled by the draft coming from an open window. He swung his legs round and was relieved to find that his feet reached the floor. Deep breaths slowed his heart rate and calmed him down. He told no one about the incident and convinced himself that it must have been a one off. He would put it behind him and move on but it wasn't long before he had another episode, this time on the way to see Charlie.

As his train approached Liverpool Street, he found himself pinned to his seat. The prospect of stepping onto a busy platform made his palms run with sweat and his legs as immoveable as tree trunks. The station roof looked flimsy against the bright sky – was it safe? He thought his fear of railways was under control but this brought back the traumas he had endured after his father's suicide. He breathed in deeply and waited until everyone else in his carriage had left. It took all his willpower to get off the train and find a space out of the way of the stream of passengers. As the crowds thinned out, he regained his equilibrium dried his palms on his trousers and made his way to the ticket barrier dragging his case slowly behind him.

He couldn't face using the tube and opted to take a taxi, an extravagance he resented but a safer bet bearing in mind how he was feeling. He didn't regret it. Being in a taxi was a helpful distraction. He felt safer cocooned inside the black box with his legs comfortably stretched out and he allowed the busy London streets to capture his attention. So much happening, so many people getting on with their lives. They all seemed to know where they were going – unlike him.

But he did know. He was going to see Charlie. Trouble was, what after that? No doubt another tricky week with his mother and Mike. He pressed the button to wind down his window and let in some air but a waft of exhaust fumes caught him at the back of the throat and he quickly closed it again. They stopped at a set of lights and another cab drew up next to him. He looked away to avoid unwanted contact with the face in the window. He wanted his space to be all his own.

Sam arrived at Charlie's room feeling marginally better but was put on the back foot before he'd even got through the door. "You look grey. What's the matter?"

"Nothing," he responded defensively. "Is that all the welcome I get?"

She kissed him lightly on the cheek. "You need some fresh air. We'll go for a walk."

There was no debate but he didn't really mind. It was easier to go with the flow and just being with her was an antidote to all the crap that was going on in his head. And he probably did look grey. A walk would do him good.

Kensington Gardens were looking at their best and already busy with local and international tourists enjoying the morning sunshine. As they made their way past the Albert Memorial towards the Serpentine Bridge, they were entertained by giggling selfie takers and snippets of conversation in a variety of languages. Charlie was full of praise for London's parks where she had spent hours improving her walking since her return to Imperial. They reached the middle of the bridge and looked down towards the Lido.

"The Serpentine Swimming Club is the oldest in Britain. There are members who go in every day of the year."

"Shit. I wouldn't fancy that."

"They say it's good for releasing stress. Maybe you should try it." She grinned.

"Thanks for the advice but no thanks."

"We'll have coffee at the café but I want to show you Princess Di's Memorial Fountain first."

The screams of children paddling and splashing in the stream of water made him smile. The wetter they were the more excited they became, and soaking dad was simply the best.

"It's become a children's play area. It's a really happy place. Just what you need." She gave him one of her disconcerting looks. "So, what's going on? You looked rough when you arrived."

She was pressing him, just as he expected, but he wouldn't mention the panic attacks. He didn't like that expression anyway. He had convinced himself that one was a nightmare (he'd had plenty of them) and the other a relapse connected with his train phobia. No need to make a big deal of either.

"Do I still look grey?"

"Not too bad, but you're obviously hiding something."

"As you said, I just needed some fresh air."

It sounded unconvincing but Charlie chose to move on. "Let's go to the café. I need some caffeine."

They were lucky to find a table outside and two coffees later Sam had begun to relax and enjoy the sunshine. "I like it here. Let's stay for a drink and something to eat."

"Fine by me."

Only a minor decision but Sam was pleased to have taken the initiative. It was too easy to be swept along by Charlie's agenda.

"I'm paying."

"Even better. So, what have you been doing since you moved back home?"

"Nothing much."

"That's gone down well then."

"It's been tense if I'm honest."

"Well, *if* we're being honest, it must be difficult for your Mum and Mike too."

"I can't get used to the idea that my life has completely changed."

Charlie softened. "I do understand that after all those days in hospital lying on my back wondering what sort of future I had ahead of me."

"And I feel tired all the time. I'm struggling to find the energy or incentive just to get out of bed."

"Not good, especially if you're living with your parents."

"No." Sam shook his head. It was definitely time to change the subject. Being with Charlie was supposed to lift his spirits. He mustn't dwell on his problems for too long. "How's Sophie?"

Charlie raised her eyebrows in surprise. "I don't see her much but she seems OK, judging by the occasional texts and photos she sends. She's enjoying being in the Sixth Form and has a boyfriend my parents don't approve of. Nothing new about that."

"I guess she's planning to go to uni."

"Yeah."

"What's it like?"

"What?"

"Being at uni. You know, on a day to day basis."

"It's good. I love it. I like my course and know what I want out of it… It helps if you enjoy studying," she added with a smile.

"What else do you do?"

"To be honest, it's mostly work at the moment making sure I'm up to speed after missing a term. I exercise a lot. I'm still planning to do a marathon and I haven't forgotten your promise to sponsor me."

"Neither have I."

"It's great to be in London. There's always something on. I do stuff with Mali and Liam. You know, the Thai girl and American guy who live in Hall. They're loving studying over here. Now I've got used to having half a leg and know I could do it, I'd like to live and study abroad at some stage."

"Maybe I should do more travelling."

"Yeah, you should, now that you've got more time."

"We'll see."

"Then there's you. The highlight of my social life at the moment."

"Do you mean that?"

She laughed. "Strangely, I do. I was planning to take you out for a film and a pizza tonight. Have you seen *Three Billboards Outside Ebbing Missouri*? I've heard it's brilliant."

"No, but I'm up for it."

*

When he was with Charlie even a routine trip to the cinema was an occasion to be savoured. Sly glances at her leg no

245

longer bothered him. She drew far more attention for her looks than her limp. Her high approval ratings had brought him respect from his mates in Bath and now he got a buzz from watching admiring heads turning in her direction while they were queueing for tickets. She had retained an edgy look with her short dark hair, the crescent of earrings and – was that a slightly larger nose stud? Hard work in the gym during recovery had ensured that she retained a figure which made any clothes look good on her. She stood tall and confident, still able to make an impact in any company.

The film made an impact too, particularly when the Chief of Police shot himself. Sam closed his eyes during the climax of the scene. Charlie grasped his hand just before the trigger was pulled and held on after the noise had made the whole audience flinch and Sam's palms sweat.

He found the incident disturbing but had managed to put it behind him by the time Charlie apologised. "I'm so sorry, I really wasn't expecting a scene like that."

"It's OK. Honestly. Anyway, it was a good film. I enjoyed it."

She reached for his hand and squeezed it affectionately. "I promise I'll make it up to you."

He grinned. "I'll have another beer to celebrate."

"You're not to have too many. I don't want you underperforming when we get back. Have you ever had apology sex?"

"I'm not sure what it is."

"You're about to get lucky."

From the time Charlie came naked out of the bathroom she took the lead and did all the things he liked best. If this was what she meant by 'making it up to you' he was all for it.

Charlie looked down at him from her favourite position. "We're good at this aren't we?"

"You sound surprised."

"It's just that too many men are under the illusion that they're good at sex when actually they're fucking useless."

Sam wasn't sure how to respond and opted to say nothing. How much evidence had she gathered? A twinge of jealousy threatened to spoil the moment. He didn't want to hear about her other experiences.

"I'm paying you a compliment, you idiot." She leant forward, kissed him firmly on the lips and then moved to make herself comfortable beside him.

"Thanks. I'm flattered." He smiled benignly at the ceiling. He must enjoy Charlie's approval while he could. She was so complicated, challenging one minute, amusing and considerate the next. Life with Charlie would never be dull. He couldn't get enough of her.

"Would you like to come to France with me?"

Another surprise. "Er, yes. That would be great."

"It'll be good to get you away from moping around at home. And you can stay in bed late, as long as I'm with you, of course."

"When are you talking about?"

"After the end of term. My parents are going to a wedding in Portugal and they said I can use the house while they're away. You'll have me all to yourself for a week with no distractions. How does that sound?"

"Amazing."

\*

"You're back early."

"Charlie had to complete an assignment for tomorrow so I left after breakfast."

"Did you have a good time?"

"Not long enough but, yes… Charlie's asked me to go to France with her."

"Lucky you."

"Her parents have offered her the house for a week while they're away."

Jill laughed and quickly apologised. "Sorry, but you've got to admit it's ironic that after all these years the trip to France is finally going to happen."

"It's a lovely place. Look." He showed her some photos Charlie had sent via WhatsApp.

"Very nice. When are you going?"

"In a couple of weeks."

"That's perfect. You can chill out in France and we can talk about the future when you get back."

"That would be good, Mum. I know I've been a pain since I came home but I'll try to be more positive. I think being away with Charlie will help."

"You're very fond of her, aren't you?"

"Do you remember when we talked about Lily after I broke up with her? You said that your first serious relationship is always something special."

"How could I forget?"

"It's a bigger deal with Charlie. I can't get her out of my head. Life seems exciting and actually worthwhile when I'm with her."

# 33

Sam was looking forward to his holiday with Charlie and the agreement with his mother not to talk about the future until his return had reduced the tension between them. He realised it was putting off the inevitable but it was a good decision in the short term. He was feeling less stressed than he had been for weeks and took it in his stride when Mum asked if he would do a little tidying up in the garden ready for a barbecue she and Mike were planning.

He surprised her when she returned home from work the following day by escorting her to the garden and showing off the newly treated shed, tidy borders and grass with stripes on.

"Wow. It looks brilliant." She gave him a grateful hug. "Mike will be thrilled."

"I owe you both more than a day's work, Mum." He smiled. "I quite enjoyed doing it. Shirt off, sun shining."

"You're in good form. Surprising what the thought of a holiday with a pretty girl can do for you." She paused and Sam guessed what was coming next. "When are you going to let us meet her? I still haven't quite forgiven you for not bringing her round when you were staying at her parents' place."

He didn't bite. "Not yet, Mum. Maybe after France. We'll see how it goes. Shall I get you a drink?"

"Why not. A glass of white wine would be lovely."

Mike arrived home half an hour later and, as Jill predicted, he was pleased with the work Sam had done. "Thanks for doing the garden Sam. Much appreciated. I fancy a lager. How about you?"

"I'll get them."

"No let me." Mike topped up Jill's wine and took two bottles from the fridge. Peroni OK?"

"Fine."

He poured them into two stemmed glasses.

"Why don't you two chat in the sitting room while I lay the table and sort out supper. I'll come through when I've done."

Mike led the way carrying the glasses and Sam got up slowly and followed him. Was this a planned move? It felt suspiciously like it.

"The shed looks new."

"Yeah. It scrubbed up well."

"It was good of you to help out. Your Mum and I have been really busy at work and we've neglected the garden."

Sam nodded. They both sipped their drinks and Mike coughed.

"I should have told you earlier but I've been waiting for the right opportunity. I spoke to Ken Jones at the conference in Edinburgh."

It took a moment for Sam to switch on. "Oh. You mean my surgeon. Good guy."

"Yes. You couldn't have had anyone better. A brilliant surgeon with no ego, unlike a lot of us who have a tendency to be a little too pleased with ourselves."

Where was this going? Sam wondered.

"Ken told me that you missed being severely disabled by a whisker. You were lucky. I understand why you're depressed about what happened and I'm really sorry that you're having to cope with your rugby career coming to an end but I hope that one day you'll be able to look back and be thankful for having had a miracle escape."

Sam appreciated Mike's concern and the way he expressed it. He nodded his approval. "Me too."

They sipped their drinks to occupy an awkward pause in the conversation. "Good news about your trip to France."

"Can't wait."

"Charlie's important to you isn't she."

"Very."

"Like your mother is to me."

"I'm glad it's worked out."

"Look Sam. I know it's been difficult for you but I am committed to your Mum... I hope you know that." Sam couldn't escape his questioning look. "I'd do anything for her."

He nodded. "Thanks Mike."

"And I want to support you too, if you'll let me."

*

Sam's main concern prior to the holiday was the Channel Tunnel. Charlie had done all the organisation for the trip and chose the route she was used to taking with her parents.

"It's easily the best way. Half an hour and you're there. Quicker and less fuss than the ferry."

He was angry with himself for getting stressed about it before he'd even set out for Folkstone but the thought of all that water above his head and no obvious means of escape was worrying. He hadn't suffered another episode since the one in Liverpool Street. He had kept quiet about the problem although Charlie had noticed that all was not well. But surely it was dumb not to tell her when there was clearly something wrong. It would mean swallowing his pride but this had to be the moment. She couldn't help him if he didn't let her.

She was understanding when he phoned to explain.

"Oh, my god. I never thought. I'm sorry."

"It's my fault for not telling you."

"I'll book a ferry."

"Too late for that, isn't it?" There was a brief silence during which Sam imagined he could hear Charlie's brain whirring.

"I tell you what. Why don't we stick with the Tunnel and face the demon together, if you can handle it. I'll look after you, I promise."

A Charlie challenge. How could he say no?

\*

They caught an early shuttle in order to do the journey in a day. Charlie described it as an eight hundred kilometre slog but worth it. There was no need to spend money on an overnight stop. With two drivers and a few short breaks they would be fine. She would do the first leg and Sam could take over when they were well south of Paris. It would be his first taste of driving abroad. Although Charlie had limited experience herself, she assured him that he would find it easy. The roads were empty compared with the ones at home.

Once they were in the train, the chocks were in place and the safety doors closed Sam felt reasonably calm inside the car reading the newspaper and listening to a *London Grammar* album. He loved Hannah Reid's voice and it was some time before he noticed that they were actually in the tunnel. Charlie reached across and gave his arm a reassuring squeeze. She followed up with a lengthy kiss and some distracting strokes of his thigh.

"If you carry on like this, I'm happy to go all the way on the train."

She grabbed his hand and held it firmly until they emerged into French sunlight.

"Job done. You alright."

"Good thanks. You've got a job for life."

"Don't get ahead of yourself."

*

Sam learnt a lot about France during the journey. His only previous visit was on a flight to Toulouse for a rugby match. Driving through it was an eye opener. So much agricultural land. So much space. Charlie drove the final stretch, hammering down the A20 from Limoges past Brive-la-Gaillarde before heading west through the rural acres surrounding Sarlat.

"There's a bijou airport near Brive. Ryan Air from Stanstead is popular with the Brits. It's only forty kms to Sarlat from here and the house is this side of it. I've packed some beers, a couple of bottles of wine and enough food for a meal tonight and breakfast. We'll go to town and do the full shop tomorrow morning in the biggest hypermarket you've ever seen."

"I've not seen that many to be honest, not from the inside anyway."

"Well, you'll have a good look at this one. The Woods family rules in France state that everyone gets involved in housework, shopping and cooking. What's the Sam Martin signature dish, apart from bacon butties?"

"Barbecued meat. There is a barbecue, isn't there?"

"Of course. All holiday necessities are available at *Le Havre.*"

"Sorry. Stupid question."

"We'll shop early. Leclerc built this giant store but the aisles are narrow and the trolleys huge. Once it gets busy it's like a traffic jam in Paris – nightmare."

They were tired after ten hours driving but the sight of the honey coloured cottage revived them. The gravel crunched as they turned into the short drive near an old piggery which was now inhabited by logs for the wood burner and a selection of garden implements and old tools picked up in the local markets.

"Dad's a bit of a collector and likes the artisan look of them. Some of the smaller ones find their way into the house until Mum throws them out. She thinks most of it is tat."

Sam smiled. No doubt he would be learning more about Charlie's parents during the next few days. He peered through the fading light at the renovated barn which had become the Woods' pride and joy. Opposite was the swimming pool surrounded by a mixture of hedging and shrubs which made it private. Not that there was anyone around. It was a tiny hamlet and as far as he could tell the nearest neighbour was some distance away.

"It's quiet here."

"Yes, that's why my parents love it. Total chill out after a busy term. But we're not far from the nearest village which has a restaurant and a boulangerie, and Sarlat is only a ten minute drive." She looked at the car temperature gauge. "It's still in the mid-twenties. They say that you have to be south of Cahors to be certain of the weather but it looks well set here for the week. You can swim if you want but I'm going to have a shower and open a bottle of wine."

They had been sitting next to each other for hours but Sam now found himself in her slipstream. While he was stretching his arms and quietly taking in the surroundings, Charlie picked up her laptop from the back seat and the cool box from the boot.

"I hope Maude has remembered to switch on the fridge."

"Who's Maude?"

"She's a neighbour who looks after the house for us and gets everything ready for whoever's coming to stay."

"I'll bring the bags," he said. It was a pointless comment. Charlie was already on her way and, of course, he was expected to carry the rest of their stuff into the house. She was putting food in the fridge and a bottle of wine in the freezer for a quick chill when he caught up with her. Double glass fronted doors led into the main living area with a kitchen bar, refectory table, benches, wood burning stove, sofa and a variety of chairs. An open staircase and first floor balcony made the space seem bigger than it was. Solid timbers and stone walls gave it a warm rustic look.

"It's lovely."

"This is what it was like." Charlie pointed out a framed photograph hanging on the wall showing a derelict barn and adjacent farm buildings in a similar state.

"Hard to believe it's now this."

"It was a long project but a dream my parents always had. They bought it incredibly cheaply and spent almost all their spare time rebuilding it before Sophie and I were on the scene. An advantage of being teachers and having school holidays I suppose. It's perfect for letting with two bedrooms downstairs and two up, all with bathrooms. They don't let it so much now. They want it for themselves, especially in the summer."

"I can see why."

"Mum's made us a lasagne."

"That's good of her."

"We'll use my parents' room. It's got the biggest bathroom and the biggest bed – two three foot singles pushed together. More flexible for letting but you have to mind the gap – like on the tube. Up the stairs on the right."

On the balcony were two bookshelves packed with holiday reading, a television, an old fashioned music system and a large collection of DVDs and CDs. The battered sofa and faded armchair had clearly hosted many hours of chilling out. In the bedroom, chunky wooden furniture, including a double wardrobe and a huge chest of drawers were in keeping with the scrubbed floorboards and exposed beams. At first, Sam wasn't sure about using the parents' bedroom but he soon got over it. Seven nights here – it was almost too good to be true. He put their bags down at the end of the bed and went to the bathroom. The shower was perfect for Charlie, a big space, wet room floor and a white plastic chair to sit on when required. She walked in just as he was finishing a pee.

"Sorry."

"It's OK. At least you weren't sitting down." She sighed with pleasure. "It's so good to be here. First time since London Bridge."

She began to undress. "The oven should be up to temperature now. Could you pop down and put the lasagne in? The beers are in the fridge. Help yourself. Did you by any chance bring my bag of books from the back seat?"

"Sorry, no. I'll get it now."

"Did you bring anything to read?"

"No, I didn't think about it."

"Not to worry there are loads of books in the house. You'll find something. Reading by the pool is one of the pleasures of being here."

*

A long journey followed by beer, wine and a large helping of lasagne had taken their toll. Sam was shattered but contented, a feeling he hadn't enjoyed for a long time. Charlie was just as tired. He fell asleep happy just to feel her in his arms. No need for more. He had her to himself for a whole week.

There was something worth getting up for in the morning.

# 34

Sam twitched and threw out a searching arm. He was caught in the moment between sleeping and waking and struggled to remember where he was. He sat up and felt the join where the beds were pushed together. A clue. It wasn't all a dream. I am in France but where's Charlie? Must have slept well not to notice her get up – a good sign. He opened the windows and stepped out onto the mini balcony to admire the view over the swimming pool and across the fields to a farmhouse a couple of hundred metres away. It was too dark and he was too tired to appreciate it last night. A bird of prey was floating high doing its morning tour of inspection and a small herd of cows ambled about in the sunshine. Some of them were already resting in the shade cast by a clump of trees. It was going to be hot. The sound of splashing water came from the pool below and Charlie swam into view.

When Sam joined her, she was sitting naked on a lounger drying her hair. She leant back to give him a better view. Her scars – pink tattoos with a story to tell – had become less angry over the months since the attack and her face had miraculously escaped any serious harm.

"You look great."

"I feel good. I love the way you look at me. It gives me confidence."

He glanced at the prosthesis by her side. "You swam without it."

"The water feels cool on my skin." She instinctively touched her stump. "You can get one specially designed for swimming if you want to take it seriously. I've been to the Lido a couple of times since you were in London and I'm thinking of joining the Serpentine Club."

"With the cold water nutcases."

"You never know. I'm beginning to see the advantage of swimming rather than running. Too much high impact exercise makes my stump sore and they say it can lead to deeper tissue wounds."

"You'll have to find something else for me to sponsor if you don't do the marathon."

"I will." She paused and smiled at him. "I like it that you remembered."

"How's the water?"

"Lovely. You don't need trunks you know. It's totally private here and you're bulging out of them. You need a swim to calm you down."

*

Apart from the enormous selection of wine and a tank full of live fish the hypermarket did nothing for Sam except to prove that his GCSE French was not up to scratch. All the vocabulary had disappeared from his memory bank whereas Charlie was able to find everything they needed without a problem and engaged confidently with the checkout assistants who appreciated the young Brit speaking their language.

"I didn't know you spoke French so well."

"Our parents pushed Sophie and me to speak French as soon as we were old enough. The basics come back quite easily." She smiled. "There's quite a lot of stuff you don't know about me."

"Sounds exciting… How much do I owe you?"

"Don't worry we'll settle up later."

After shopping, coffee and a croissant Charlie wanted to chill out and enjoy the house on the first day. It had been a long time since her last visit. She promised they would venture further afield during the week (the full programme was posted on the fridge door before lunch) to make sure that Sam went home with a good feel for the area. There was a lot to see.

"So, you'd better find a book if we're going to be lazing by the pool."

"Any suggestions?"

"What do you like?"

"I'm not sure. To be honest I haven't read much since I left school."

Admitting it to Charlie was embarrassing but she just nodded and smiled benignly.

"My Dad's an academic snob but he loves a good crime novel or historical fiction for his holiday reading. There's a lot of Ian Rankin and Robert Harris on the balcony shelves. Try one of them."

Sam was intrigued by Charlie's comment about her father but it was not the right moment to discuss it. "Sounds good. I'll have a look."

He found *Conclave,* a Robert Harris he remembered Prof reading on the team bus. He always had a book on the go.

"Dad enjoyed that. He's got a thing about the Catholic Church so it neatly re-enforced his prejudices."

Once they had settled down by the pool Sam tried hard to concentrate on his book but with Charlie lying naked next to him, he found it difficult. She was engrossed in *Normal People* and could have done without being asked what she thought of it.

She sighed. "The author's a young star in the making according to the critics but I'm not sure yet. Sometimes I want to scream at the two main characters but there are some pretty graphic sex scenes so you might want to give it a go." She went back to her reading but then looked at him over her shoulder. "Could you rub some lotion on my back please?"

He was more than happy to adopt the role of masseur and soon his hands, strengthened by hours of passing practice, were prompting moans of pleasure.

Charlie rolled over. "Your bloody good at this. You can do the front now if you want but don't get too excited. I want to finish this chapter." She saw his disappointment and smiled. "It's OK, there's only a couple of pages to go."

The curved steps at the Roman end of the pool were the perfect venue and the combination of sex, sunshine and cool water was irresistible.

They relaxed sitting next to each other on the side of the pool. He had to ask. "Have you done it in here before?"

"There's never been the chance… Good wasn't it." Her eyes were glinting with excitement. "Let's have another go if you're up to it."

In the afternoon, they went for a gentle walk around the hamlet. Charlie held on to his arm while they ambled along. It made him feel as if they were meant to be together.

"I had a good chat with Mike the other day."

"That's encouraging."

"Yeah, it was. He's changed since he first moved in."

"People do."

"At first I thought he was arrogant and I resented him being there."

"So, what's changed?"

"He's convinced me that he loves Mum… and I've grown up."

"Big news of the day. I've finally found myself a grown up man."

He unhooked his arm and pulled away from her pretending to be annoyed. They both burst out laughing.

"Peace has broken out at home then."

"It's better. Mum's more relaxed but I'm still going to get grief about the future when I get back."

"So you should but let's not talk about that now. We're almost home and it's time for games."

After a cold drink and another swim, the 'World Series' darts and table tennis competition began in the half dilapidated open barn on the other side of the house which had escaped Sam's notice the night before. He went ahead in the table tennis – "you ought to with me wearing a prosthetic leg" – but Charlie was too good for him at darts and amazingly competitive about it. He would have to take tomorrow's round more seriously.

Charlie put Sam in charge of the evening meal so while she went up to take a shower, he tinkered with the gas barbecue to make sure he knew what he was doing. He had already started cooking when she came down looking cool in a white linen slipover dress. She stood by him but soon stepped back to avoid being splashed by fat and barbecue sauce from the chicken and burgers.

"You'd better get an apron if you're going to stay there."

"Don't worry I'll lay the table and light a couple of candles to keep the bugs away. They're starting to bite."

They talked about their families during the meal. Sam prompted the conversation by asking why Charlie thought her father was an academic snob.

"Something you don't know about me is that I had a place at Cambridge but wanted to go to Imperial. Dad was at Cambridge and horrified that I decided not to take up the place. For him, it was all about the Oxbridge kudos and being able to brag to his friends. Fuck all to do with the course and what I wanted."

"But Imperial's one of the best isn't it?"

"In the world," she said loudly. "And I wanted to live in London not boring Cambridge."

"Has he forgiven you?"

"Yes, he's moved on but now he overdoes his praise of Imperial and it's so obvious he's trying to compensate."

"How was your Mum about it?"

"Very supportive. She was at uni in London and has never been over impressed by the Oxbridge hype." She paused. "Is talking about your father off limits?"

"Not with you… I have vivid memories of him and he's often in my dreams – nightmares mostly. I still have my problem with trains."

"But you've cracked the Channel Tunnel."

"Thanks to you."

"It's better now you're talking about it."

"It's because of you that I am. I've always found it hard to open up about things. It got worse when Dad died. I tried to bury the trauma but it still springs to the surface when I'm down. Discussing him with Mum has been hard. We've sort of skirted around it. They were unhappy together for a long time, hardly agreed about anything. Now she's with Mike she's building a new life for herself and I'm pleased for her."

"Did you love him?"

"I was in awe of him when I was young. He spent hours with me practising ball skills. As I got older, I began to find him embarrassing. He drank too much and all he thought about was his business and my rugby. It was as if he was living life through me. It changed when I went to Bath. I found the confidence to speak to him more like man to man. We were getting on as well as we'd ever done when he died. That made it even harder to take… What about yours?"

"He's a pain at times, I suppose most parents are, but, yes, I do. He's had to cope with three difficult women ganging up on him but we know he still loves us all. He deserves a lot of credit for that."

Charlie laughed but her attempt to lighten the conversation hardly registered.

"The suicide changed everything. Whatever you think of someone you can't feel anything but deep sadness when they've been driven to do something so horrendous. I felt guilty, still do. So did Mum. We were both getting along without him and never imagined such a thing could happen. He texted me just before he jumped you know." He tried unsuccessfully to hold back the tears. "I honestly don't think a family ever gets over a suicide."

Sam was drained. Charlie stood up, nudged him to move his chair away from the table, sat on his lap and wrapped her arms around him. "That's enough for tonight Sam. I'm taking you to bed."

# 35

"Do you want to have children, Charlie?"

"I'm too selfish. I think I'd be a terrible parent."

A bold question. Sam thought he must have been lulled into complacency by the lazy feel of being in a canoe swept along by the Dordogne current.

"That might change."

"So, you think I am selfish."

"Well, that's not quite what I meant. I'm saying that you could change your mind about being a mother when you get older."

"Unlikely, but who knows. What about you?"

"Maybe one day, if I sort myself out and find the right partner."

They paddled over to a stony bank to have their picnic – fromage et jambon baguettes et une bouteille de rosé – Charlie was working hard to improve Sam's French. They watched canoes and strong swimmers go past in the deepest water and listened to the screams of overexcited children playing on the other side of the river.

"You'd have to put up with noise like that."

Sam topped up their glasses and took out two peaches from the cool box.

"So, what are you going to do about it?" She asked just as juice started to run down his chin.

"Having children," he slurped.

"No, idiot. Getting yourself sorted out."

"It's not as simple as that, Charlie. Your injury hasn't stopped you doing what you want to do."

"You mean like walking. Like a normal person."

"I'm sorry, Charlie. Don't take it the wrong way. I'm talking about your work. All your plans can still happen, and I'm sure they will. You can't see my injury but it stopped my career in its tracks. Bad luck mate, they say. You can't play rugby anymore but you're young. It'll be OK. There are plenty of other things you can do."

"And there are. The world is full of people who've changed their jobs. Some because they wanted to but plenty who had to."

"The problem is that there's nothing else I want to do. I was a really good player. There was so much more I wanted to achieve. Now I don't have a future to look forward to."

"Look, I can do my best to support you, Sam but you'll have to deal with the 'what next' problem. You've got to find something or you'll go bonkers."

"My head's already full of demons."

"Don't you think there were demons in my head, nightmares with white vans coming at me?"

"You've recovered from something far worse, I know, but not everyone's like you."

"I saw a counsellor and sought help, including from you as it happens. You've given me confidence in myself and made me feel attractive again. I'll never forget that but depression is a cruel thing. It needs expert advice as well as friendship to get you through it."

"I don't feel depressed when I'm with you."

"Sam, I can't *be* the solution. You have to find that from within yourself."

"We're good together."

"Yes, we are but that doesn't change what I just said. It's not fair of you to put all the responsibility on me to get you through this."

"That's not what I'm doing."

"It's what it feels like. You're just not seeing it."

They sat in silence for what seemed like an age but it gave Sam time to think. He was expecting too much. Burdening her with his problems would ruin everything. It dawned on him while staring at the water wondering what lay hidden under the dark surface that losing Charlie would be worse than losing his ability to play rugby.

*

For the next few days Sam was swept along by another current – Charlie showing him her favourite Dordogne jewels. He would never have believed he could find a garden interesting until he toured Les Jardins de Marqueyssac and took in the views across the valley. The medieval squares and buildings in Sarlat were impressive too and he found himself looking with genuine interest at the food and gift shops, tourist traps of course but they did catch the eye. There were even things that he might have been tempted to buy if he could afford them. The Chateau de Castelnaud was the castle on the hill that small boys dream of and Rocamadour confirmed the power of the Catholic Church to make men do extraordinary things, as did reading *Conclave* which he had to admit, he was enjoying more than he expected.

Difficult conversations were instinctively avoided for the next few days while they concentrated on enjoying the holiday, exploring the area and improving Sam's knowledge of French history and culture. Charlie was a good teacher. Must be the family genes, she said, when Sam complimented her. They relaxed in each other's company, read their books and talked routine stuff about where they had been, what they had eaten and whether they should put comments on Trip Advisor. Charlie was suspicious of the platform but they posted a complimentary paragraph about *Le Havre* to amuse her parents.

Their sexual adventures were less hurried and more satisfying, an advantage of being together for a whole week. They wanted to do their best for each other and took time to explore the places where and when a gentle touch or more urgent pressure would give the most pleasure.

On the final day it hit Sam that time was running out. They lounged by the pool and completed the final rounds of their World Series. Charlie won the darts but Sam was too strong in the table tennis. Honours even then, but she reminded him that things might have been different if she'd had two good legs. These diversions could not disguise the fact that a special week was coming to an end. He could feel the heaviness in his limbs as his mood changed.

It was a stifling evening and when Sam came downstairs after a swim and a shower Charlie was preparing a salad to go with the local fish and a bottle of champagne she had bought to celebrate their last night in France. She was wearing nothing but a *Vive la France* apron and came out from behind the work surface to ensure that Sam could enjoy its full effect.

"I thought this would cheer you up but don't expect it every time I cook for you."

"You look stunning."

"I was hoping you'd say something like that. Champagne's in the fridge."

Sam popped the cork and slowly poured two glasses, taking care to avoid any spillage in his excitement. "I don't want this to end."

"Cheers." Charlie raised her glass and chinked it against his. "It's been brilliant hasn't it?"

"Awesome." He looked straight into her eyes and kissed her while they skilfully held their glasses out of the way. "Will we be able to do this again?" he asked.

"I hope so but it depends."

"What on?"

"You."

Sam nodded. He knew what was coming.

"Look, you're a lovely, kind guy and being with you is special but you know how important my work is to me and that's not going to change. You'll have to find something else that floats your boat other than hanging out with me. It won't work for us otherwise."

He nodded again. "But we do have a future if I sort myself out," he said nervously.

Charlie took Sam's glass out of his hand put it down next

to hers and took off her apron. She moved forward to kiss him and eased her hand down the front of his shorts.

"The food can wait. I need you to make love to me."

The meal tasted all the better for having been delayed. Sam felt the sense of calm that comes after urgent sex and half a bottle of champagne – but there was more to it than that. Charlie had given him hope and the motivation to pull himself together. He would prove to her that he could. A life with Charlie would have to be one in which they also had lives of their own. He must find his.

\*

They were making steady progress up the A20 when Charlie casually announced that she had some good news.

"Liam's invited me to America."

Sam wasn't at all convinced that this revelation was good news. "When?"

"Not sure exactly but soon."

"Why didn't you tell me before?"

"He only contacted me a couple of days ago and I wasn't sure I could afford it."

"Can you?"

"I can now my parents have agreed to pay for the flight."

"Lucky you." It was a prickly response but he couldn't help himself. "Will Mali be there?"

"What difference does that make?"

"I just wondered."

"As it happens her father is undergoing cancer treatment and she's gone back to Thailand to be with her family."

Sam said nothing and fought to put memories of Lily and her climbing instructor out of his mind.

"So, I'm going to look at the possibility of doing a post-grad in America. Liam's family live in Boston and his father is a Professor at Harvard. He's offered to help me. It's a great opportunity."

"Sounds it."

"I thought you'd be pleased for me."

"I am."

"You don't sound very convincing."

"I was hoping we'd have more time together before next term."

"We will… Look Sam, this isn't a good sign. Don't spoil everything."

Sam's heart sank. "I've fucked up already, haven't I?"

"Nearly."

*

Charlie drove the final stretch north of Paris and nursed Sam through the tunnel without a problem. It was a relief to feel her holding his hand after his pathetic reaction to her trip to America. Perhaps she had forgiven him. He hoped so. Why was he so stupid? He could have ruined his chances forever.

It was slow round the M25 and they arrived at Sam's forty minutes later than expected.

"Are you going to come in and see Mum and Mike?"

She leant over to kiss him on the cheek. "I'd better get home. Mum is bound to have cooked something for me. I'll call you tomorrow."

# 36

The front door closed and Sam's bag dropped heavily to the floor. Jill glanced nervously at Mike, held up two crossed fingers and went to greet him in the hall.

"Where's Charlie? I was hoping to meet her."

"She was running a bit late and thought she ought to get home. Her parents got back from Portugal this morning."

"You look well."

"We had good weather."

"Do I get a hug?"

Sam nodded, put his arms around her, squeezed tight and planted a loud kiss on her cheek.

She grinned. "That's a good sign. Are you hungry?"

"Yeah. I could do with something."

"How about a cheese toastie and a beer."

"Perfect."

He grabbed his bag and rushed up the stairs. "Sorry Mum, I need a pee."

It wasn't long before he came back down. The smell of toast was irresistible.

"Hi Sam."

"Hi Mike."

"Good trip?"

"Great thanks."

"Becks or Peroni."

"Becks please."

"Any highlights."

Vivid images of moments in the bedroom and by the pool immediately sprang to mind but he wasn't about to mention them. "Lots. It's a lovely place and it was good to be with Charlie." He paused. Might as well tell them now. And don't sound disappointed he said firmly to himself. "She's going to Boston for a couple of weeks."

"Great city," Mike responded enthusiastically. "What's taking her there?"

"She's going with a friend from uni whose Dad's a Professor at Harvard. She's thinking of doing a post-grad in America and he's offered to help."

"What an opportunity. She's a lucky girl."

"When's she off?" Jill asked.

"Soon but she hasn't booked her flight yet. It was a bit of a last minute offer. She's ringing me tomorrow. I'll know more then."

The conversation moved on to the Woods' cottage, the beauty of the Dordogne area and the pleasure of canoeing on the river. Sam was enthusiastic about all three and succeeded in creating a more relaxed atmosphere around the kitchen table than at any time since he came home. He retired to bed happy with the way the evening had gone but although he was tired after the long journey he slept badly. Memories of those special nights sharing a bed with Charlie were distracting. He kept reaching for her and managed to knock his glass of water off the bedside table in the process. After mopping up he lay wide awake flat on his back with thoughts about the future whizzing round in his head. The immediate worry was that phone call. Would Charlie change her mind and decide that a week's fun in the sun was not the basis for anything more serious or would she stick with him and give him the chance to sort himself out. He thought about texting her first but decided against it. She said she would ring so he must let her do it.

When he appeared at breakfast, Mike had already left for work.

"Well, this is a turn-up. Coffee."

"Please Mum. Black and strong."

"I'm not working this morning so we've got some time on our own. You were in good form last night. It was obviously a really enjoyable trip."

"Yes, it was."

"Do you want to talk about it?"

"Is that code for talking about Charlie?"

She laughed. "Fair cop. Her and the future. It'll be easier without Mike although you seem to be getting on better."

"I think he wants the best for me."

"He does, and he wants to help. You should let him."

Sam nodded and Jill produced a powerful cup of coffee. "So, the million dollar question. How was it with Charlie?"

"Good."

"Is that it?"

"Better than good." His broad grin spoke volumes.

"You're really hooked, aren't you?"

"I guess I am."

"The trouble with having a son is that you have to be ready for the day when another woman comes along who's more important to him than you are."

Sam thought it was best to move on from that minefield. "Charlie's really into her academic work. She's determined to do her PhD so she'll be studying for years."

"You support that, don't you?"

"Yes, I do."

"That's important. One of the things that went wrong with Dad and me was that he spent every waking hour on his business but didn't respect the fact that I wanted my own career."

Mention of Dad caught Sam unawares but it was an opportune moment. "We didn't talk enough about him after he died."

Jill shook her head. "No, we didn't… I wish we had."

"I felt guilty."

"So did I. It was painful and I think we both tried to bury it to cope."

"We used to talk about a lot of stuff when I was young. What happened?"

"You became a teenager. Then you went to Bath and I found Mike. A triple whammy."

"At least we're talking now."

"Yes. It's good. I feel I'm being a useful mother again."

"Charlie expects us to have lives of our own if we're going to continue our relationship. She won't commit to anything until I've sorted myself out."

"Clearly she's an independent woman."

Sam gave her a knowing look and smiled. "Definitely."

"You *must* let her have room to breathe." She paused to let the point sink in. "So, what does she mean by 'sorting yourself out'?"

"She liked Tony our scrum coach's advice. Remember the good times you've had, crack on and find something new."

"I like it too. What are you going to do about it?"

"I've got to get the rugby monkey off my back first. Then we'll see what happens."

"That's easier said than done."

"Yes, but Charlie's given me the motivation to do something about it."

*

The call came just after Jill had left for work. There was some disappointing news.

"I'm sorry Sam, I won't be able to see you before I go. I've managed to get a seat on the same flight as Liam so I'm off tomorrow and I've got loads to do."

His mother's advice was still ringing in his ears and he managed a sensibly upbeat, "I'll miss you."

"I'll be in touch while I'm away… There'll be plenty of time for you to do some thinking about the future," she added with just the right emphasis to make sure that Sam paid attention.

"Don't worry. Mum's been on the case already."

"Good for her. My Mum was chatting to me about you until quite late last night."

"That's sounds ominous."

"Actually, it was pretty positive. She thinks you should focus on all the things you enjoy other than rugby. You never know, they might point to something."

"I'll try."

"She also mentioned that you're A Levels were good. They give you options too."

Charlie sounded enthusiastic and Sam took note. She'd reminded him that those results were one of the most satisfying achievements of his life. He'd surpassed expectations. "Your Mum got me an A."

"I know she did but you had to do the work… I had an amazing time in France, Sam."

A sudden but welcome change of tack. "Me too."

"I wondered if you'd be able to collect me from Heathrow when I get back. Mum and Dad will be in France."

"Of course."

"I'll text my flight details."

"OK."

"Must go."

"Lots of love."

"You too."

Charlie's reassuring request to collect her from the airport gave Sam further encouragement to think about the future and to reflect on Mrs Woods's advice. What else *had* he enjoyed apart from his love affair with rugby? His immediate answer was cricket and basketball. Come to that, any sport. He chuckled to himself at the thought of how Charlie and his mother would react to this narrow assessment. They were a powerful team without having met each other.

"You'll have to find something or you'll go bonkers." He could hear Charlie's voice as clearly as if she was sitting next to him. Being with her was number one on the list but he couldn't make a living out of that. Sport. He had enjoyed coaching rugby on his courses and speaking about the demands of professional sport to the PE group when he visited his school. He got a buzz from being with the students. Food for thought, but first he must face down his rugby bereavement.

His great ambition had been to play at Twickenham. It was his Holy Grail, and his Dad's too. He took him there to see a match when he was ten. "It'll be the proudest day of my life when I watch you play here." He should visit the stadium and confront that demon – his London Bridge. It sounded pathetic to make such a comparison but it helped him to get the issue into proportion. Imagine what Charlie had gone through when she walked again across that murderous stretch of tarmac. If she could do that, surely…

Mum had told him that he needed to get back into the company of his rugby mates. He had isolated himself from the very people who would understand how he felt. Stubborn, self-pitying, defeatist, sulky – not her words (although she probably thought them) but ones which he had used many times against himself as he went through hours of depressing analysis. He'd had a few texts from the lads inviting him to Bath. He hoped to be ready for that one day but not yet. He couldn't face seeing the pitch where it happened or the close group of mates who had been with him day in day out, on and off the pitch from his time in the Academy. It would be too intense.

It struck Sam that he could combine his attempt to lay the Twickenham ghost with a visit to Chris Kenny, a rugby man whose company he could enjoy without the emotional baggage that he would carry on a return to his old Club. He had stayed with Chris after his lunch in London with Charlie. Perfect. It was almost as if it was meant to be. They hadn't been in touch since an exchange of texts after Sam's injury but Chris was solid gold, a formidable back row forward on the field but an easy going and unflappable personality off it, the kind of guy who wouldn't mind being asked a favour out of the blue.

# 37

Sam dropped his bag and joined Chris in the main living space. It was surprisingly tidy (perhaps a slightly unfair assessment) and bigger than he remembered. A functional kitchen area and a pine table with four chairs tucked under it were separated from a huge television by a twin sofa and an armchair. A range of well-known posters brightened up the walls but there were few other clues to indicate the personality of the tenant apart from a photograph of the Harlequins Academy which Chris had joined after he left school. He was big then but now he was enormous and looked like a bulked up superhero although he had retained his boyish facial features which were remarkably unscarred considering the fearless way in which he approached the game.

"It's good of you to have me Chris."

"No problem mate. It's good to see you. Bung your grip in the spare bedroom. Do you want a beer?"

"Great."

It wouldn't be cheap to rent this round here, Sam thought. "No-one sharing the flat now Chris?" he asked.

"I wanted the place to myself. Living with a teammate helps the cash flow but it isn't always the best option." He winked and handed Sam his beer. "I'm on the diet coke. I promised myself I'd keep off the booze during pre-season. I thought I hadn't lost too much fitness over the summer but training's been knackering this week. It doesn't get any easier."

"I don't have to worry about that anymore."

Chris glanced at Sam's waistline. "You haven't run to fat yet."

"I was in danger of it for a while."

"So, it's been tough."

Sam had decided when he called Chris that he had to be honest about the situation. There was no point in contacting him if he wasn't. In order to move on, he had to talk.

"Yeah. Fucking awful at times. I've been depressed but I'm hoping I've turned a corner. Charlie's helped. She's been through a lot herself."

"Sounds quite a girl."

"She said that if I couldn't face up to the future, we didn't have one. They weren't the exact words but you get the drift."

"Tough call."

Sam nodded. "It certainly gave me the kick up the arse I needed."

"The word is that you were lucky not to end up in a wheelchair."

"Very lucky, but at first all I could think about was what I'd lost. It felt like I'd been cast adrift. My job, all the routines, structure and your mates gone, just like that." He clicked his fingers… "Are you enjoying your rugby?" he asked tentatively.

"Not all the time but enough to keep me going. I don't think I'm as in love with it as you were."

"I had the piss taken out of me at Bath for being too keen," Sam confessed.

"Doesn't surprise me, you were intense when we were going through the age group system. To be fair most of us were super keen at that stage – starry eyed at the thought of earning money for playing sport. The reality hits after you've been doing it for a while."

It was disconcerting for Sam to discover that he had acquired a reputation so early in his career. "I wish I could be as laid back as you."

"It's all an act mate. Underneath the water my feet are paddling like fucking crazy."

"I don't believe you."

"It's true and I'll tell you something else. What happened to you made me think more about my future."

Sam decided to change the subject. They had already gone further in a short time than he could have imagined but he wanted to avoid the visit being all about him. "What's the plan tonight, Chris?"

"We're meeting my little sister, Sara. She's a student at St. Mary's. On the Primary Education course. I've booked a table for the three of us."

"Sounds good."

"I'm starting a course there next term."

Chris seemed slightly embarrassed to admit it and Sam didn't help by looking up in disbelief and grinning.

"What in? The art of the choke tackle."

"Cheeky bastard."

"Sorry. Couldn't resist. Which course is it?"

"Piss off."

"Come on… The meal's on me tonight."

Chris smiled happily and quickly accepted the peace offering. "Now you're talking. Business Management – part-time. There'll be clashes with my rugby commitments but it'll be great to get out of the bubble for a few hours a week."

\*

They arrived early at the restaurant. "She's always on time, never misses, so we need to be there. She's changed my habits," Chris admitted before Sam had a chance to comment.

'Little' Sara was tall, bright eyed and attractive with the glowing skin of someone who took regular exercise outdoors. Chris had said that she was a keen sprinter and long jumper who had been a serious competitor at national schools level and she looked the part. She seemed to disappear into Chris's large frame when he put his arms around her. Sam enjoyed watching her emerge from his affectionate embrace and wondered what it would have been like to have a brother or sister.

Sara took him by surprise when she leant forward to kiss him. "Hi Sam."

She smelt fresh, almost edible. "Hi Sara. Good to meet you."

"I've heard a lot about you. I'm sorry you've had such a difficult time but I'm glad you've talked to Chris about it."

Sam wasn't sure how much Sara knew or how much he wanted her to know but he had rarely met someone who gave out such immediately positive vibes.

"She knows the story Sam. We're not going to spend the evening catching up with the past."

And they didn't. It simplified matters to be told what to do and when Sara challenged them not to mention rugby for at least the first half hour Sam found it much easier than he expected. They warmed up with routine chat about local places to eat and drink and the advantages of living in London. He was amused to see Chris's embarrassment when Sara sang his praises.

"He's fierce on the rugby field but a real softy off it. He's always looked after me and my friends think the world of him, not just because he's good at rugby but because he's kind and thoughtful. One of Mum's friends calls him a real gentleman. She'd like her daughter to go out with him but I think she fancies Chris herself."

"A wide fan base then Chris."

"Oh yes. I'll be a social media star in no time."

Chris and Sara were great company and not in the least inhibited by discussion of Sam's 'condition' as Chris described it with a wry grin. If he was asking for their help, they were going to give it in their way without the constraints of being family, Bath teammates or, dare they say it, Charlie.

Sam was reserved at first but gradually loosened up. Talking to Chris and Sara was refreshingly uncomplicated. He felt he could drop his guard and say what he wanted. He was as much to blame as anyone but he had experienced too many recent buttoned up conversations dominated by difficult and unresolved issues. It was liberating to be able to discuss his problems with comparative ease. Their advice had its share of clichés but coming from Chris and Sara they sounded authentic. They actually applied them to their own lives.

"Chris is training tomorrow and I'm taking you out for coffee after you've completed your mission at Twickenham."

"So, you know about that too. It sounds sad but I just need to get the place out of my system. It seems a small thing after talking to you guys but I want to tick it off as a job done."

"Remember, it's just a ground, Sam. Don't big it up too much. I was talking to one of the old players, I mean really old – in his seventies. Back in the amateur days 'Quins used to play their home matches before Christmas at Twickenham. It held about fifty odd thousand then. There would be a few hundred there if they were lucky, plus a few dogs on leads. He reckoned you could hear people in the crowd coughing and farting."

*

By ten o'clock the next morning Sam was standing near the South Stand imagining the scene on a big match day. He walked past the RFU shop and stared across the car park towards the Lions Gate stationed proudly under the lee of the West Stand. What a place to play – running out, the anthems, the roar of a full house. He might not have made it but it would have been good to have had the chance. The stadium was as physically impressive as ever but without the crowds it looked unloved, a concrete and steel edifice lacking the energy to bring it to life. Sam was disappointed to see it like this but pleased that it had not brought on the kind of negative feelings that he feared.

He took a slow walk to the café in town where he was due to meet Sara. He was looking forward to seeing her again. More than that. Admit it. He was excited at the prospect and slightly unnerved by the effect she had on him. It wasn't just that she was good looking. She was so engaging and full of enthusiasm. He imagined her in a classroom with a group of children eating out of her hand.

She was waiting outside when Sam arrived and he instinctively looked at his watch to check that he wasn't late.

"You're OK," she said with a smile.

He was ready for her kiss this time. Just a brief peck on the cheek but he would have been disappointed if it hadn't happened. He went to order the coffees while Sara found a table.

"This place is absolutely buzzing during term time."

"Aren't you here a bit early for the start of term?"

"Yeah, but I'm sharing a flat with two other girls this year and we had to take it on from August. It's more fun being here than at home with my parents."

"I know just what you mean. Home's in London, you said."

"Streatham, so I haven't come far."

"Didn't you want to get away somewhere else to study?"

"No, I love London. It's got everything and it's convenient. I've got a friend at Edinburgh and one at Durham. It's a mission for them at the beginning and end of term. Anyway, St Mary's has a good reputation for my course."

"It's good that Chris is starting one."

"I'm so pleased. He's totally into rugby just like you were. I had to work hard to convince him but I'm sure he won't regret it."

"I'm guessing you're pretty tough to shake off once you've taken on a challenge."

She beamed and nodded her agreement. "How was Twickenham?"

"It doesn't have the same aura when it's empty."

"Or after Chris's farting story."

He laughed. "It must seem pathetic to you but it's a box I'm pleased I've ticked."

"No, it doesn't. Anything that helps you move on is worth doing even if it is a bit weird." She gave him a cheerful smile. "So, what's the next major challenge?"

He found Sara's gentle teasing helpful rather than undermining. Last night her face was so unjudgemental and the wine had so mellowed him that he began to tell her about his father's suicide and that somehow moved on to his difficulty with trains and his career ending injury. Looking back, he realised that the evening had become almost entirely about himself. Genial Chris kept topping up his glass and they both listened patiently while he got things off his chest. It was a self-centred performance but at no stage did they tell him what to do.

"The next challenge is what to do next."

Sara looked thoughtfully at the logo on her coffee cup. "Tell you what. Why don't I show you St Mary's? I've got nothing else on until this evening. You're not rushing home, are you?"

"No. I was just hoping to see Chris before I go."

"Perfect. He'll be home from work at about three o'clock so we've got time for a look and some lunch."

*

Sam switched on his car radio and picked up Heart London. He needed some background music while he tried to make sense of the last twenty four hours. His departure was

288

quite emotional especially during his farewell man-hug – a powerful one with much back-slapping to emphasise its importance. They had talked until far too late in the evening for someone who had to go to work for a hard session next morning.

"I won't forget this Chris. You've been a star."

"No problem mate."

"You too Sara. I can't thank you enough."

Sara's hug was warm and affectionate and her kiss on his cheek disturbingly close to his lips. "Don't be afraid to ask for help," she said quietly.

It was a significant parting shot. Too often he had suffered in self-imposed silence and made things worse. Why hadn't he taken the plunge sooner? He had Charlie to thank for forcing the issue but it was telling that he had found it so easy to talk to someone he'd never met before. Perhaps that was the answer. People less close to you were better placed to give advice. If you went to see a counsellor there would have to be a first meeting. Of course, there would… But that wasn't the point. He was dodging the issue. This was about Sara.

For months now he had been consumed by his relationship with Charlie so it was unsettling to find Sara so attractive and attentive. This was not part of the plan. He felt a twinge of conscience when they exchanged details but he added her to his contacts list having convinced himself that there was no harm in keeping in touch.

He had enjoyed telling her his A Level grades when she raised the possibility of going to university.

"ABC – that's bloody good."

"Don't sound so surprised."

"You'd have no problem getting a place here or plenty of other universities come to that. At least you ought to do a bit of research so you know what the options are."

He was sceptical at first but Sara's description of her first year as a student sounded a lot of fun. Sam wasn't a natural academic like Charlie – not many people were. Nor was he stupid, but he would need something other than a lab and a lecture room to make him tick. University for Charlie was all about the academic challenge, working with the brightest and best and moving on to a PhD whereas Sara was driven by her desire to be a teacher, the opportunities her course provided for practical training and the enjoyment of a lively social life. As far as he could tell they were both committed students who had different priorities in their approach to university but for Sam it was Sara's model that had greater appeal.

As he ground his way along the M25 there was plenty of time to consider this new scenario. His mother had never made any secret about her wish for him to go to university. In his desire to play rugby he had resisted and she had given him her support but he hadn't forgotten the promise he made to her to get the best A Levels he could because "they might be useful one day". Maybe they will. If Charlie was going to be studying in London for the foreseeable future, and with Sara at St Mary's he could see the sense of joining the bandwagon. He smiled to himself. God, Mum'll be so over the top if I go ahead with this…

But it wasn't that simple. Which course would he do and how would he pay for it? What would he do between now and next September? There was much to discuss. He would have to bite the bullet and broach the subject with Mum and Mike but decided to wait until Charlie got back before talking things through with her. This was too important to discuss on the phone.

Thinking about these potential problems was stressful but at least he was looking ahead and that made him feel better about himself. Seeing Sara and Chris had been a great help and he arrived home feeling more optimistic about the future than at any time since receiving the bad news from his consultant. He picked up his phone to check his messages before going in.

*You should look at this course at Mary's. BA Hons 3 yrs Phys Ed Sport and Youth Dev. Perfect for you 96-112 points no problem AND you're a post A applicant xx*

Sara was on his case already.

*Thanks. Will do. x*

There was also one from Chris.

*Good to see you mate. You're always welcome here especially if you buy dinner.*

*Ha. Thanks*, he replied.

And his daily one from Charlie.

*Had a great day looking round Harvard Medical School. Awesome x*

Sam toyed with the idea of mentioning his great day looking round St Mary's but it sounded rather underwhelming by comparison.

*Just got back from my stay with Chris. Very helpful. Miss you x*

# 38

There was a note for him on the kitchen table.

*Shepherd's pie ready to put in the oven. 40 mins at 180c.*
*Mike's taken me out for dinner. Back about ten.*
*Baked beans in the cupboard. You know how to do them!*
*Mum*

Sam smiled. Baked beans were a must with shepherd's pie. How convenient he thought. No need to face an interrogation tonight. He would be able to collect his thoughts and be better prepared for the inevitable session round the table tomorrow evening. He put the shepherd's pie in the oven as instructed, nipped upstairs to fetch his laptop and settled down to do some research on the St Mary's website.

It was good to be feeling positive. At his worst he had found it hard to get out of bed let alone do anything useful. His hopes had been dashed, life was unfair, the future was bleak. The trip to France with Charlie and seeing Chris and

Sara had made him think there was a way forward if he chose to look for it. He would never forget the misery of being forced to give up rugby but maybe there were other fulfilling things he could do. There were also people who cared about him. He risked losing them unless he stepped up. Self-pity would get him nowhere.

Reading through the details of Sara's recommended course made him think of Mrs Woods and that day with the PE students. Certain phrases caught his eye: 'ensures you are equipped for many different roles within the sports industry', 'undertaking work-based opportunities and additional sporting qualifications', 'links with a range of National Governing Bodies in Elite and Disability Sport'.

There was some trumpet blowing about St Mary's having an incredibly strong reputation for PE teaching and sports performance but he could forgive them for that having toured the place and listened to Sara's enthusiastic comments. He began to imagine himself being there. He could become a sports professional again, admittedly not a playing one but still with plenty to give to the sector if he put his mind to it. He poured over every aspect of the St Mary's experience, enjoyed his meal and decided to have an early night. He added a message to the note his mother had written.

*Gone to bed. Getting up early to go for a run.*
*See you after work.*

Chris and Sara had stressed the importance of getting back into an exercise routine and seeing Chris go off to his day's training reminded Sam of how much he enjoyed the feeling of being physically fit. Charlie had worked incredibly hard 'to get back on her feet' – an expression they had both agreed should be part of their black comedy collection. He promised himself he would follow their advice.

*

Sam felt good after his run and made himself a bacon sandwich for breakfast with the satisfaction of someone who felt he deserved a reward for his efforts. He made a cup of coffee and continued his research on St Mary's prompted by a text from Sara asking if he had looked at the course. He replied that he had, but her keenness encouraged him to view it again. He had been mildly addicted to playing too many games online during his off days at Bath but this was proper research and he was energised by the thought that he was using his time purposefully. Having read through the details for the second time, he was more than impressed. It was a good fit for him and he texted Sara to say so.

*Great!! x* she replied within seconds.

While he was in the mood, Sam revisited a website explaining the symptoms of a panic attack. He hadn't suffered one since arriving at Liverpool Street and with Charlie's help had successfully negotiated the Channel Tunnel so he felt more confident about addressing the problem. It helped to be reminded that although an attack was frightening, it was unlikely to harm him. The site made a series of recommendations for dealing with anxiety including regular exercise, healthy diet, breathing exercises, and talking to friends, family members or a health professional. It also had a list of don'ts, one of which stood out – *do not focus on the things you cannot change.* When he first looked at the site he was not in the right frame of mind to respond to the advice but this time things were different.

*

When Sam confirmed that he would be applying to university and talked enthusiastically about the course at St Mary's the expression on his mother's face was a picture. She seemed almost overwhelmed.

"I can't believe what I'm hearing," she said on the brink of tears.

"I think you've pleased your Mum, Sam," Mike added with a smile. "You'll have our one hundred percent support."

"Thanks Mike."

"And before you say anything else, that includes finance."

"Mike and I have talked about this Sam. We know you have some money from your insurance but we want you to keep as much of that as possible for security in the future."

Mike chipped in again. "I've been living in your family home for a long time now so the least I can do is to help with your living costs."

Sam was touched by their warm and generous response. "Thank you... both," he said diffidently. "It means a lot."

"I'm so thrilled, Sam," Jill said happily before moving on to other practical matters. "Does Charlie know about this?"

Sam was ready for the shift in emphasis after the initial excitement of breaking the news. "Not yet, Mum. I wanted to be with her. It's only a few days before she's back."

"What are you going to do between now and next September."

Sam laughed. "The thought of having me at home for another year must be horrendous."

She reached out to give him a playful slap on the arm. "That's a wicked thing to say."

"I've not even applied yet and I need to talk to Charlie before I decide anything."

"You ought to get in, surely."

"I've got more than enough points so I should be fine. It helps to be a post-A Level candidate."

"All that hard work was worthwhile."

"Definitely."

"So, what made you decide to apply?"

"I've always known I *could* go and in the end the injury and Charlie's ultimatum forced me to think about it seriously."

"And St Mary's…"

"It's in London."

"Is that it?"

"There are one or two other things," Sam replied with a grin. He was enjoying himself.

"Come on. Stop winding me up."

"The course. Having a look at the place. Seeing Chris and finding out that he's starting there part time this September."

He left it at that. It will complicate things if I mention Sara, he thought.

There was a pause in the conversation. Jill put the kettle on to brew them some coffee while Sam cleared the table and loaded the dishwasher.

"You know, we wouldn't mind having you at home for a bit longer now you're better company and being useful for a change." Jill grinned. "Just getting my own back."

"Have you thought about travelling?" Mike asked.

"To be honest I've only just decided to try for uni and I haven't thought much beyond that."

"You'll never have a better chance."

"He's right Sam."

"I've got some good contacts in South Africa and Australia. I'm sure they'd help if you're interested."

Mike's offer was tempting. It didn't feel as if he was forcing the issue or that they were trying to get rid of him but perhaps that was because he had become more willing to think about the future. Either way, he knew that living at home for the next year would not be a good idea for any of them.

"Thanks Mike… I think South Africa would be my first choice," he added, by way of encouragement.

# 39

Sam was nervous on the way to Heathrow. Charlie had kept in touch while she was away largely through short sharp texts without much elaboration other than exclamation marks and smiley faces but a couple of calls had confirmed how excited she was about the academic opportunities there were in America. Twenty days she had been away, that was all but a lot had happened since those blissful days in France. He had some ideas for the future but wondered how they would fit in with hers.

He managed to negotiate the complex short stay parking arrangements and walked slowly towards the arrivals hall. He was early – this was definitely not the day to be late. The flight was on time but had he put enough money in the machine? He checked his watch. It would be close but he couldn't be bothered to go back. Coffee was needed. He queued for a latte in a paper cup and splashed out on an exorbitantly expensive biscuit which was almost the size of a CD and much thicker. He found a seat from which he could see the exit point and settled down to do some people watching.

Seeing the bustle of passengers made him think about travelling himself. He had seen little of the world – Majorca and France were his limit – but now had an opportunity to put that straight. He preferred the idea of seeing a country properly rather than flitting from one to another ticking them off like a train spotter. South Africa and Australia were huge. You could spend years in either of them and still have plenty to see. What would Charlie think? He already knew the answer. She would definitely encourage him to go.

As soon as he saw her come into the hall, he felt proud to be the one lucky enough to be picking her up.

"You look great," he said as they unwrapped themselves.

"I scrubbed up a bit before we landed. Didn't want to let you down."

"Flight OK?"

"Fine. Good to have it done though. I'm longing for a shower. You are staying at mine tonight, aren't you? My parents aren't back until tomorrow evening."

"I've got my tooth brush and a clean pair of pants in the car. And a shepherd's pie. Don't ask… Mum insisted."

After some routine chat about the weather in Massachusetts, the size of meals in American restaurants and the number of adverts on TV out there they quietly listened to an Amy Winehouse album. Neither of them felt the urge to tell their stories. Charlie dozed, happy to be safely back in England with her journey almost over and, although Sam was keen to tell her about his plan to apply to university, he held back. It would be better to talk about serious matters once they were relaxed at home. They stopped to get some shopping on the way but still arrived in good time to cook the pie and enjoy their evening together. Charlie sighed with pleasure when she opened the front door and took in the familiar surroundings of the entrance hall and the old prints of London buildings that had been hanging in it since she was a child.

"Come up and shower with me." She laughed at Sam's wide-eyed expression of surprise. "I've been looking forward to saying that ever since we took off from Boston."

"Do you mean it?"

"Yeah. I do. Aren't you the lucky one?"

Charlie took her clothes off in double quick time as soon as they were in her bedroom. "Come on. We can shower afterwards." She knelt on the bed and demanded entry from behind with no frills. "Just get on with it, Sam."

There was no emotion. Charlie was noisier than usual and Sam was rougher. He felt like a ram in the tupping season. There was an intense feeling of physical release at the end but it was too short and clinical to be truly satisfying.

"OMG, I needed that," Charlie said. "Three weeks off after so much indulgence in France was tough."

Sam extricated himself and rolled on to his back. He should feel grateful after such a rampant start to the evening, but he felt odd, almost used. It wasn't what he was expecting. Was this some sort of signal or was he looking for problems that weren't there?

Charlie flopped down next to him, reached for her phone from the bedside table and began to ping off texts to announce her safe arrival at home.

"I'm going to have a shower. Are you joining me?"

"I'll be there in a minute. Just let me do these."

He had already showered and dried himself by the time Charlie arrived.

She looked surprised. "Aren't you staying?"

"I thought I'd go and put the shepherd's pie in the oven."

"God, so that's what rejection feels like."

"I'm hungry."

"Clearly not for me."

*

By the time they'd had a glass of wine and were sitting down to eat, they had laughed about the shower incident and moved on.

"I shouldn't be so demanding," Charlie admitted. "So, have you made any progress?"

It was the moment he had been waiting for. He started by telling her the Twickenham story, mentioned what a good friend Chris had been and then surprised her with his plan to apply to St Mary's.

"That's amazing. The best news... Why St Mary's?"

Sam sensed a slightly disparaging note in her voice. "It's right for me if I want to continue to be involved in sport," he replied defensively. "Chris's sister showed me round and I liked it. Mum and Mike have agreed to help with the finances," he added to prove that there had been serious discussion at home.

"Awesome. Mike's turned out OK hasn't he?"

"Yeah, and he's suggested I do some travelling. He's got some contacts who will help."

"Where?"

"South Africa and Australia."

"Cool. A belated Gap year."

"I'm not sure I want to go."

"What. I can't believe it."

"I'd be away from you."

"You would anyway, for chrissake. You're not expecting to come and live with me in London, are you?"

"Well, no but…"

"Look Sam. I'm still an undergraduate and now you're going to be. It will be four years before you graduate. I'm definitely going to do a post-graduate course and will spend some time in the States at some stage. It just depends on when and for how long. The opportunities there are amazing and I want to take advantage of them."

Sam nodded. What she was saying was no surprise.

"So, like it or not, ours is going to be a distant relationship. Why don't we just enjoy the sex and each other's company when we can and stop worrying about all the long term stuff. Neither of us is ready for that… It's too soon. Please take the chance to go abroad. You may never get a better opportunity."

Sam was reduced to silence. If their relationship was going to continue it would be on her terms. It made sense, especially now he had plans and opportunities of his own.

She reached across the table and took hold of his hand. "I've got a confession to make. I knew I was going to America before we went to France."

It took him a while to take it in. "When did you know?" A pointless question in the circumstances but Sam felt the need to say something.

"The day before. I'm sorry, Sam. I was going to tell you

on the way out and then I kept putting it off. I didn't want to spoil the holiday. We were having such a wonderful time."

"Yeah, we were." He smiled. "It doesn't really make any difference. To be honest, I'm still embarrassed about the way I reacted."

Sam's calm response encouraged Charlie to continue. "When I was away, I decided that I couldn't go on taking advantage of you. I needed to be honest about the future. I'm so happy now you've got plans."

"Me too," he said quietly.

"Have you ever thought what brought us together?"

"Your Mum?"

Charlie laughed. "Yes, I always felt that you were one of Mum's projects but I wanted to join in and we became a joint project. Then I fell for this lovely man who rescued me, built up my confidence and helped to get me through my trauma. I was so lucky to find you when I needed you most." She held his hand tighter. "But we're different, Sam. I'm scared of total commitment. You want it. I'm selfish. You're generous. I don't want children. You do."

"If I find the right partner, I said."

"I'm not that person, Sam. I was the right person to help you through your depression. The hard bitch who forced you to realise you were ruining yourself. The job's not done but I'm confident that you can handle it now."

"But I love you, Charlie."

"I love you too but I'm not a happy ever after person. I'm too complicated. It would all end in tears." She was still holding his hand.

"We're in tears now."

"I know but it's better this way."

"Will we stay friends."

"Always."

"Can I stay tonight?"

"I'd be upset if you didn't."

# 40

"They're boarding for Cape Town. I've got to go."

"Oh, Sam. Give me a hug. I'm going to miss you."

"Don't cry Mum. It's only six months. You weren't like this when I went to Bath."

"But it's thousands of miles away and I've got used to having you at home… You'll be away for Christmas," she added randomly.

"It's overrated. Anyway, you'll be with the girls and Mike and I'll be on a beach in the sunshine."

"You be careful. It's a dangerous city."

"I can't wait."

It was true, he couldn't. The feeling of freedom once he had found his seat and stowed his hand baggage was palpable.

He took out *The Cape Town Book*, a guide to the city which Charlie had bought him for the journey and the

Moleskin traveller's journal she gave him after he received confirmation of his place at St Mary's.

She made him promise to use it. "I want to read it when you get back. When you're old and grey you'll thank me for making you record the memories."

Bossy as ever…

He checked his phone before switching to airplane mode. There was a text from Sara.

*Hot news. Chris has had an offer to play in France. A lot more money! Have a great time. Looking forward to welcoming you to St Mary's xx*

Sam settled into his seat ready for take off and smiled. It felt good to be making a fresh start.

# SOME FACTS ABOUT DEPRESSION

Depression is more than just a short period of sadness. It is a consistently low mood lasting over two weeks which may be accompanied by other symptoms such as: sleep disturbance, a loss of energy, changes to appetite and feelings of anxiety. Left untreated it can go on for months or even years.

Depression is one of the leading causes of disability and, in its most severe form can be fatal – more than 6,500 people took their own lives in the UK during 2018. It is also linked to a range of other illnesses including heart disease.

One in four women and one in seven men will be diagnosed with at least one episode of depression during their adult life. The number of antidepressants prescribed by the NHS has more than doubled in the last decade.

# ACKNOWLEDGEMENTS

My thanks to the players, coaches and staff at Bath Rugby who welcomed me to their exceptional training facility at Farleigh House, in particular, Henry Thomas who has had to endure more than his fair share of injuries and months of rehabilitation.

Mr Roland Walker, surgeon at St Thomas's Hospital who was on duty on the night of the London Bridge terrorist attack and gave me a disturbing insight into the carnage that occurred.

Peter Skivington ex-paratrooper who helped me to understand the mental and physical strength it requires to cope with the trauma of losing a leg.

Peter Smith at the Help for Heroes Recovery Centre in Tidworth where the support for victims and their families enables them to achieve remarkable things.

Wanda Whiteley, editor, critic and mentor par excellence from whom I have learnt so much.